MW00850334

Director Guy

By Edward G. Gauthier

i

Copyright © 2017 Edward G. Gauthier

All rights reserved.

ISBN-13: **978-1-7320824-0-3**

No part of this publication may be reproduced, distributed, or transmitted in any form or by any means, including photocopying, recording, or other electronic or mechanical methods, without the prior written permission of the publisher, except in the case of brief quotations embodied in critical reviews and certain other noncommercial uses permitted by copyright law. For permission requests or large quantity purchases by educational institutions, corporations, associations, and others, write to the publisher at eggchess@yahoo.com with the subject line: "Attention Director Guy Coordinator."

This novel, Director Guy, is a work of fiction. Names, characters, places and incidents are the product of the author's imagination, or are used fictitiously. Any resemblance to actual events, locales, or persons, living or dead is coincidental and unintentional.

DEDICATION

To Anna, Andre' and Gabriel Emile, who scratched their heads and wondered at my perpetual scribbling, typing, pondering and waking in the middle of the night to write down some new idea. You are the loves of my life and no writer could wish for better allowances and encouragement than you provided to me.

CONTENTS

ACKNOWLEDGMENTS

First, my thanks and friendship to Da Grils: Kathleen Oshaughnessy, Nettie McDaniels and Lisa Meaux (deceased), the writing group that has always encouraged me and pointed out my "rusty barges" since 1999.

Secondly, to four of the professors at University of Louisiana, Lafayette. They are: Ann Dobie, Professor Emerita, who rekindled my writing practice through participation in the Acadiana Writing Project; to Darrel Bourque, Professor Emeritus and Louisiana Poet Laureate, who can delicately explain any element of the English language and then challenge me to match it; to Ernest J. Gaines, Professor Emeritus, Pulitzer Prize nominee, who critiqued my stories for two semesters; and to Jerry McGuire, PhD, whose poetry instruction taught me the sound of wonderful sentences.

And then my thanks to Mary Allen for many hours spent on the phone as my writing coach.

Thanks to the workshop lecturers at University of Iowa Summer Writing Festival who include, Paula Morris, Anthony Varallo, Anjali Sachdeva, Gordon Mennenga, Ian Stansel, Katie Ford, Patricia Henley and Wayne Johnson, and to all the wonderful fellow participants.

And I bow all the way to the ground to Jeanne Cavelos, director of the Odyssey Writing Workshop and the six weeks of training I received during the summer of 2017 with my fifteen fellow attendees. There is no finer writing teacher than Jeanne and no finer writing workshop than Odyssey.

And finally,
To Mom, Nicole, Byron and all the baristas at Johnston Street Java. May the cloaking device I stole time-traveling to the future continue to disguise my main writing office as a coffee shop.

Chapter One

{ I found myself piggybacked in someone else's mind . . . }

Tuesday, May 5th

Odd as it may seem, I'm not sure I actually exist. I couldn't tell you who my parents are or whom I'm related to. I am unaware of my birthday or hometown. I'm at a loss to even tell you my name. Those kinds of things don't describe me. I'm not certain they even matter. Like I said, odd.

Straight away, I found myself in another person's head. A teenager's head at that. I saw through his eyes, heard through his ears and felt the warm joint his big muscular friend was handing to him. Darkness was all around. I felt the cold steel railroad track he sat on, his feet on either side of a railroad tie. The sky lit the evening with stars, a dark, clear, cool night. The quality of the air fostered a familiarity which I thought to be late spring or early summer.

At first, complete disorientation inhabited my mind. How was this possible? I found myself piggybacked in someone else's mind, a stowaway in another's consciousness. And where had I been before? Who had I been? I had no other starting point except this present moment. I strained to bring up any, absolutely any, past image, but nothing arrived. Frustrated, I realized that I possessed no memory at all. Something had startled me awake. Everything before that very minute just wasn't there.

Focusing on the senses of the body I now occupied, I could tell he was a guy. There seemed a normality to it. Maybe I'd been a guy myself? Who knew? He felt energetic, new, so he must be young, perhaps younger than I had been. Whatever, whoever I had been. Nevertheless, I was trapped. When he reached out to take the joint, he controlled his hand. I could only watch. Yeah. Trapped.

He sat between two of his peers, the big muscle guy and a rather pretty girl. Two other boys sat on the other track facing him. The group conversed as they passed the joint.

"Damn jaw-boned mother of mine has been riding my ass endlessly," the kid I inhabited whined. "Parents. You'd think grades are the end-all in life. I could do without parents." He took a second toke.

"Man. Pass the friggin' joint, Von."

The name Von was directed at my guy and so I learned his name. "Ok, Moby Dick," this Von answered, "Next in line is Julia and she just may decide you don't deserve another toke." So the pretty girl was Julia.

"You'd think Mrs. Keife might realize someone in her English class is named Moby and that could cause problems, for me at least." So that kid across the way was Moby.

Von did not realize I was there, present in his head, using his senses. I also discerned that I could think a thought that he would sense, but only if I intended him to. His thoughts were unavailable to me and I felt certain he couldn't read mine, or else he would have already sensed my presence. I knew the necessity to declare myself would eventually arise. But for now, until I got oriented to this strangeness, silence seemed the best option. I quietly studied the situation.

Von liked marijuana. I could feel the high. He handed the joint on to Julia and let the back of his hand rest high on her leg. She took the joint, gave him a scant smile and slid his hand off.

"It's on the way, Moby." Then after she hesitated a second or two. "Dick."

2

Everyone laughed.

"Freakin' English teacher," Moby Dick mumbled.

They laughed again.

"Teachers. Just another set of parents plus homework. Bossy bastards," Moby said, taking the joint. "You're lucky, Derrick. Parents rich as hell. I could put up with my folks if they were rich." Moby passed the joint to Derrick.

Derrick puffed on the joint and leaned forward handing it off to Von's muscular friend. "Poor little you, Moby Dick. Charlie, rip off Moby's dick so we can use it as a sacrificial offering to our English teacher, please. 'Here Mrs. Keife. Here's Moby's dick. Do I still have to read the novel?'" Everyone laughed as Charlie took the joint.

"Man. Could we just leave my dick out of the conversation?" Moby said smiling.

I strained to orient quickly to these uncanny circumstances; living in someone else's head would be no vacation. I ran their names through my mind. Moby and Derrick on the other railroad track facing me. Charlie to my left, beautiful Julia to my right. Me inside Von's head. Damn it! The only one I couldn't name was me.

As Von laughed and looked around, I noticed that the railroad tracks they perched on came to a blunt end a hundred feet up the line. There were two other sets of tracks that ran parallel to theirs. Three numbered yellow signs jutted up from the ends of the tracks. Track one where they sat was clear of all rail cars. On track two rested an old caboose only ten feet from the sign at the end of the line, its paint peeling from its dark red wooden sides. Track three bore two rusting flatcars still coupled together, just sitting there. An overturned coal car lay in the weeds past the third track like some big buffalo shot dead, its rigor mortis wheels stiff in the air, most of its coal strewn across the ground. Trees, high grass and lots of underbrush stood just past the numbered signs. In the other direction all three tracks faded off into the distant darkness. The inky night's slight breeze rattled the tall reeds and cattails that grew on either side of the tracks.

But how long could I occupy Von's head without him discovering me? If he suddenly realized my presence, that would probably produce anxiety or extreme anger. I had no idea how to maneuver the situation or how to prepare him for such a mind bending introduction. Experimentation would force itself upon this situation. I dreaded some kind of shocked reaction but I decided I simply had to try it.

Ahh Von, I hope you understand this. Please don't panic.

"What?" Von yelled out loud. He jumped to his feet, spun around looking at his friends and then at the area around them. He searched the tracks, nearby rail cars, even the sky. "What the hell?"

His friends watched him, curious, waiting. Derrick pointed at him and laughed. "Boy. You are so stoned, Von,"

"Charlie, did you say that?" Von demanded.

"Say what?"

"Something about hope you understand and don't . . . I think my brain just tuned in to some radio station. Did you say that?"

"He didn't say anything. Nobody did," Moby added. "You just jumped up and started babbling. It's the weed, fool. You're stoned."

They all giggled. Von slowly smiled and then giggled too, shook his head and sat back on the track.

"I don't know what that was. This voice. It talked inside my head.

4

I don't know."

I could feel Von forcing the smile, his nerves on edge. Well, at least he'd had his first exposure. This introduction would obviously necessitate a gentler manner. How to initiate a relationship with someone as a new consciousness in their head? Good gracious.

Von sat down, hunched over and rubbed the back of his neck, then sat up straight and glanced around. The group watched, waiting to see what he'd do or say.

"I don't know . . . like a voice . . . like a thought, but I didn't do it." Von looked at Charlie and raised his palms. "Charlie, is this one of your practical jokes?"

Charlie smiled, laughed and shook his head. "Space cowboy rides the smoke pony."

Julia rubbed Von's back. "You have been smoking a lot of pot lately."

Von spun toward her and I was struck by her look of concern.

"Yeah, well you would too if your mom hounded you like mine. Nothing satisfies her." I felt Von's blood rise into his cheeks.

"We got loaded yesterday out under the football stadium, for sure." Derrick held up one finger.

"And this morning before we walked to school. Maybe it's time you enter smoking pony anonymous," Moby bellowed. Everybody howled. Moby and Derrick slapped palms.

"Your butt, Dick Moby," Von called. "Besides, there's no such group."

"So? You could start it up. Stoned Pony Anonymous. The most stoned cowboy wins. You could associate with Alcoholics Anonymous and claim your stoned ponies pull the AA sobriety wagon." Moby stood and waved his arms wide, proud of his announcement. "My dad has been through AA three times. Fell off the wagon so many times, I told him he could use my bike helmet."

Moby sat back down and the group took in the quiet night around them and fell into studying the starry sky above them. Charlie leaned back.

"The universe is just so freaking big," he said.

I could feel the effect of the marijuana pulling Von down into a calmer state.

"Yep. Most of what you see is Milky Way," Von pointed, seeming to run his finger along the starry night cloud. "They estimate between one hundred billion and four hundred billion stars in this galaxy."

"Is that one of your research facts?" Derrick asked.

"Nope. Neil deGrasse Tyson. I love all his Space Talk videos," Von said.

"Oh. And I wanted to ask you, Von," Derrick said. "Was that explosion in physics lab, you? Because like on Monday morning, Mr. Howard started washing his hands as he usually does at the start of class. The flame coming out that drain pipe hit the ceiling tile. He barely got his hands out of the way. Was that you, Von?" Derrick repeated.

Every head turned toward Von. "Elaina started crying the other day," Von answered. "She told me Mr. Howard embarrasses her all the time and he keeps touching her. He might be young and handsome but she's already asked him to leave her alone. So, after school, we snuck into his lab. I used sodium out of the storage room, wrapped it in tissue, stuffed it down the lecture table drain pipe and we were out of there."

"Von strikes again," Charlie announced laughing out loud.

"Yeah, but in one way Von's right," Julia said. "Mr. Howard keeps coming on to Elaina to the point she's afraid of the guy. How the heck is she supposed to pass his course now? He likes to think he's all that, with his big college degree and all."

"Yeah. More adult crap," Von said. "They tell you the rules and then they break 'em." Moby and then Derrick reached forward and tapped knuckles with Von.

Everyone grew quiet again and went back to star gazing. As they peered over the heavenly orbs, I worried about having alarmed Von. At least observing the Milky Way felt very familiar to me. I had no idea why. But it was quickly becoming obvious I would need to get accustomed to a minimum of certainty. No identity, no method to my arrival, no memories, and now I've set Von on edge. How does one do this? I didn't want to be in someone else's head but where else could I be?

"You think there's a god?" Charlie asked still watching the stars.

"Oh man. Not another freaking authority figure, alright," Von responded.

"If I were a god, I'm not sure I'd make all those stars," Derrick said. "I mean, what's the point?"

Julia quickly leaned forward. "Oh, I would. They're beautiful. We need beauty. Just think. If we didn't have the stars, all that sky would just be empty black. With nothing out there to wonder about, that would be freaky. It would feel so cold and lonely."

Von nodded. "Yep. Have you seen the Hubble telescope pictures of the Horsehead Nebula? Fantastic. I think it's in the Andromeda galaxy."

"We have the moon. Isn't that enough?" Derrick said. "I'd rather

7

another moon or two. Put colonies on them. We can't really use stars."

"Is there a smoking pony nebula?" Moby stood up, smiled and pointed at Von, who chose not to respond. Moby stretched, walked around a little and sat down, this time on the other side of Julia.

Von glanced over at Moby, leaned forward and stood. "I gotta piss." He walked around the far end of the caboose out into the high weeds and unzipped his pants, relieving himself.

Without his friends there, I decided to give it another try. Just as he finished zipping up his pants, I sent another thought.

Actually Von, the Horsehead Nebula resides within the Orion spiral arm of our own Milky Way.

"What?" he whispered, spinning around. His hands clutched the sides of his head. "Who is that?"

I apologize Von. This must be disconcerting. But, I'm here and having difficulty—

He whirled around again, hands flailing the air around him. "I can't see you. You sound like you're in my head." He hissed his words, fearful of his friends hearing him.

Unfortunately. I'm afraid that's correct.

"What? That's impossible. I mean that's crazy!" he whispered.

Suddenly Von drew silent. He stepped back, took a deep breath and checked that his pants were zipped. He walked out of the weeds, went around the caboose and approached the group. The muscles of his face pulled like metal wires drawing tightly across his skull. He was so shaken by our exchange, the marijuana now had little effect on him. He stood with his hands in his pockets and noticed Charlie had scooted over, taking Von's place next to Julia. He huffed, pushed pebbles around with his toe and listened to the group's conversation, which had moved on to something in their common past.

"Yeah, remember Sister Gills? She assigned you those ten thousand lines to write . . . by the next day." Charlie said to Derrick. "She's still at Perpetual Peace Elementary."

"Good ole Perpetual Peach." Derrick nodded and held his first finger in the air.

'Man, dealing with her was a trip," Moby stood waving his arms wide. "Remember her angelic army?"

Julia was immediately on her feet. "Christ, guard me today against every poison, burning, drowning or fatal wounding."[1]

Derrick and Charlie both jumped up joining Julia, the three of them reciting in unison. "Please have your angelic army bind up Satan, his demons, all forms of witchcraft, of divination, of sorcery, the Ouija board, astrology, horoscopes, fortune telling, palm readings, and anything else associated with the occult of Satan and baptize us, your disciples, on the day of Pentecost."[2]

"Damn right!" Derrick concluded sending high fives all around.

Overhearing their Catholic nun story made me chuckle. *Yes. Nuns. Every kid that ever survived Catholic school must have a —*

Too late I realized I'd sent my thoughts so that Von received them which made him suddenly jump sideways, his hands flying out of his pockets. He grabbed his temples again.

_____ *Take it easy Von. Your stress levels are off the charts. Take a*

[1] St. Patrick's Breastplate (Long version), http://spiritofthesword.net/?page_id=508, 11/11/2016. (Note: Incomplete version of this ritual used for the sake of brevity).
[2] The Catholic Warrior, Spiritual Warfare Prayers, Denouncing the Occult, https://www.catholicwarriors.com/pages/warfare_prayers.htm, 11/11/2016. (Note: Incomplete version of this ritual used for the sake of brevity).

breath. Try to relax.

"Relax!" he screamed, bending over yelling at the ground. "Something's in my fucking head and you say relax? Shit!"

I will not harm you, Von. I'm not mean or harmful. Calm yourself so we can speak with each . . .

"If you're in my head, you've already harmed me. GET OUT!"

"Von? What's up man? Who are you talking to?" Charlie said as he stood.

"IT'S IN MY HEAD, CHARLIE," Von yelled.

I went silent realizing my attempt to get him used to me was failing miserably. There had to be a rational method to ease myself into his awareness without this total meltdown, but right now I let him be so he could catch his breath. There was the sound of feet scrambling across railroad ties and gravel as Charlie, Julia, Moby and Derrick quickly surrounded Von, worried looks on their faces. He stood there with one hand entangled in his hair and the other feeling the space around him. Charlie grabbed both Von's shoulders steadying him, trying to get Von to stand upright.

"What?" Charlie asked.

"Von, you ok?" Julia said with a hand on his back.

"No. It's . . . it's a voice. It didn't go away. It's in my head. It spoke to me. I'm telling you, it talks to me. Calls me by name. IT'S IN MY DAMN HEAD!" Von began poking his temple repeatedly, harder and harder. Julia's eyes registered complete shock and her jaw muscles tensed. She took a quick step back and swung. The slap hit Von square across the right side of his face and I felt it full force.

Yeow! I told Von. *She hits hard. Calm down. She might do that again.*

Von froze. He stood straighter, took a deep breath gazing at Julia. "You hit me," he said.

"Well yeah, Von. You were totally panicked," Julia fussed. "My goodness, I've never seen you so freaked out."

"Yeah, but it's this voice. It keeps talking in my head and I'm not doing it. It's like . . . it's someone else."

He'd gone so out of control that I had no choice but to try again. *Von. Do you really want to scare your friends? Do you want to terrify them? Please. I'm not here to hurt you. We're just going to talk. That's all. Now take a deep breath and calm yourself, ok? You're acting like some little scared child. Get a hold of yourself.*

Slowly, Von stood up straight, put one hand against his forehead and sent a thought back to me. *But, how the hell . . . I mean . . . we're supposed to talk to each other?*

Excellent, Von. That's the method you and I have to use to communicate. We think thoughts back and forth. No need to overreact and horrify your friends. I mean, look at them. Your reaction is totally freaking them out. Von took in the expressions on his friend's faces, all four with serious worried looks.

"Hey man. You ok?" Charlie asked putting his hand on Von's cheek.

Von nodded. He huffed a breath in and out and nodded again. Julia continued to rub his back.

"Sorry if I hit you too hard," she said. "Are you alright?"

"Yeah. I'm sorry. Just need to catch my breath. I freaked. Completely lost it there. Never happened to me before. I just don't know what to make . . . "

Good. You're much calmer. Just deal with your friends right now. I'll give you a second to collect yourself. It's important to breathe, ok?

Yeah. But, I don't understand. I mean . . .

The thing is Von, I don't understand either. But I won't hurt you. That's the main thing. So, there's no need to panic. Be with your friends right now. We'll talk more in a little while.

"Yeah," Von said taking another very deep breath, "Yeah. Let's go sit down again. Whew. Let's sit down."

"Maaaan, Von. I've never see you so loaded," Derrick giggled and shook Von's shoulder. Everyone moved slowly to where they'd been sitting on the tracks. Just as they rearranged themselves again on the tracks, Von responded to me.

Talk? Talk about what?

Yes. But not talking. By thinking. We should communicate by thought, not by speaking aloud. Simply orchestrate your thinking toward me.

Orchestrate my thi . . . ? I've never had anyone else in my head! What the fuck!

Take a deep breath. Stay composed. Somehow, we'll reason this situation out, I said trying to stay composed.

Reason it out! I don't want it figured out. Get the hell out of my head!

Yes, that's complicated. I tried to be calm. *I seem to be incapable of leaving. And besides, I don't have a proper place to go.*

No, no, no, no. You can't stay. You can't get stuck in my brain, Von responded sliding toward panic mode again. *You get out. You . . . Aw,*

12

what the hell am I doing? A freaking voice in my head? Now I'm talking to it? No. I don't want to hear your voice again. Shut up! Go away!

Damn it! I kept torturing this young man. I retreated into silence again.

"You still look a bit shook up man," Charlie said. "You ok?"

Von looked around and managed a smile. "Yeah. I'm just tired. And that damned voice. It bugs me."

"What. You heard it again?" Julia's brows furrowed. Her smile barely clung to her face.

"Yeah. I think I'm frazzled. And ya'll are right. I've been getting wasted way too much. I'm ok. I just need rest. You guys mind if we get going?"

Derrick checked the time on his cell phone. "Oh wow, it's after midnight. Yeah, my mother is the local rooster every freaking morning."

With that, the group rose and walked past the caboose and down the path through forested woods back to Derrick's car, a red Mini Cooper. Von, then Julia and then Charlie piled into the back seat all squeezed together. Moby got the front passenger seat. Derrick swung his car around and started up a gravel one-lane road that snaked from the abandoned railroad spur to a nearby two lane highway. Because Von sat gazing out the right side back window, I got to see a Louisiana highway 541 sign go by. Shifting through the gears, Derrick got up to seventy mph. We were cruising along when they came to a crossroads where another highway intersected highway 541. A JCT 18 sign went by. Derrick glanced both ways, slowed to thirty-five but then started accelerating again. Von still gazed out the back right window but, deep in his own thoughts, he wasn't responding to what was out there. Luckily, I saw it.

Truck! Look right! I screamed in Von's head.

Then Von saw it. "Truck on the right! Truck on the right!"

Derrick's head twisted right and he hit the brakes hard. Tires screamed, everyone pitched forward and Derrick's Mini Cooper skidded to a smoking halt. An eighteen-wheeler zoomed past right in front of us, air horns blaring. It missed us by inches.

"Shit!" Derrick yelled hammering his fist against the steering wheel. He flipped on the inside cabin light and turned toward us. "I'm sorry you guys. I didn't even see that thing."

"That was ahhh . . . SCARY." Moby sat with his hands and forehead still on the dashboard.

Julia's head slowly came up off her knees. "Good call, Von. I didn't see it either," she muttered.

Von nodded. For seconds everyone sat silently in their own fear, but then Von spoke. "The voice warned me."

"What?" Charlie leaned forward looking at Von. "Von, man, are you serious?"

"Yes. Totally serious. I wouldn't have seen it in time," Von whispered.

Nobody moved as Von's words sunk in. Derrick and Moby turned in their seats to stare at Von.

Finally Julia spoke. "Maybe someone should tell that voice thanks."

Charlie nodded. "Yeah, really."

"A voice," Derrick repeated. "I don't think I'm stoned at all, now" he added as he turned off the cabin light, shifted into gear and eased forward. Moby nodded his agreement.

Yeah. Thanks for the warning, ahhh . . . I don't know your name, Von told me.

It took a second for me to answer. *A name? My usual designation isn't . . . ahhh . . . available right now, Von. However, I should apologize for scaring you earlier. I want to assure you again that I'm no threat. I don't know the rationale of how this has occurred. But, I'm not your enemy. I'm not evil. I just need . . . to . . . investigate . . . to reason this whole thing out. Ok?*

Well. You just saved my . . . our lives. I still need something to call you. How could you not have a name?

I presume I had one once, but I don't remember it now. I can't conjure any distinct memories, although certain feelings arise automatically.

So what do I call you?

I . . . don't know, Von. You must be feeling invaded.

It feels like a weird movie, with someone else calling the shots. Some kind of director guy controlling everything.

Well, I guess that would suffice.

What? Oh. Director Guy?

Certainly. It'll do for now.

Von nodded. Everyone sat wrapped in a scared silence, the car's motor the only sound breaking the quiet. Charlie glanced over past Julia at Von with a worried look. He started to speak, even raised his hand to point, but deciding against it, sank back into his seat.

Chapter Two

{ Hmmm. I think I just retrieved a memory. Fished it out of oblivion. }

Wednesday, May 6th

"Von. Get up. It's almost seven," my mother called from downstairs. "You've got school. No excuses."

"Yeah. School. Got it," I mumbled and then added, "Jaw-boned witch."

I opened my eyes, but in my head I saw the blaring eighteen-wheeler roar past again, its huge tires whirling a storm of dust just a few feet in front of us. Freakin' lucky, that's what we were. If he hadn't warned me, I'd be dead. In such a small car, we'd all be dead. I felt rested after a good night's sleep.

Now that I wasn't stoned anymore, would that voice still be there? I wanted it gone. Completely gone. I hesitated testing to see if it still lodged in my head. But how else to find out?

We agreed on Director Guy, right? I asked.

Yes Von. That'll be fine.

Yeah, he was still there so I may hang myself before sunset today. I waited. No response came from Director Guy. And so I began to see that I could think my own thoughts that Director Guy could not sense. Well then, at least I had some mental privacy. The possibility of no mental solitude had scared me. But when I wanted him to hear my thoughts, he did. Weird. Now I'd have to make up new rules for operating my own brain. This was gonna be trouble. At least I controlled my mind. Control.

Yeah, control would be very important. So far, I was sure I controlled my body, all of me. I worried a bit that maybe that could change. I'd have to keep a close eye on control.

Man, I thought you showed up in my head because of the marijuana.

Oh no, Von. All indications are otherwise. For one, I sensed your being high but I never discerned me getting . . . high, stoned, or whatever its designation. I honestly don't know what forced this situation, but we must determine how this has occurred. Somehow.

Oh, you think? I started climbing into my pants, school shirt and running shoes. *So you don't remember anything of your past? That's weird. There's gotta be something.*

Actually Von, I'm afraid it's miniscule. I obviously have a past because feelings, emotional responses, those keep occurring. That angelic army prayer tickled my fancy. I obviously know English so I had to acquire that somewhere. I knew about the Horsehead Nebula. With stargazing a certain familiarity arises. I sense a science background of some kind. But memories are just beyond my grasp. I try casting my mind backward in time but everything is blackness.

I grabbed my toothbrush and started scrubbing my teeth, thinking about what he'd said. I spit out, swished my mouth with water and then looked up into my own eyes in the mirror. So weird, there being one of me and one of somebody else in there.

Together, we ran through a quick list of his traits. He had a bigger vocabulary than me, he definitely sounded older and he had the presence of a man, not a woman. It all pointed toward lots of experience but in what field neither of us could tell.

I nodded, wiped my face and headed downstairs for breakfast. I figured my chat with Director Guy was finished, or at least that's what I wanted.

"Where's my kiss young man," my mother barked as I entered the kitchen. I gave a blunt peck to her temple as I grabbed a cereal bowl from the cabinet. Dad was already at the kitchen table working on eggs and sausages, his usual financial page next to his plate. I sat next to him and he nudged my shoulder with his fist, his usual way of trying to buddy up to me. I used my usual tactic of ignoring him as much as I could.

He chuckled. "Let me know when you think you're ready for that wrestling match, child." Was Dad going senile maybe? Dad and I hadn't wrestled in three years. I ignored it.

"You kids better get down here and eat. You're not missing your bus," Mom hollered up the stairs. Seconds later, a small herd of horses came stampeding down the stairs. They were Harper, my twelve-year-old brother and Oma, my ten-year-old sister.

Your family?

I didn't like Director Guy butting in, me being with my people and all. *Ahh, yeah, family.*

Your father. He engages in what kind of work? What's his name?

I sat up, irritated. Somehow, Director Guy's asking about them felt like an invasion. I glanced at Dad. *Welder at an Irish channel shipyard. Everyone calls him George but his name is Giovanni Gialanto.* I looked at Mom scraping a spatula across the skillet on the stove. *Legal secretary. She's Martha Gialanto. Harper is fifth grade and Oma is fourth grade.* I started to take a bite of eggs.

And you?

I hesitated, my fork in mid air, and considered ignoring Director Guy, but this guy was in my head. *About to finish up junior year at Mid-City high school.* I finished the solitary bite of eggs and pushed my plate away. I scraped my plate bare, rinsed my dishes, stuffed them into the dishwasher, draped my backpack over my shoulder and headed for the door.

"Hey, my kiss," my mother called. "You sure didn't eat much."

"I'm requesting you learn to study, kid," Dad added.

"Or give away everything to your little brother," Harper yelled. Oma just ate her breakfast. I ignored it all.

Dieting? Superior eggs your mom scrambled. Director Guy observed. I ignored him. Even if he was in my head, I didn't feel like giving special treatment.

My regulars were on the sidewalk two houses down. I tightened my back pack and trotted to catch up with them. They began to walk toward school four blocks away, their backs toward me.

Inform me about this Julia. Her eyes are intensely green.

I stopped, letting my friends walk away without me. *Look Director Guy. You gotta understand. I don't like having you in my head. Thanks for saving our butts last night, but that only bought you a little time. If it keeps up enough, I'll go crazy with it. I mean I'll get in bed, cover up with a blanket and not come out till one of us dies. I'll try to help you but—*

I am sorry Von. I—

No. Listen. You gotta understand. I'm so tired of parents, teachers, priests, nuns, the cops, anyone telling me what to do, when to do it, how to do it, why I should do it, what they'll do to me if I don't do it. You getting this? And now I have some older adult inside my freakin' brain!

19

The only damn place that was safe? Could drive me ape raving nuts. You've gotta observe. I'm not explaining everything. They're just my friends, man. Just my friends.

Suddenly, my own ranting bothered me so I shut up. Director Guy was quiet. I turned and trotted to catch up with the gang. Once among them, they turned toward me and stared.

"Well?" Moby snapped.

"Well what?" He'd caught me off guard.

"Oh, I don't know," Moby said flailing his arms to the side. "Everyone has new voices in their heads. What do you mean what? Are you still hearing that thing?" The nervous worry in his voice was obvious. I stood there just looking at him and then saw the same look on Derrick, Julia and Charlie as they waited.

"What voice?" Vivian asked looking around.

"Von. Did you sleep well last night? Are you ok this morning?" Charlie said as though speaking to a small child. Julia looked at me, stayed silent, and just cocked her head a bit expecting a response. What was I supposed to say?

"Yeah. I slept well," I finally answered. "But it's still there. It just asked about you guys as I walked up."

Everyone but Vivian seemed frozen. "What the hell are you guys talking about?" she asked.

"A voice? Don't get me wrong Von," Charlie said with both arms outstretched. "I appreciate you saving us last night. We'd have been smashed to soup under that truck, but a voice? I mean, if you actually are hearing voices, maybe that's not so good, you know?"

"You're hearing a voice?" Vivian cut in, her eyes expanding. "Whoa.

20

You ok, Von?"

"Yes. I'm fine," I tried to reassure them. "They thought last night I'd just been smoking weed too often. I'm not crazy. I'm fine. Really."

"A voice," Vivian mocked, thought about it a second and then shook her head. "I don't have time for this. Did anybody study for that first hour math test?" Everybody's shoulders dropped. No, I didn't study. I'd been out at the railroad spur getting an extra voice in my head. Vivian turned toward the side entrance of the school building near our math class. "Well great. The last test of the year and none of us prepared. I'm not cheating off any of you guys. "

The group fell into our usual talk about who had done what homework. Charlie and Julia traded papers for Biology and American History, an old agreement between them. I watched Julia smile receiving Charlie's homework. Director Guy was right about her eyes. Her eyes had hypnotized me many times. Shit. What do you do with an extra mental voice? It hit me that Director Guy had been the least judgmental toward me that morning.

Ok Director Guy. You asked about them. Julia is of course beautiful. Known her since second grade; all the guys dream about her. She's smart, studies and has the coolest mother, who does Voodoo and reads fortunes. Julia can bargain like nobody's business. She'll go somewhere in life. Charlie there is the tough silent type. And he is tough. He's really strong, played linebacker for the football team till he got in a severe argument with the coach. He can handle himself, runs his own life and everyone around him knows it. Moby is easiest to set off so we pick at him. Luckily, he takes it well and can give it back pretty well. He has an active sense of humor and loves to argue with teachers. But his home life is death defying. Nothing funny about that. Vivian there scares me. You don't dare her to do anything because she will immediately try it, no matter how insane it is. In fifth grade, Derrick dared her to ride her bike through this big bonfire. She still has scars on her arms and ankles from that. Her bike actually melted. She drives her parents crazy; they worry so much about her. Julia thinks Vivian does all that just to get back at her parents. They argue a lot. So that's your local newscast about this bunch.

Thank you Von. I'll attempt to be less intrusive. Getting acclimated to all this is challenging.

Yeah. Acclimated, huh? You keep using all those big words and my English grade might improve. I guess I'm adjusting too. Well, somewhat. Part of the run down on me is I can be a real crank. A part of me I don't like. Catch myself at it now and then.

Not to worry Von. My feelings aren't hurt.

Moby started daring Vivian to make an 'A' on the math test and let him cheat.

She shoved him. "Cheat off me all you want. Just don't expect to pass."

At that moment the bell rang for the beginning of first period. We had five minutes to be in our seats. Once in class, Mrs. Dillman reminded us about the test and had us put everything away.

"As I said before," Mrs. Dillman went on, "this test is from material presented earlier this school year. Many of you needed the review, especially with final exam approaching so soon. Now we find out if you understand division of polynomials. Please adhere to the school rules concerning cell phones." She handed out the tests and began her slow march up and down the aisles between desks, watching our every move.

The ten problems on dividing polynomials using long division got harder and harder as they went. I basically didn't like math, found Mrs. Dillman's explanations difficult to follow and I didn't like things she'd said about the way I wore my clothes. The first four problems, a simple review of linear equations, I could handle. But the fifth problem began the polynomial equation section. Dog-man Dillman stood right there next to me, hawking over my work with her thick, black, horn-rim glasses low on her nose, watching me sweat. I looked up at her, gave a sappy smile and went back to work.

The fifth problem was $(2a + 22) \div (a + 8)$. I knew I had to rewrite the problem in long division form, which I did correctly. And my estimate that $a + 8$ would go twice into $2a + 22$ was ok. But I thought my remainder of 6 would be placed over 22, which reduced to 3/11. So, my answer came out to 2 + 3/11. What a bitch of a problem. I looked it over again suspicious of I-don't-know-what. I snuck a glance to my right where Dog-man Dillman still glared down her smug nose at me.

Hey wait Von. That's the wrong answer. Director Guy's thought caught me cold.

Oh? You know a better way? I caught a glimpse of Mrs. Dillman turning toward the other side of the isle, looking down at Charlie's work.

Your denominator for the fraction you ended up with has to be a + 8, don't you think? Director Guy had me erase my answer and some of my work. He slowly described the process and his much clearer explanation made sense. For once I got it. Redoing the problem the way he suggested, I came out with 2 + 6/a+8. Dog-man Dillman had turned back toward me and out of the corner of my eye I saw her lean forward and nod. A tiny smile showed on her dog mug.

The next problem, $(16v^2 + 64v) \div (v + 4)$ took me a minute or two longer to figure out and Director Guy tossed in one hint, but I put down $16v$ with no remainder as my answer and Mrs. Dillman's eyes got bigger.

You're doing well, Von. Keep it up, D.G. told me.

Within twenty minutes and only three more hints from Director Guy, I was done and handed in my paper. Mrs. Dillman assigned a review graph sheet of sine function problems to the class and graded our tests as we worked on the assignment sheet. In fifteen minutes, she stood and began handing out the graded tests. I saw Charlie's seventy-five percent as she handed it to him. Julia got hers and flashed it at me, an eighty nine percent. Moby had a sixty. Vivian showed us a sixty seven. The Dog-man stood before me saving my test for last. That deadpan smug look of hers gave credence to Moby's claim that he knew a junk yard dog with the very same expression. She plopped my test before me. One hundred percent in red covered the top of the page. Charlie, Julia, Moby, Vivian and three others craned forward with shocked looks.

"Nailed it Von. You the man," Carl, who sat right behind me, said pressing the back of my shoulder.

"Let me see your cell phone," Mrs. Dillman recited in monotone.

I froze. Silence filled the room. I slid my phone out of my pocket and handed it to her. She glanced at it. The school rule required all cell phone to be turned off and out of sight. I remembered turning it off in the hallway on the way to class.

"Ok," she said placing my phone back in my hand and walking away. "You get to keep that grade."

I smiled and looked at Charlie. He mouthed the words, 'A hundred?'

Julia was just past him looking at me too. I mouthed back at them, 'The voice,' and pointed at my head. Charlie's eyes grew huge and Julia's jaw dropped. Just then, the bell rang for second period.

Everyone stood, gathered books and backpacks and started herding toward our next class. I could hear Derrick coming down the crowded hallway making his usual low moaning cow call. Someone bleated like a sheep in return. He caught up to us and Charlie whispered to him.

"You made a what?" Derrick knew about my D average in math for the first five grading periods. "Seriously. The voice? Aww Von. Don't give me that. You must have studied your ass off last night after I dropped you off," he whispered.

Charlie and Julia crowded in close. "We gotta talk, Von." Charlie grabbed me and tugged me into one of the locker coves. Moby and Vivian followed right behind. "Voice. You're telling us that that same voice got you that grade?" Moby demanded while Julia and the rest closed in, pinning me to the lockers.

I shrugged. "He told me I had a problem wrong. And he explains it a lot better than Dillman. I got it. I understood. After that, he only needed to give me hints."

"Voice. In your head. Von, knock it off," Vivian said pushing on my shoulder.

"In math, of all things," Charlie said. Charlie always did better in math.

"Yeah, really," Julia added. "If you're messing with us, ok, ha ha, you got us."

"So the voice that just showed up in your head just happens to be a math genius," Derrick blared out at the top of his voice. "Bullshit. You saw that truck coming yourself. We were just so freaked out at the time that nobody thought to call you on it."

"Hey. Hey guys," I panicked, "let's just keep this between us. I don't need the whole school thinking I'm nuts." I tugged on Vivian's sleeve for emphasis. I knew some of her bad habits.

Suddenly, they were all launching questions at me. Other students around in the hall began to look our way. I raised my hands stopping them. I didn't seem to have a choice, so I launched into telling them everything I knew about Director Guy, including the name I'd given him.

"Director Guy?" Julia bowed her head and giggled. "Von. Seriously? You are so funny. I mean, you're certainly sharp enough to trick us."

"Look, I'll give you that you saved our bacon last night," Charlie said pointing. "And you pulled out an 'A' today in math. I mean, maybe we believed you last night because we were scared, not to mention stoned. Today though, it seems fishy. If you have a voice in your head, better hope he sticks around for finals next week." Everyone laughed at Charlie's remark.

"What are you people waiting for? Get your second period books and move on. You'll be tardy." Mrs. Dillman stood there, arms crossed, her usual junkyard dog expression bearing down on us. We started moving and spread out toward our various upcoming classes.

Julia and Charlie walked along with me a few steps, skeptical grins still showing. "I feel like you're trying to get me to believe in Santa Claus again. This isn't even possible, Von," she said.

I shrugged my shoulders. "It's the getting-used-to-it part that racks my nerves. It's like being possessed. For all I know, I am."

Charlie and Julia both stopped and looked at me, skeptical grins fading. "Ok, ok. We've got class," Julia said. "But I want to talk later."

Vivian had English III with me during second hour. Mrs. Keife's lifetime of teaching had turned her freckled face into a permanent straight line non-expression. No one could remember her smiling or frowning. She seemed to me always neutral, often turning any question you asked right back at you. Her tricky reputation sponsored stories from every student I knew at the school. She loved to net students in their own embarrassment because they hadn't done the assignment. Though our long term assignment for the six weeks revolved around reading the novel Moby Dick and writing a report on it, our present in-class responsibility involved completing Hamlet. I strained to get meaning from Shakespeare's language and hadn't yet gotten past Act One.

Vivian and I sat across rows from each other and we'd just sat down when Mrs. Keife aimed her first question right at me. "So Von, explain to your peers how Mercutio greatly complicates the overall plot of Hamlet. What did he do to turn things into a more difficult situation for our poor Hamlet?"

I blinked. The sounds of pages flipping came from everyone around me. Vivian looked down, avoiding Mrs. Keife's eyes.

Refrain from answering that, Von. It's a trick question.

Huh? Trick how?

Mercutio isn't even in Hamlet. He's in Romeo and Juliet.

Romeo and Juliet? I read that. And I saw the movie. Which one was he?

He meets Romeo in the town square and initiates that big conflict with Tybalt. Remember? He engages swordplay against Tybalt because Romeo refuses to fight. Mercutio claims his 'fiddlestick' sword will do his bidding. *Mercutio dies when Tybalt stabs him under Romeo's arm. It leads to the fight between Romeo and Tybalt resulting in Romeo killing Tybalt. Remember?*

Suddenly I could breathe so much easier. Trying not to smile too broadly, I said, "I realize you are the Shakespeare expert here at the school, Mrs. Keife," and then as if stepping over the edge of a cliff, "but you're wrong."

All the page turning immediately stopped. The room went totally silent. Moneen, who sat right behind me, whispered, "God Von. Don't piss her off." Mrs. Keife's hand halted inches from the chalk board never finishing what she had started to write. She slowly spun on one toe and took a few steps toward me.

"I'm wrong? Well, aren't you uncharacteristically courageous? Please explain."

"Mercutio isn't in Hamlet. He's in Romeo and Juliet. He claimed his sword was his fiddlestick. He died when Tybalt stabbed him under Romeo's arm. And I just remembered his line, 'A plague on both your houses.'"

Nothing about her face changed, but she did blink twice. Her head tilted to the side, just like my neighbor's German Shepherd. She held the chalk in the air. "Vivian, come here please. I need you to write on the board for me."

Vivian hesitated but when Mrs. Keife looked directly at her, she got up.

"Please make a list on the board of those who agree with Von's explanation. Everyone who agrees with Von, raise your hand."

Just about everyone knew I had a C minus to D average for the year.

Only six people raised their hand. Vivian, willing to stand by a friend, put her name first and then wrote in the other five.

"Thank you, Vivian." Mrs. Keife took back the chalk. "Now, those of you with your name on the board will have no homework tonight. The rest of you are hereby assigned to re-read Act three of Romeo and Juliet." Then she winked at me so quickly I almost missed it. She spun and added my name to the list on the board.

How the hell did you know that Director Guy?

Oh, I love Shakespeare. Always have.

It suddenly hit me what he'd just said.

Oh yeah? What was the occasion?

Just like here. We covered it in high scho . . . . Well. Isn't that something. I couldn't tell you my teacher's name, fellow students, the name of the school, or any of that. But, I definitely liked Shakespeare a lot.

Well, thanks. Again. Once you reminded me, I began to remember Mercutio. Far out, man.

Well, since I occupy such an opportunistic location, I may as well take on some utilitarian purpose. Besides, that woman scares the hell out of you. I felt you panic inside.

Yeah. She has that effect on people.

Mrs. Keife quickly went on to the final bloody scene of Hamlet and to tricking other students into exposing if they'd actually read the play or not. But I'd made my mark for the day with her and she didn't call on me again.

Vivian, however, stared at me like some orangutan occupied my chair. "You don't know Shakespeare that well. I don't know Shakespeare that well," she whispered in a huff. "You reread Romeo and Juliet last night?" I tapped my head three times and went back to taking a few notes. Slowly Vivian's mouth opened and she mouthed, "The voice?" as she tapped her head. I shrugged and went back to my notes.

Toward the end of class Mrs. Keife called out, "All of you may want to consider reading over stories and notes from this year. Finals are next week and I won't be giving out review material for a few days. Best to prepare early." A few seconds after that the bell sounded for third hour.

Between classes, Vivian and I drifted along with the hallway herd. We could make out Derrick somewhere ahead coming toward us, his low cow moan bellowing away. Vivian quickly spread the story about my answering Mrs. Keife's trick question and saving six people from an extra assignment. When they heard about it, Julia, Moby, Charlie and Derrick pressed in close wanting details.

"Von. Don't tell me," They stood there gawking at me.

I nodded. "Yeah. He likes Shakespeare. I'd forgotten about Mercutio. Keife tried a trick question on me but Director Guy caught it."

"Director Guy," Moby muttered slowly turning a circle. Von, when we go to lunch, we have to talk," he added.

"No. No, we talk now," Julia said pushing me up against a locker. "You look at me Von. You and I have known each other since childhood. We've clowned around, we've played tricks on each other, but when we're done with that, we tell the real straight truth. Now you give it to me straight. Are you hearing a voice in your head?"

I'd seen her like this before. I said nothing but exaggerated my nodding.

"Is it something you're controlling? You making it happen?" she

30

added.

My nodding changed to shaking my head side to side. Julia with her hand on my chest, Charlie leaning with his hand on the lockers, Moby behind Julia with his chin resting on her shoulder and Derrick behind them, all four of them gawked at me. They seemed to want to say something but they didn't.

Moby reached past Julia pointing at me. "Von, you have to get this. There can't be an extra voice in your head."

"Yeah. Like you can even figure out what's happening in your own head," I reached forward and pushed his shoulder catching him off balance. He nearly fell. After we finished laughing at Moby, we broke up and headed for our next classes.

For a while, third hour American History turned out uneventful. Mr. Benedict always enjoyed the sound of his own lecturing voice and talked about the relationship between the United States and Japan that led to the beginning of WWII. We saw pictures from the 1927 Depression and took notes in preparation for a test. I purposefully laid low. But Director Guy was on to other things.

Von, I think I've scrutinized some of your memories. I find I'm able to access some of them.

What? Memories? Like what memories?

For example, that girl Moneen seated immediately behind you in English. First girl you ever kissed, correct?

The shock of Director Guy finding his way deeper into my head ran chills up my spine. I put down my pen, leaned forward with my fingers shading my eyes and forgot about taking notes. I feared some bug-like creature boring its way through my brain breaking into my past. I didn't

31

want him to know that it scared me. I tried to steady my breathing.

How did you do that?

Unknown. I'm unaware of the method. But I'd describe it as walking in a huge utterly dark cavern. One outstretches a hand to touch things but finds no resistance. There's nothing to feel or see. So, one wanders randomly. Without warning, a light shines but I can't say where the light is coming from. It's just present. Then, I can see and witness some bygone event, a memory. Only the area proximate to the memory glows and images associated with that memory make themselves known. A scene plays itself out, right there in front of me. It can flash by for just a second or endure for long minutes. There's no chronological order. By context, I come to understand what part of your life it originates from. I see things, listen to voices. Sometimes they multiply into the hundreds. I believe Mr. Benedict's video of the 1920s depression must have stimulated something. I couldn't tell you how to repeat the experience.

What other memories of mine have you found?

Oh, nothing really profound. Experiences that occurred during your growing up. You crashed in a big ditch when you were learning to ride your bike. Your father slid down to retrieve you. You both came out of it covered in mud. And then there's the time you caught ringworm from the cat and your parents decided to shave your head. You hid under the house. It took them two hours to find you. Oh. At one year of age, your mother and your Aunt Inez bundled you up to play in the snow. Your first exposure to snow, you were elated. You assisted in building a snowman the size of an adult.

What? Wait a minute. I don't have any aunt named Inez. And I'm pretty sure I didn't see snow until I was seven years old. This is New

Orleans. We hardly ever get snow.

But Von. I can see it in great clarity. You, your mom and your father's sister Inez. She lived right next door and . . .

My father has two brothers. He has no sisters. For a long moment, we were both silent. *D.G., I remember learning to ride a bike and falling into the ditch and all, and the ringworm infection I really hated, but I made my first snowball and threw it at my little brother when I was seven. Mom took a picture of that. Maybe that memory is yours?* Again, silence invaded our thinking.

But Von, it materialized by the same method that sponsored the other memories . . . and . . . well, I can't say you're wrong. Hmmm. How odd. Maybe I just retrieved a memory of my own. Fished it out of oblivion. Shazam, Von. Now what?

Now what? I don't know. I guess get more. But hey, as far as digging around in my stuff, don't go rewriting my history. No tampering, you know.

It wasn't intentional, Von. An inadvertent occurrence. I doubt I could change anything even if I wanted. Please don't agonize over this. When it started happening just now, I thought I should report it to you.

Yeah. I get it. Yeah. Let me know when anything changes. I need to know.

I played it off like it wasn't that important but deep inside I worried that Director Guy could tunnel so deeply into my mind. Suddenly, the bell went off for fourth hour.

I have P.E. this hour. Gotta go, I told Director Guy.

I didn't usually participate much in P.E. But today I felt like running, doing exercises and exerting myself, just so I could clear my head. I needed my blood to flow fast. Mostly, I wanted to make sure that I alone controlled my body. I had to make sure.

We chose teams for basketball and my team managed to squeak out a three point win. It ended up being lots of fun. None of these guys were part of my crew. None of these guys knew or cared about the latest weirdness in my head. After the game, we showered, sat in the bleachers and waited for the bell. When it rang, the herd thundered toward the cafeteria.

Chapter Three

{ Does a thought prove a person is alive? Cogito ergo sum? }

I couldn't believe Von's agility. Feeling his basketball maneuvers, feeling his wiry leg and calf muscles tense and release as he feigned, dodged, sent and received passes, feeling the ball's grid surface with each dribble, I marveled at his physical abilities. He had talents that any basketball coach would drool over. I remained silent, stupefied at what the kid did without thinking. When he charged the goal dribbling past defenders, he changed speed and direction with such dexterity I felt like I rode a rollercoaster.

Von sat in the bleachers after the game talking with Moby. As the bell rang for lunch break, he and Moby bolted for the cafeteria, scampered through the lunch line, slid around groups of students wrapped in conversation, grabbed a brown bag lunch from the cafeteria lady in line two and darted outside in time to call dibs on their favorite wooden picnic table on the outdoor deck. The shade of three mammoth oak trees protected them from the early May sun. I could tell this was a regularly practiced routine for this tight knit group because within a minute Charlie, Vivian and a new kid named Nick also claimed their places on the table top. Suddenly Julia showed up and stood before Von appraising him, up and down, very carefully.

"Vivian just told me what happened in English," she said. "Mercutio? You hate Shakespeare. This voice again? I'm getting a little worried about you." I felt her touch Von's forehead.

Von nodded as he sat chewing his ham sandwich. He reached up and grasped Julia's finger, still against his forehead. Though he chewed and smiled simultaneously, I sensed he was about to speak, but he didn't. Julia must have sensed it too because her eyes flashed expectation, a slight smile on her face. But just then, three more friends, Derrick and two girls I didn't yet know, joined the group, sitting at or standing next to the table. As they arrived, Von let go of Julia's finger.

"Yeah, what voice?" Cherry, one of the new girls, asked. "I've been hearing eerie stuff about you Von."

"He thinks he has this extra voice in his head. But it's smarter than him . . . as if," Derrick said waving a hand at his own head. "I got to thinking Von. Suppose it's a dead guy? AAAHHHH."

Is he always so obnoxious? I asked Von.

Oh yeah. Never stops, came Von's reply.

Nick, the new kid, smiled. "Yeah. Derrick told me about this voice. Suppose it starts slowly taking over more and more of your mind, controlling you. AAAHHHH." Nick high-fived Moby and Derrick.

"Biting us on the neck in the next few days," Cherry added grinning. Four of the group hollered 'AAAHHHH' in unison.

"I'll make sure to brush my teeth if it gets to that point." Von answered in a drab monotone.

Your friends are having a bit of fun with this.

Clowns. What do you think? Are you a ghost? A dead Director Guy?

No. No. I have a functioning mind, which is obviously alive, with math and language abilities. If I were dead . . . there'd be . . . well . . . no response at all, I guess. It again struck me that I had no evidence, certainly no proof of what I was telling him.

36

But who's to say the feelings you're having are yours? Von reasoned. *Couldn't they be mine? Like you picked up some of my memories?*

Overall, I'm uncertain. I answered, a bit confused. *But if I go by my awareness, I feel separate from you, with my own sensitivities and very few memories. Does a thought prove a person is alive? Cogito ergo sum? I think, therefore I am?*

Oh yeah. I've heard that before. Who said that? Von asked.

René Descartes. He was a French philosopher. And you're the only one that can sense my thoughts. So, I'm alive to you. For now, at least. If I'm dead, then I'll probably just waste away and disappear. Honestly, I can't prove anything.

I noticed Vivian sitting on the other side of Charlie intently typing into her smartphone. *What's Vivian doing, Von?*

Von watched her for a second before catching on.

"Vivian, Director Guy wants to know what you're doing?" he asked, his gaze focusing in on her phone.

"Well, tell him I just put him on Twitter," she perked up.

"What? Twitter! Are you nuts! I told you to keep this just between us. I don't want the whole school thinking I'm out of my mind. Don't send. Delete it."

Vivian had already pressed send. Kids at other tables checked their phones. A few turned toward Von and voices began calling out.

"Voice in your head? You mean you finally figured out thinking?"

"Extra voice? Is that like a spare tire?"

"Director Guy? You gave it a name?"

"Coo coo. Coo coo. Dat boy loooosin' it"

Ok Von. Remind me. This Twitter thing sounds . . . well . . . ominous.

It's social media, on the Internet, he answered with a huff. *It's mostly bullshit, rumors and stuff like that, but it can destroy a person's reputation.*

Von lowered his head and glared toward Vivian. "You know Vivian, I know you have personal stuff you don't want told."

"Oh, you don't want to get in a broadcasting contest with me baby. I got stuff on everyone here. Everyone," Vivian squeezed off a smart ass wink at Von.

"Vivian, play nice," Julia said.

"Oh y'all. It's all in fun. Who's gonna take it seriously? An extra voice in his head. For real? He's playing us for all its worth." Vivian slammed her phone case shut.

Charlie sat looking sideways at her. "I saw you put it on Facebook before you did Twitter."

Von jumped to his feet. "Facebook!"

Wow Von. Slow down. Is Facebook like Twitter?

Yeah. But you don't understand. Three students got 'doxed' in 'cook sessions' by Vivian, all of them since Christmas. She used texting, 4Chan, Yik Yak, Kik and just slammed their reputations. Vivian can be hardcore man.

Von stood glaring at Vivian. His brown bag lunch still contained an apple and milk but he slammed it into the trash can as his temper ramped up quickly.

"I guess having my trust doesn't matter to you," Von growled at Vivian as he took steps toward her.

Charlie quickly came off the table blocking Von's progress toward Vivian. Von stepped back, slung his backpack on as he continued glaring at Vivian. Charlie kept one hand out toward Von as he cautiously finished his milk. Julia stood and stuffed her apple into her pocket. Vivian sat rolling her eyes, now suddenly silent. All the other students stood watching dumbfounded, the grins gone from their faces.

Perhaps you shouldn't give out information about me, I told Von.

He turned and stormed down the sidewalk along building two. I heard footsteps behind Von and assumed it would be Charlie, Julia and Moby about to catch up with him, but just then Von turned into the boy's rest room. The others waited outside.

Throw some water in your face. Cool down, I suggested. *I'm glad you didn't hit her.*

I wasn't gonna hit her, Von ranted. *I just wanted to get up in her face a bit.*

But suddenly, he was at me full force.

You see what I mean? This ain't fun, Director Guy! Having you in my head. I don't know how to handle it. I have absolutely no idea, no experience with this at all. And now big mouth Vivian who loves to embarrass people . . . I don't know why I even hang around with her.

Maybe you could use a cover-story? I told Von. *Start denying everything. It's all a funny joke you pulled on your friends. You could claim Vivian was the most gullible.*

I could tell the idea had some kind of appeal to Von. He hesitated, took a deeper breath and looked into the mirror. The silence of the rest room seemed to hum as he peered at himself. He didn't answer, but dried his hands, tightened his backpack straps and walked outside.

"Ok guys. I'm gonna need your help," he told Charlie, Julia and Moby. "I need only you guys knowing that the Director Guy voice is real.

Yes. I'm actually really hearing a voice. Yes, it helped me in math and English. But I need your help to tell everyone else it's a hoax. Just a practical joke I used to fool my friends. You guys think that'll work?"

Charlie stood up straighter and took a deep breath. Julia took a step closer to Von, staring into his eyes.

"Ok. So you really are hearing something . . . a voice. It talks to you," Julia recited.

Von nodded looking directly into her very green eyes.

"Look Von. If that's what you need, I'll do it," Charlie said, a serious look on his face.

"I'm down with that," Moby agreed. "We'll have to watch out for Derrick. He's been blabbing his head off about it. He loves the latest 'news'."

"Count me in," Julia said. "But you have to make sure to keep us informed on how this is playing out for you. You know? I'm . . . worried, Von. I want you to be ok."

Charlie nodded and put his hand on Von's shoulder. "We can do this. And yes, Derrick has been talking all morning."

Moby nodded. "Yeah, and I have serious information on Vivian that'll shut her up."

The bell rang. Everyone touched knuckles and split up for fifth hour class.

Chapter Four

{ "Von. If you're having mental difficulties, I'd suggest we talk." }

"It has come to our attention that you may have some kind of problem, Von," Mr. Tomblyn, the head guidance counselor, said to me as he and I stood alone in the hall. It angered me that he'd called me out of Art II class for this. Controlling who knew about Director Guy was proving difficult.

Von, who is this guy? You just tensed. I ignored Director Guy. He'd have to wait.

I snuck a glance through the little classroom door window at Nick, Cherry and Sammy Daxtal; we all shared the same classroom table. They looked back at me, no longer paying attention to the Stephen Hawkins' video, Mrs. Wrathe's presentation for this hour. They probably wondered what kind of trouble I was in.

Mr. Tomblyn's eyes went from my head to my feet. I knew he didn't approve of what he saw. Tomblyn and I had argued lots of times and I wasn't planning on taking any crap from him over dress code.

"No Mr. Tomblyn, I don't have any problems you need to worry about. Why would you say that?"

Von, who is this? D.G.'s curiosity had him on high alert but I still ignored him.

"Well, we've counted over two hundred and fifty Twitter messages so far about you having some kind of extra voice in your head," Tomblyn insisted in that bossy voice of his.

"Twitter. Really? Your source is unreliable," I answered in my own bossiness.

"I can show you all the messages, Von," Tomblyn said as he drew his smartphone from his pocket.

"Teachers tell us Wikipedia and other Internet sites are not reliable sites for research, that we shouldn't use them, that they can't be trusted. But here you are using Twitter as though it knows the inside of my head better than I do."

"Von. If you're having some kind of mental difficulties, I'd suggest you come in and we talk about . . . "

"Mental difficulties? Really? Would you quit talking about me like some kind of sicko. We simply joked around. They had played practical jokes on me. I played one back. I don't have any voice in my head. And, exactly how are you planning on proving what, if anything, is going on inside my head?"

Careful Von. If you overreact, that could just make him more curious.

D.G. Shut up.

"Proof? Von, this isn't a trial. I'd like you to tell me what's going on. Volunteer the information. You know. Counseling."

"Ok. Fine. I have nothing to volunteer. Now if you don't mind, Mrs. Wrathe is presenting a really fine lesson right now that I'm interested in. Ok?"

With that I reached for the doorknob but Tomblyn's hand came up and rested against my shoulder.

"Von, you should come in and talk to us. Mrs. Frans is also very concerned."

I shrugged Tomblyn's hand off my shoulder, stepped past him and closed the door behind me. Mrs. Fran of all people. She treated me only a little better than Tomblyn did.

Von, you have to understand that your temper can fuel their intrusion into . . .

D.G. Really man. Back off. It's my issue . . .

To be exact, it's not just yours, Von. They are talking about me. Being in your head. Which I am. I simply think a cooler temper would serve you most effectively. Overreacting will drag them in on top of you. That's all.

Says the guy with no memory? With no body? No past? I got this. Tomblyn is always on my case about something. Let me watch the video.

I took my place back at my table, Sammy, Cherry and Nick giving me questioning stares. We all went back to watching the video, but then I noticed Cherry, just to my right, with her backpack on her lap. Deep within the backpack her phone glowed as she scrolled through Twitter. She glanced up at me and showed the screen my way.

"What gives, Von?" she whispered. "There's nearly three hundred tweets at #Vonsheadvoice."

I leaned right and gave the phone a closer look. "Really? What are they saying?"

"Mostly, the usual wisecracks. But one guy, some psychologist, says he has a practice treating people like that." Our eyes met and Cherry shrugged her shoulders. "Just saying, Von. I mean, could it be some kind of condition?"

Something in me stepped back. I kept my thoughts away from D.G. Looking at Cherry, I wondered if she had a point. Had some virus invaded my brain causing me to generate the voice myself? Was I delusional or schizophrenic? The bell for class change brought me out of my thoughts long enough for me to gather my things. But then my worrying started up again as I dragged along following Nick, Cherry and Sammy Daxtal to last hour class. Bi-polar disorder, psychosis, let's see, maybe schizophrenia, hmmm. I wonder.

We all had the same last hour class, Biology II, and just as we reached the doorway, Julia and Charlie met up with us. Charlie bumped me against the doorframe by forcing himself through the doorway with me.

"Oversized loads should use the loading dock, klutz," I barked at him.

Charlie laughed. "Hey, you ain't big enough to talk to me like that."

"I don't know these two children. Never seen them before," Julia said from behind us.

In class, Ms. Jourst stood leaning against the lecture desk, surveying the group, a slight smile on her face. Her fingers fiddled with the ends of her hair falling across her right shoulder.

Whoa. Von. Is that your teacher? D.G. asked right away.

Yes. Ms. Jourst teaches Biology II. What do you think?

She demonstrates quite a sexual presence, I'd say.

Did sexy women get to D.G., I wondered? But I didn't ask. Ms. Elaine Jourst was smoking hot and had her own way of doing everything. She was twenty-five years old, beautiful, fresh out of college and into her first teaching assignment. Her usual short skirts and cleavage had gained everyone's attention throughout our Junior year. All her students had been amazed at how wildly she danced at prom with one of the football coaches. Our principal, Mr. Sears, once stood in the hall trying to explain why she should dress more conservatively. With the classroom door wide open, we'd all listened and giggled as she'd put her hand on his chest and said, "But Donald. Tell the truth. You like how I dress." Sears had gone silent and just walked off.

"Good afternoon," Ms. Jourst began. "I have a PowerPoint lecture that will compare and contrast the differences in the reproductive processes between plants and animals. Take notes everyone. Information given here will be all over your final exam."

Everyone began searching their backpacks for notebooks, laptops or iPads. Ms. Jourst, impatient as usual, started right away. She strolled around the room lecturing and as she passed next to my desk, quietly slid an index card note under my opened Biology book. It read: Von. I'll need you to help with inventory after school today.

A jolt of surprise grabbed me. I had completely forgotten that last Friday Ms. Jourst had approached me after class saying that she needed someone to stay after school now and then to help her in the biology lab storeroom. "I'm thinking you could use a few extra points," she had told me.

The offer had surprised me. Something about her smile, those gray-blue eyes and the coy expression, yeah, it made me hesitate, but only for a moment. I admit I agreed to it because she was so much fun to look at. And for sure, I could always use the extra points.

Wow. The hottie teacher and you, alone after school? And the principal allows her to dress in such a provocative fashion? How can a young man learn at all? I just ignored D.G.'s surprise.

45

I smiled back at Jourst to disguise my forgetfulness and nodded that I understood. But then I noticed that Sammy Daxtal, Charlie and Nick were turning and glaring at me. Julia stopped digging in her backpack, slowly turned toward me and, I don't know, her eyes were bigger and more serious. Charlie closed his eyes and slowly shook his head. Sammy developed a smirk on his face.

These kids know something, D. G. muttered.

Umm hum. They often do. I can get Charlie to tell me later.

Ms. Jourst's PowerPoint lecture used up the entire class period. As class ended and the others left the room, I shouldered my backpack and happened to notice Julia's pink spiral Biology notebook still on the rack under her chair. She'd left quickly and forgotten it. I picked it up, planning to get it to her on my walk home. I moved to the front of the classroom where Ms. Jourst waited. She stood, put her hand on my shoulder and handed me a clipboard. She told me where to start and what to record in each column. I left my backpack and Julia's notebook on the lecture table and got started in the storeroom.

The biology lab storage room's layout was long and so narrow that only one person could walk through at a time. I found the glass beakers in a lower cabinet, sat cross legged on the floor and started counting. Through the storage room doorway, I saw Ms. Jourst working at her desk grading papers.

The janitor, an older guy named Bill, came through. She greeted him, they talked just a bit and she went back to grading, him to sweeping. After fifteen minutes, Bill told her he was done and said goodbye. She followed him to the door, said thanks and clicked the door shut.

Moments later, she entered the storeroom and I thought she

wanted to get past me to reach the far end of the storeroom. I stood, squeezed forward, my stomach against the counter, to allow her space to go by. She stopped, looked at me and her smile grew wider. She turned her stomach toward the wall and began to slowly squeeze past, our rumps rubbing slowly across each other's.

"Oh well goodness Von. You must enjoy pressing up on me like that," she said just as she got past.

"Sorry. It's such a small space," I said deciding not to deny it. Hell, it had felt good.

"Sorry, you say? I think you might have enjoyed it," she answered quickly. "Huh? Tell the truth."

Oh oh, Von. What is she doing?

I couldn't help but grin. I shrugged and wobbled my head around.

"Go ahead. Admit it," Jourst kept on. "You liked it."

I chuckled, giggled. "Well, what can I say. I am a guy."

Careful Von. Try not to encourage her. I smell a rat.

"A guy, huh?" Jourst repeated. "Maybe less guy and more man."

I chuckled in response and recorded the number of test tubes in the lower cabinet.

She turned, took two steps away and slowly bent over, reaching down to a lower shelf for a calibrated cylinder. As she bent, her short skirt rose higher exposing the backs of her thighs. The way she moved had me hooked and I liked seeing her smooth legs.

"You're not looking me over again, are you?" she said as she slowly stood upright and turned toward me.

She has a hidden agenda, Von. Get out. You can't run with these dogs.

"Just doing inventory, Ms. J." I said as I sat on the floor again and started counting test tube racks. But then, she stepped toward me and just stood there looking down at me.

"You're not trying to trap me in here, are you?"

I looked up at her staring down at me. I smiled. "No. No. I'll be glad to let you pass," I chuckled and stood again.

Von, she's dangerous. This isn't a high school girl. Von! Von? But she had my attention and I couldn't answer D.G.

She pressed her hand to my chest and started to squeeze by, this time face to face. She stopped midway and leaned into me, her breasts pressing into my chest.

"You know, this little job might turn out well for you. It only requires two things. First, be discreet and secondly, be a man. You know what discreet means, right Von?" she whispered and leaned her face closer to mine.

Von, you're dealing with dynamite. Get out!

"Yeah. I'm not great in English, but I know that one. Like keeping things to yourself. Secret like."

Are you kidding me. Leave! This woman will chew you up and spit you out.

"Good Von. And, you are a man, right Von? "You've had girls before, haven't you?" Our noses were only an inch apart.

"Well, I've had them but they haven't had me." I muttered with no idea what the devil that meant.

What! Concentrate. You have to go. Just go. Run.

"Oh," Jourst smiled. "Well, we could take care of that ourselves." Jourst said as she pressed her cheek against mine. I could smell a slightly berry flavored lip gloss. Our lips met and then pressed against each other. She began to pull my shirt up, un-tucking it from my jeans just as her tongue pressed between my lips.

Oh no. Not the clothes. I'm telling you, Von, leave the clothes on.

I dropped the clipboard. My hands went to her back, pulled her blouse upward out of her skirt. She pressed against me, kissing me hard. She held one hand behind my neck pulling me down toward her. The other hand began to edge down my stomach toward my crotch.

Do you really want to be known as this teacher's sex toy! D.G. demanded.

I grabbed her lower wrist stopping its downward progress. The way my friends had looked at me flashed across my mind. I forced my head to the side making our lips slide across each other's and managed to break the kiss.

"Some of the others gave me a funny look when you handed me that note," I whispered to her.

She pulled back a bit and looked at me.

"You've had other guys in this closet, haven't you?" I went on.

I felt her shoulders sag and it was her turn to not answer.

"Hey Von, are you here?" a voice called from the classroom.

"Yeah, I'm here. You forgot your notebook," I hollered back.

Jourst's expression went serious and she shook her head at me. But I started sliding sideways, got away from Elaine Jourst and stepped through the store room doorway. Julia stood there smiling, her books cradled against her chest.

"You forgot your notebook," I said as I picked it up and handed it to her across the lecture table. Though she took the notebook, curiosity

49

crossed her face as she looked at me.

"What's on your face?" she asked.

I wiped my mouth. "Ahh . . .   yeah. I've been doing   . . . inventory," I muttered pointing into the storeroom.

"Where's Ms. Jour . . . ?" Julia's eyes flicked to the storeroom doorway and her smile melted from her face.

"Julia," Ms. Jourst said leaning against the doorway.

I glanced at Elaine Jourst, wishing she would have stayed in the storeroom but, no, there she stood with her blouse twisted to the side and her berry flavored lip gloss smeared. I looked back to Julia but she'd already turned and headed for the classroom doorway. She was gone in a second.

I turned toward Jourst. She seemed unaffected with her messed up hair, her blouse twisted and her smeared lips. The doorway Julia had just disappeared through felt as hollow as the pit of my stomach. The sexual heat I'd enjoyed turned to ice in my veins.

"Damn it. Aww hell," I grumbled.

I slung my backpack on and jogged toward the classroom doorway.

"Oh, come on, Von," Jourst called from the storage closet. "Honey, high school crushes never last anyway."

I drew up short, turned and walked back a few steps, facing her. "I won't do that inventory job. Not me. I don't want it. I can get by on my own points." I turned, jogged out into the hallway and looked both ways but couldn't see Julia in either direction.

Oh boy, D. G. muttered. *Julia looked distraught.*

Of all the crap luck. I gotta find her.

I fear she won't be happy, D.G. said.

I stormed down the hall checking the side entrances, looking in the locker coves. What was she feeling? Would she hate me? I turned and kicked the brick wall. "Shit," I screamed. "Where did she go?"

Look, I am cognizant you're frustrated. I doubt that . . .

Shut up! D.G. Man. Shut up. Just shut up. Damned extra voice in my head crap.

I huffed my way down the hall, kicked the exit door open and stomped down the steps, my fists clinched. I scanned the campus in every direction but only saw three small groups of students standing around waiting to leave. Julia wasn't anywhere. Suddenly, my name blasted through the air.

"Von Gialanto, report to the guidance counselor's office right away please." I stood there. The cone-shaped speaker bolted to the side of the building hollered out again. "Von Gialanto to the counselor's office. Your parents are here, Von. Please hurry." I stepped back a few steps still taking in this electronic bull horn mouth that kept blaring out my name. How could they know so fast? Jourst and I were only together in the lab closet for a minute or maybe two.

Von, that's your name, right?

Yeah. But how could they know? Did you see a security camera in that lab closet? How could the office know so quickly?

I don't know Von. I didn't see any camera.

Suddenly my feet froze to the sidewalk. *Oh my god. You don't think Julia would have . . . told on me . . . would she?*

I hesitated saying this earlier Von, but might Julia have left her notebook on purpose? If she suspected Ms. Jourst and you might . . . ahhh.

51

Well, returning to get the notebook would provide an excuse to go back and check on the situation, as it were.

I froze. D.G.'s idea scared me so much that I didn't even try to answer it. Could Julia get that angry at me? Anyway, however the office had found out, they must know. Well great. Jourst wants to manhood me and I get blamed for it. Just great. I slowly started marching toward the office.

Chapter Five

{ "I've been talking with it. Is that bad? Should I just start ignoring it? Is it like, poisoning me?" }

As Von trudged across campus toward the administrative offices, I attempted to inform him of my latest development. *Von. I got another image. I'm rather sure of it,* I told him. *Back there in the biology lab storeroom, when Jourst kissed you.*

Leave me alone, D.G. If they saw me and Jourst together . . .

Jourst hugged and kissed you, Von. She did it. If they saw it, she'll be the one in major trouble. But listen, please. When she kissed you, I saw a woman's face. It just appeared without notice. Not Ms. Jourst. Some other woman, attractive, somehow familiar. Someone I cared for. I saw the side of her face clearly, as if she were really close, maybe hugging or kissing me. I think I just had a second memory. Maybe I'm starting to rememb . . .

Congratulations, D.G. Now if you'll excuse me, I have to go get expelled or suspended or whatever.

It thrilled me that I'd discovered another memory, but to convince Von to join in any celebration of the fact would be impossible. He was approaching panic. His pulse pumped much faster than usual as he entered the counselor's office. Mr. Tomblyn led Von into the counselor's meeting room where his parents, George and Martha, sat, along with a woman and man I didn't know.

"Von, this is Dr. Raoul Kalchavic, a neurological pathologist from

Tulane University," Mr. Tomblyn said gesturing. "We've asked him to join us today. Please have a seat."

Von stood silent, not moving toward any chair. "Neurologic. So brain scientist, right?"

"Very good, Von. That's correct," Dr. Kalchavic said, smiling so intensely that his lips drew back exposing the gums of almost every tooth in his mouth. His brown corduroy coat with leather patched elbows and green bow tie blared intellectual nerd.

"Pathology, as in disease, right?" Von added with suspicion.

"Very good, Von. Correct again," Dr. Kalchavic said, his smile still radiating.

"Ahhh . . . and of course you remember Mrs. Yvonne Frans, your junior class counselor," Mr. Tomblyn said smiling. There was a lot of excessive grinning going on and I could tell it made Von nervous.

"Please Von. Sit here," Mrs. Frans said sliding back the chair next to her.

"You feelin' ok kid?" George, Von's father, chirped.

"Yeah Dad. I'm fine." Von gave his mother a look, shrugged and moved to the chair next to Mrs. Frans. He strained to appear relaxed, but inside his stomach churned and his left hand trembled though he hid it by gripping his heavy backpack.

As soon as Von was seated, Mrs. Frans started. "Von, Mr. Tomblyn and I have had it brought to our attention that hundreds of students, many your close friends, are reporting that you have some sort of extra voice in your . . . ahh . . . brain. This concerns us. We've spoken to your parents here and they were not aware of this. They report no such statements from you about it. So, first of all, we'd like to hear from you. Could you just speak freely about it?" Everyone stared at him.

Take a deep breath, Von, I told him. *You can do this.*

Von breathed deeply and I felt a tiny grin starting on his face. *Well hell, Julia didn't tell on me. This isn't about Jourst and her touchy feely session.*

Concentrate on this, Von. We'll handle Julia's feelings later.

"Well, it's just us chickens in here, you know?" Von said pointing to his head.

"No! NO!" his mother hollered across the table. "You are not gonna just pitch this off as some silly joke. You are NOT going to just ignore us again. You show us no respect and ignore us at least half the time. You will answer, or so help me, I'll have you put in a hospital, do you understand me mister!"

"Martha. Martha. Please. Let's keep our shirt on here, ok?" George cautioned. Martha gave a side glance at her husband, slid back in her chair and got quiet.

"Yes. We must let the boy speak," Dr. Kalchavic cautioned. "He is the only one that actually knows what occurs in his mind. Even parents cannot know this. So, please Von, tell us what you experience."

"Look, it was just a practical joke that got out of hand, that I played on some friends," Von began. "Of course, now, they've figured out a way to turn it back on me by putting it all over Twitter and Facebook, pretending it's serious. I'm not having any actual trouble with my mind, I'm not attacking people in the hallways, I'm friendly with teachers, I won't go home and hurt anyone. I'm fine. I'm fine. It was a joke. That's all."

At this point, I sensed Von's breathing calming a bit, his heart rate approached normal and his left hand loosened its grip on the backpack.

"Von, several of the comments on Twitter stated that you've been using marijuana, going out somewhere smoking with friends, that you first experienced this voice while you were high and that's when you told your friends about the extra voice in your head," Mr. Tomblyn said tapping his fist softly on the table.

Von's hand started jittering. He made sure to keep it on his lap below the table. I felt the muscles on his face tense and his eyes widen.

"Von. I found three marijuana cigarettes a few weeks back in your sock drawer," his father said, his face downcast. "I figured it for teenage indiscretion, so I flushed them."

"Ahh, this now becomes interesting," Dr. Raoul Kalchavic interrupted. "Tell me Von. Did you use the marijuana first or did you hear the voice first? It's very important to know the order things happened, you see. If the voice occurred first, you may have been attempting to self-medicate. To try to reduce the effect of the voice in your head by getting stoned. Some people try alcohol, some LSD, cocaine, all kinds of things. So, Von. Which came first, voice or marijuana?"

I could tell the room was closing in on Von. His nerves were so on edge that his left foot, left knee and left hand all were shaking.

"No no. You don't understand. I used the marijuana first. Then . . . I heard . . . "

Careful Von, I jumped in quickly. *He's crafty. That was a trick question.* I waited for a response from Von but none came.

"So then. You have been hearing a voice. Yes?" Dr. Kalchavic leaned toward Von, eyes sharply focused, bearing down on him.

"Von. Don't keep it from us son. We're your parents. We love you. Just let us help you with this," George said offering an outstretched hand.

"Does this voice occur mostly when you are feeling down? Maybe depressed about something?" Dr. Kalchavic asked. "And have you felt stressed out lately?"

"No. I mean, I don't know. What stress?" Von said stiffly. "I get up and go to school. Go to classes. I'm passing. I know my grades could be better but I am passing. It's all one level of stress, all the same. Just plain ole everyday life. Nothing I can't handle."

The psychiatrist leaned over the table an inch more. "Von. I realize that you are nervous, suddenly getting a lot of unwanted attention and to add to that, I, a complete stranger, show up and ask crazy questions. But you must understand. This can be very serious.

I am from Switzerland, graduated from University of Zurich and I have studied illnesses of the mind for over thirty years. I receive many phone calls from other such experts asking me to help them with different cases. Voices occurring in a person's thinking can indicate schizophrenia, which usually develops in late high school or early college. Or it could indicate general paranoia, bipolar affective disorder, early onset of dementia, severe depression or several other mental conditions. So, this conversation we're having at this table right now is a very important point in your life. If you lie about this, if you try to hide it, it could harm you in a most horrible fashion. I've seen it. I have many patients that hear voices in their head. I'm quite familiar with this. So please. Even though we've just met, please trust me. I'm certainly not here to harm you or put you in a straight jacket or lock you up in some hospital or anything like that."

Dr. Kalchavic's piercing eyes made Von's forehead muscles wrinkle. I couldn't hold back. *Von, I think this guy will figure you out even if you don't want him to. He's practiced at this. He's good. Remember what I said earlier about drawing too much attention to yourself? Maybe just tell him a little bit, just enough to . . . .*

He's telling me you could be a disease, Von responded. *Like, you could be a poison. You already dug into some of my memories. What next?"*

A pin dropping would have made the sound of a baseball bat hitting the floor. Von leaned back in his chair, his eyes still locked onto Dr. Kalchavic. He looked over at his mother and father. His eyes moved around the room, over shelves, the walls, the table's surface. But his attention wasn't on things outside himself. His thinking plunged far out of my reach and I sensed he didn't want my opinion right then.

Suddenly, I became nervous. This could be a really bad turn of events for me. If this psychiatrist was able to root me out of Von's consciousness, what would become of me? I would have no way to discover how my landing in Von's consciousness had occurred, or how to reverse it.

Dr. Kalchavic broke the silence. "The main thing I need to know, and that you need to be most honest about, is the nature of the voice you are hearing. Tell me the kind of voice it is. First, is it two voices talking about you as if you aren't there, as if you don't matter? Or second, is it one voice commenting on your actions, your behaviors? Or third, is it like hearing your own thoughts pronounced in your head as though spoken aloud?"

"Well, it's definitely not the third one," Von said right away.

"That's just thinking. That's normal for me. I have my own thoughts, so what?"

"So, is it the first or the second?"

"It's not two people talking."

"So then, it's the second situation. The voice comments on your behaviors?"

Von didn't answer. Instead, he glanced at Mr. Tomblyn and then at Mrs. Frans. Then he sat back and looked hard at Dr. Kalchavic. The psychiatrist straightened. I could tell the shrink had recognized Von's body language. He smiled.

"I would like to have the room alone with Von, please." Dr. Kalchavic smiled at all the others as they gathered their things, stood and left the room. George, the last to exit, closed the door behind him.

"Don't worry Von. I am quite used to protecting people's privacy. Everything is completely confidential."

Von nodded and leaned forward onto his elbows. "It's one voice. I've been talking with it. Whole conversations. Is that bad? Should I just start ignoring it? Is it like poisoning me? How do I handle . . . "

"Relax. Relax. Relax Von," Dr. Kalchavic said, one assuring hand in the air. "Now tell me this. Are you making the voice say the things it says, or does it seem independent of you?"

"I have no control over it at all. It has its own free will. Some of the things it says really surprises me. It's a man, older than me. He's smart and . . . I don't know what to do."

"Listen to me carefully, Von," Dr. Kalchavic went on. "As I said, I have many patients that hear voices in their head. Sometimes, I cannot completely cure these people. The voice still remains. But, some of the time we have been able to arrange things so that they are able to live a productive, happy life even though it's still there. Most of their friends and work associates don't even know my patient has a voice in the head. Some of these patients just do face-to-face counseling, some take medication, well, we'll see about that much later. So, please, don't start obsessively worrying about all this." The doctor thought a moment and then went on.

"Now, I want you to say nothing to these school counselors about our conversation," Dr. Kalchavic continued. "They don't need to know any more and they aren't trained for this kind of thing. Also, it's not good that fellow students know of this voice. Don't speak with your friends about it anymore. Most people will judge you harshly about this because it scares them. They aren't trained for this. But I have years of experience and I'm quite used to it.

"We will start with once-a-week sessions," Dr. Kalchavic said nodding. "You and me. First, I must get much more information from you about what is happening in your head. So, once a week we will meet. I'll arrange it with your parents. Ok? You have any questions?"

"Yeah. Should I talk with the thing? I mean, I even gave him a name."

Actually, Von, we agreed upon that designation in the heat of a very nervous moment. I wouldn't exactly call it a name.

"Well, does this voice ever just take over your life? Make you do things? Control what you say to people around you?"

"Oh. No. In fact, he apologizes for being in my head."

"It doesn't sound like it will harm you. So, if you speak with it, that's fine for now. But if it attempts to control you at all, you should tell your parents and have them call me. Ok? Anything else?"

Hummph. Suddenly, I'm an 'it', I complained.

Von shook his head. The doctor reached over and shook Von's hand, picked up his briefcase and exited. Left alone in the room, Von took in a deep breath and slowly let it out.

Are you ok, Von? I asked. The only answer was a bleak silence. *I assure you Von. I'm not trying to poison you and I would never harm you. Please believe me.* He looked around, found his backpack beneath the table and strapped it on. I could tell he considered answering me but he didn't.

As he exited the meeting room, we both saw Mr. Tomblyn behind his desk and Mrs. Frans, across the room behind hers, both with serious looks on their face. Von aimed his eyes straight ahead and marched between the two desks.

"We have a few more questions, Von," Mr. Tomblyn said. But Von ignored the man and walked out of the room. In the hallway, Dr. Kalchavic finished a conversation with George and Martha. He shook hands with each of them and left the building. Von's mother looked at him with big sorrowful eyes, his father with a small grin.

"We're headed home. Hop in the car," his dad said.

Von shook his head. "Naw. I need to walk. It isn't far."

"Oh Von. Couldn't you just get in the car?" his mother fussed. "I'd rather you not be gallivanting around all over the roads . . . "

Von did an about face and walked away leaving his mother speechless. He used a back exit to leave the administration building and started walking home.

Director Guy

Chapter Six

{ "You could be under attack by Satan or one of his minions." }

Walking home, I couldn't stop my mind from going over and over what Dr. Raoul Kalchavic had told me. I thought about schizophrenia, bipolar disorders and all the mental illnesses that might be happening to me. Now and then, D.G. would speak to me but I was in no mood. I ignored him. How could I trust some voice that had just arrived and wanted space in my head "to figure things out." It seemed to me that Dr. Kalchavic already had it figured out, had plenty of experience at this and maybe I was very lucky that the counselors had brought him in to warn me. As I walked down Esplanade, I arrived at Margarita Paris' Voodoo shop. I looked through the open shop door for Julia. I just stood there on the sidewalk trying to decide if I should enter. Julia gradually emerged from out of the shop's darkness, her large eyes and pursed lips showing disappointment. Her cheeks looked like she'd been crying. I stepped toward her but she shook her head and raised her palm at me. For a moment or two we stood just looking into each other's eyes. Slowly, she turned and walked back into the dark regions of the Voodoo shop. She didn't want to talk. What a day this had been.

Pushing through the back door at my house, I snuck through the little mud room where sweaters and hats hung on hooks and came upon Mom in the kitchen. Her eyes were red and I knew she'd been crying. Well, that or it was the onion she sliced on the cutting board. Right away she put the knife down and approached me.

"You can't just keep ignoring your father and me. We are your parents. You have to tell us when something like this happens. You can't just leave us out of your life. We can't just guess that you're ok while you're hearing voices in your head." We stood there looking into each other's eyes for a few seconds. "And we've arranged for you to see Dr. Kalchavic tomorrow afternoon. You must go, Von. Please don't avoid . . . "

"Ok. Ok Mom. I'll go. Just let me know when and where. I'm not afraid of the guy," I sidestepped around her and headed for the stairs.

"Why wouldn't you tell us? Why hide it? We're your parents. You have to inform us if you're having trouble with . . . "

"Because," I said angrily turning toward her, "I don't like you awful-izing everything about me. You turn it into the end of the world, like I'm gonna crash and burn in the next few seconds, like I can't think or handle any situation at all, like I'm completely stupid. That's why. Believe me. I would have never told you any of this if you hadn't found it out on your own. Just let me know where I have to meet the shrink."

As I started up the stairs, I realized that Harper and Oma stood at the top landing and had been watching Mom and me argue. I climbed past them and went into my room. Within seconds, Harper and Oma stood at my door silently watching me. Oma's poker face hid her feelings as usual, but Harper's worried look seemed to explode off his face. I sat on my bed and patted the mattress next to me, my signal that they had permission to enter. Harper lost his flip-flops, hopped on the bed and sat Indian style, ready to talk. Oma liked to sit on the edge and dangle her feet.

"Mom's been crying since she got home," Harper complained. "She keeps whispering to herself about voices in your head. What

64

voices?" Oma's poker face hadn't flinched.

"Ok. Look. I'm not really changed or any different from before. I'm still gonna be the same big, mean brother that picks on you and will still sometimes tell you stuff Mom and Dad won't. Ok?"

"But," Oma added. These two could act as a tag team against me at times.

Talk to them on their level, Von, D.G. said.

Butt out. You don't tell me how to talk to them, I fired back. *This is my family. If it weren't for you, I wouldn't have to explain anything.* D.G. got quiet. But my face had flashed anger and Oma had noticed it. I dropped the frown and smiled again. She squinted slightly, reading my every emotion like a hawk.

"But," she repeated.

"Ok. One night ago, this voice started up in my head. It has a mind of its own. I don't control it at all. It isn't mean, but it doesn't belong there. It's new. Just started. So, I'll go to a brain doctor tomorrow and talk with him. He knows how to handle these kinds of things. I don't know. Maybe he'll give me a shot or something. Don't worry about it, ok. I'm fine."

"Does it hurt?" Harper asked, his nose wrinkling.

"Naw. No pain at all. I'm fine. Really."

"Does it bother you?" Oma asked. "All that talking in your head?"

"I've told him to shut the heck up a few times."

"Does he?" Harper said.

"Yeah. For the most part. He even apologizes now and then for landing in my . . ." I suddenly caught what I was saying.

"Is he talking to you now?" Harper asked, watching me closely.

65

" . . . for landing in my head. And no. He's not talking to me now," I added. "So Harper, have you noticed Oma looking at any boys?"

"No fair trying to change the subject," both of them recited in unison.

"No. No. I just thought it would be more interesting talking about boys that Oma is inter. . . "

"Von," my mother suddenly appeared in my doorway. "I just got off the phone with Father Winnlyn at Perpetual Peace. He's very willing to help."

"Help? What?" Where was she going with this?

"Father Winnlyn says this voice could be a demonic possession. He says he's seen this kind of thing before. A few times, in fact."

Oh for goodness sakes. I am NOT a demon trying to possess you. Of all the silly . . . D.G. ranted.

Hey. Chill D.G.

"Mom. Call off the priest. I'm not possessed. If I wanted Voodoo, I'd go see Margarita Paris, Julia's mom."

"You need to start going to church again, young man. He could be right. Father Winnlyn has always given good advice to our family. You could be under attack by Satan or one of his minions. And I insist you attend that ritual."

"Ritual? What ritual?"

"He happens to be trained and certified in the rite of exorcism which he will perform for you at midnight this Friday night. You'll have to sit up there by the altar. He says, basically, he'll blow a lot of incense smoke and sprinkle a lot of holy water. You don't have to say or do much. Just sit there."

"Oh, cool! Remember the movie, the Exorcist? I was so scared," Harper called out. "I gotta see this."

"No, No, No. No Harper. Don't get all excited. I'm not going to any exorcism, especially mine. Mom, what the hell were you thinking? Exorcism? Exorcism. Really?"

"Plan on being there, my boy. I've already spoken with your father about it and he agreed."

"What! Dad? He doesn't even believe in god. Why the hell would he want to . . . "

"Your father absolutely does too believe in God. And he's certainly more open minded than you. So, yes. You're going. Friday night at midnight," Mom said as she waved a finger at me and walked off.

D. G. broke out in a long laugh. *What are you laughing at?* I growled at D.G. *This isn't funny. These people want to make a joke out of me.*

Actually, it's hilarious, Director Guy came back. *And the psychiatrist told you to relax. Even if you go to it, it won't mean a thing. Or are you afraid you'll levitate into the air and float across the church?* He went back to laughing.

"So cool," Harper said shaking his head. He retrieved his flip flops and followed Mom downstairs.

"Yeah, I guess," Oma droned as she followed Harper out.

For long moments, I sat there stunned at the tidal wave of reactions building up over all this.

Von, there's been a change, D.G. blurted.

Change? Haven't you paid attention! There's been nothing but change today. Now what?

67

You were distracted earlier, worried that they had seen you and the Biology teacher kissing, but when she kissed you, an image arose within me, a memory. I saw the side of . . .

Yeah. Of a woman's face. I remember.

Yes. A woman I cared deeply about. I'm sure of it. In fact, maybe my wife.

So?

So when you got home and argued with your mother in the kitchen, another memory appeared, of my mother. I saw her. Director Guy's passionate tone got my attention. *Old, sick and dying, but it was her,* he went on. *I remember now that she died in my arms. I even remember the nurse using a stethoscope and then telling me that my mother was dying, right then. I'm starting to have memories, Von. Memories of my past. It's progress. This is good. The more I can remember, the closer I'll come to figuring this whole thing out. Don't you see?*

Yeah, I see. I guess you're right, I tried to reassure him. *That might be important for you. But what if you're a disease? If I'm mentally ill, schizophrenic or something, your memories won't matter at all.*

The memories I am able to recall will add up to something, Von. They'll point to something, some conclusion or some process that'll answer the question of how I ended up in your consciousness.

Of how you 'landed' in my head? When I said that to my brother a while ago, it struck me that that's what you did. You 'landed', as if you were going somewhere. Like a guy with a parachute, landing. You were going somewhere, but where and how?

Well yes, Von. But only the memories I can recall will answer those questions, of where and how. That's why the memories become very important. I don't think anyone else can figure this situation out. Not a psychiatrist and not an exorcist. I think it depends on memories that I'm able to collect.

Maybe. We'll see, I told him. *But I can tell you this. If that psychiatrist says he has some pill that'll get rid of you, I'm taking that pill.*

Yes? Gee thanks, Von. Self preservation comes natural to all of us. I have no choice but to try to survive too. So, try not to be too bewildered if you take that pill and I'm still here afterward. His voice had turned sharp.

Whoa. Is that a challenge? I felt my anger kicking in. *Look D.G. It's my head. It's my body. This is my territory. You're the invader. Possibly an invading disease. You don't get to jump in and take over.*

Believe me Von. If I could leave, I would. Whatever happened to land me inside your head wasn't my choice. That's for sure. I would have selected someone caring, intellectual, studious, with unquestioning integrity who could appreciate his family and the woman that loves him.

My mother doesn't love me. She just needs me around to dominate.

I wasn't speaking of your mother, Von. Grow up.

Grow up! I hated people telling me to grow up. As if anyone could possibly hurry that process along. Now I was pissed. I wasn't gonna have any extra mind voice talk to me like that so I went down to the kitchen for supper. Dad had come home from work and I found out he too wanted me to attend the exorcism. Made no sense to me. My father was no friend of religion. But, if Dad wanted it done, I wasn't gonna get out of it. Looked like I'd be un-demonized. I ate my food. Hardly any conversation happened at the table. After excusing myself, I took a shower, read a science assignment and decided I was tired. I climbed into bed and fell asleep. But sleeping that night got weird.

Usually I fall asleep once and wake up once around seven a.m. or when Mom yells up at me. But this night, I must have woken up a bunch of times, each time bothered by a dream I'd just had. The first dream contained a thread. Not a regular thread but one made of silver that passed through a point in the middle of my back and attached to something inside me. The part of the thread outside of me reached out so far away that I couldn't see the other end of it. It followed me everywhere I went, magically untangling itself when I went around a tree or post. I never did find out what the other end attached to but I did have some feeling that whatever occupied the other end held an important meaning in my life. I got frustrated and pulled on the thread, thinking I'd learn if the other end had some kind of effect on me. That's when I woke up.

After going to the bathroom, I lay on my back wondering about the dream. It didn't take long before I fell asleep again, but this time, I dreamt of a locket. At first, I thought I saw an old pocket watch like my grandfather used to carry at the end of a little chain that hooked to his belt. His watch had a gold cover that popped open. The shape of my dream locket was the same but the size of this locket was gigantic. It seemed big enough to fill a clock tower, maybe like Big Ben in London. It floated in the air in front of me. I reached out and touched the cover and it slowly swung open. The cover contained a giant clock and the base also held a clock. Both clocks showed a regular analogue face and were identical in every way, that is until you observed the second hands. The clock on the left registered 2:47 a.m. which seemed like the correct time of night. The one on the right showed a second hand that ran backwards. It read 3:00 o'clock. As its second hand swept past the twelve, it clicked to 2:59. All its hands, second, minute and hour, moved backwards. I remember feeling confused. It was counting down, running backwards toward twelve o'clock. Did that mean there was three hours left before reaching 12:00 midnight? Did I have three hours left to accomplish some task? Why would it be going backwards? I had no idea what to make of this strange sight. It confused me enough that I woke up again.

I glanced at my clock radio's red digital readout. The numbers 2:48 glowed back at me. My confusion doubled. Did the clock dream have anything to do with the thread dream? I yawned and rolled over. I'd figure it out in the morning. Or so I thought.

The third dream started the same way the second dream had. A large round locket-like container hung in the air before me. I touched it but this time its cover disappeared altogether and was never seen again. The whole device moved from being upright to being horizontal. I could tell the surface of it underwent some change. To understand the change, I stepped up onto the surface and realized it now featured a compass. I looked over the compass rose and saw that I stood almost directly on East. I walked across to the West side and counted seven strides as I did. The great compass and I floated in space. Everything around was darkness. I reached down and touched the compass face. Its markings were nothing different from any Boy Scout compass I'd ever owned, except that it was so much larger. Then I noticed the thread. The same silver thread, this time only a foot long, lay there close to the West pointer. I tried to pick it up but when my finger touched it, I woke up.

My clock radio now read 3:37. I turned onto my back, slowly went over all three dreams but remained clueless as to what they meant.

Chapter Seven

{ Why not make fun of what they believe? Screw them if they can't take a joke. }

Thursday, May 7th

Von and I woke simultaneously to a shrieking local D.J. trying to sell us toothpaste, Von's clock radio blaring away. He shot out of bed into his jeans and shirt. I observed him freshening up in the bathroom, standing before the mirror combing his hair. His shoes on, he hoisted his trusty backpack and clamored his way downstairs for breakfast. I wanted to tell him about the strange dreams I'd had during the night. I wasn't sure what they meant, the nature of dreams being so obscure much of the time, but his body language and overall attitude told me he didn't want to talk. Our contentious conversation the previous evening seemed to have created an emotional distance between us. I remained silent.

"Oh Von, your appointment with the psychiatrist got changed to this morning," Martha informed him. "He has classes to teach at Tulane in the afternoon. I'll drive you there in a half hour."

"This morning?" I could feel Von's nerves tense. "What about school?"

"It's an excused absence," his mother answered. "You'll only miss an hour. You'll be fine."

Great! Thanks a lot, D.G., Von said sounding angry.

I found myself cross with him now. I decided I didn't have to hold back.

Let's see, Von. You're alive after avoiding a fatal car wreck, I fussed. *Your math grades have improved, oh, and your English grade, oh, and you may recall I recommended you leave early before your Ms. Jourst smeared her boobs all over you. And now you demonstrate appreciation by playing the pouting wounded teenager. You're welcome anyway.*

Yeah, well maybe I am the wounded teenager, Von growled back. *And maybe you are the wound.*

Well, it seemed definite now that we were angry with each other. I decided to hold my tongue.

Minutes later, I observed Von and his mother reading Dr. Raoul Kalchavic's name imprinted on the large mahogany entrance door to his office. Von pushed the door aside. There stood Dr. Kalchavic and Susie, his receptionist. Introductions were quick and Dr. Kalchavic escorted Von into his inner office to begin the counseling session while Susie had Martha fill out family health history forms.

A large brown leather couch sat at one end of the finely decorated office bookended by two overstuffed lounge chairs. I liked the walls of finely grained real-wood panels. Floor-to-ceiling maroon curtains surrounded the edges of each window and the rug covering the floor seemed inches thick under Von's feet. It all struck me as very tastefully arranged.

Von approached one wall, attracted by the many degrees and diplomas boasting Dr. Kalchavic's certifications. I found myself greatly impressed by Dr. Kalchavic's Ph.D. from John Hopkins School of Medicine. But as I read the writing on his degree, the script began to move, rearranging itself and suddenly transforming so that it read as a Ph.D.

degree in Astrophysics from Massachusetts Institute of Technology. When I tried to read who this new degree was issued to, only the first letter "J" showed. The other letters of the name became too blurry to read. In less than a minute, the writing switched back to its original version. What was that? Why would the letters rearrange themselves like that? Who's 'J' I wondered?

Von, did you just see the letters on that degree shift? I'd forgotten we weren't speaking just then.

D.G. Leave me alone. Especially now, of all times. Go away.

But Von. Those letters repositioned themselves into a completely different . . .

I don't care D. G. Shut the hell up. You're probably making it up anyway. I was about to argue with Von but Dr. Kalchavic needed to begin so I decided to wait.

"Ok Von. Let's start," Dr. Kalchavic beckoned for him to sit on the couch. Von sat down and they considered each other. Dr. Kalchavic then asked about the voice and how it first began. Von told of him and his friends at the abandoned railroad spur smoking marijuana, of my first speaking to him and his reactions. He told of the close call with the eighteen-wheeler and about my apologizing for being in his head.

"Humm. Yes, you mentioned that before. Very interesting. I've never heard of a voice in the head apologizing. Keep going please." Dr. Kalchavic then learned about my helping Von on the math test, on the trick question in English class and about my accessing some of Von's memories, even finding out that one of them was a memory from my own life.

"What? This Director Guy, as you call him, he has memories separate from you?" I enjoyed seeing this doctor become surprised by Von's description of me. Von nodded and told the doctor of the woman's face that might have been my wife, and then spoke of my memory of my mother dying. I watched Dr. Kalchavic's eyes squint in stern concentration. Von's statements certainly had the good doctor's attention. He made copious notes on a yellow pad and typed on a laptop computer like a man possessed. He muttered to himself as he typed, "Unique. Very unique . . . not the standard patterns. A rather balanced personality . . . too civilized. Usually more contentious, more discontent . . . even grumpy."

Von ignored the good doctor's mumbling and went on, telling him how we got along for a while and lately argued. This caught the doctor's attention.

"Ahh. You argued," Dr. Kalchavic said, writing quickly.

Argument? I jumped in. *A minor thing, Von. Nothing severe about it.* But Von ignored me.

"Argued about what?" the good doctor wanted to know.

"About survival. I told him that I would be willing to take medicine to get rid of him. He said he might still be around afterward. We got mad at each other. Do you have any pill that would just wipe this voice out? You know, a quick route?"

"Oh. We have very good medicines. But they just make you relax. It is too early for medication, Von. First, we discover things by asking lots of questions and getting you to talk about things. We must not take the quick route. No. We must take the careful route, so, no medicines yet. But, let me understand. Does this voice seem to be judging you, or tormenting you, or being mean to you, or trying to shame you, or taking over your life, anything like that?"

"Ahh, well, no. Nothing like that. I just get mad at him for being there. Taking up space in my head, that's all. If I just ignore him, will he go away?"

"I'm not sure but you could experiment with that. Let's give you a small experimental assignment. Try not talking with this Director Guy for a few days. See if the voice is reduced. Or if it goes away. And, of course, inform me of results, ok?"

Dr. Kalchavic then brought out some forms and began asking a series of questions concerning family dynamics, which I found completely boring. Had Von ever been abused? Sexually mistreated? Spanked or struck? Did he love his mother, father, siblings? And the questions went on and on and took up most of the meeting and I felt relieved when all the routine first-visit questions were done. Toward the end of the hour when the questions finally subsided, Von asked about exorcism. Oh, this is gonna be good, I thought.

"Exorcism?" Dr. Kalchavic's nose wrinkled.

Von quickly explained his parent's plans for the exorcism. Dr. Kalchavic listened intently for half a minute. Abruptly, lines appeared across his forehead, his eyes slammed shut, an enormous grin broke across his jaw and he howled with laughter. He slapped his knee and almost doubled over. Yep, just the reaction I'd have predicted. He reared up and laughed more, howling to the ceiling. After two more times like that, he removed his glasses and wiped his eyes. Then he laughed some more. My feelings exactly.

"Well. It won't hurt you," Dr. Kalchavic chuckled. "I certainly doubt if it will make any change at all. Perhaps, just go along with it, so it doesn't make arguments." And then he giggled.

"I'm also concerned, Von, about the other kids at school teasing you. Teenagers can be mean sometimes. They haven't learned to be graceful yet. Are they taunting you?"

"Some," Von answered. "They put a bunch of things about me being crazy on Twitter. Most are just jerks seeing how much attention they can get. Some are just teasing. Lots of it makes no sense at all. Anyway, I don't care. I have a small group of friends that I hang with. They'll stick by me no matter what."

"No. No. Don't talk with them about this voice. If they bring it up, ignore them. Force them to talk about other things. This is usually the best defense from teenagers."

With that, the doctor stood and they shook hands. "This session is over now. I'll arrange for us to meet in one week. If things get too difficult for you, have your parent's call me. Ok?"

His mother waited in the outer office and after a few minutes of talking with Dr. Kalchavic, she drove Von to school.

Well, that wasn't too bad. He seems well trained and concerned, at least, I told Von. But Von gave no response. I waited. Still no answer. *Oh. The silence experiment. You're gonna force me out by not responding. I can assure you Von, that won't work.* But, he still didn't answer me.

Arriving at school a few minutes after second period began, Von walked into Mrs. Keife's English class. The low murmur of students working together in pairs filled the room. Von handed off the admission slip from the office to Mrs. Keife and she suggested working with Moneen, who up till now had been working in a group of three.

Oooh. The first kiss girl. Lucky you. I whispered. Von didn't

78

answer, but I could feel his nerves tense slightly. I could tell he was right on the verge of saying something but held back.

Moneen retrieved a worksheet from Mrs. Keife and moved to a seat next to Von.

"Here's the review page, Von," Moneen said. "Since finals are next week, this might help us prepare. So we're to complete it. And Von."

"Yeah?"

Moneen put her hand upon his. "Are you ok?"

Von looked at her fingers on his and then at her face. "Yeah. Why? You been reading all that trash talk on Twitter?"

Moneen shrugged just one shoulder. "I just wanted to make sure. To ask, you know?"

"I could be a lot better if we went out together this weekend," Von said.

Right on! I virtually yelled into his head. *Two points. Field goal. Keep it up Von.*

Moneen's smile rose slowly and her head tilted a bit. Her eyes went back to her worksheet. "Yeah. You're ok. No different. But, I'm going to see my Aunt in Texas this weekend. So, no date. Now about this worksheet."

Rats. Nice effort though, I said. But again, Von gave me no response. This silence had me concerned. I would have to do something strange, something that might catch him off guard. Moneen explained the assignment and before long, they'd both handed in their papers. The bell rang minutes later. Von winked goodbye to Moneen and avoided Vivian as he merged with the hallway crowd. Charlie and Moby came up from behind him.

"Where were you first hour, Von?" Moby asked.

Greetings Charlie and Moby. I hollered. *Why, Von took part in head shrinking, his own, thank you. And I, the invincible Director Guy, always willing to converse, always willing to communicate, am still in attendance, right here in his head. However, a bit of jumping up and down and hollering may be required to achieve some KIND OF RESPONSE from ever obstinate, Von.*

Von hesitated, then smirked. "I overslept."

"You mean you can't get that extra voice to wake you up on time?" Charlie leaned in and whispered as I felt him push against Von's shoulder.

Hey, of course, Von. An unforeseen advantage of my fantastic presence. Just set your friendly inner voice alarm clock and presto, I could broadcast GET UP, SUCKER through every cell in your body. That might go along well with the personality I need to manifest IN ORDER TO GET A RESPONSE. Von stopped walking, rolled his eyes, pretended to stretch his muscles but he didn't answer.

"What new surprises has our local head voice got for us today?" Charlie asked.

Excellent question, Charles. The Kalchavic head shrinker has declared that Von ignore any comments or questions about that invading terrorist heathen inner voice. The tension builds! I wasn't particularly enjoying taunting Von. But if he wanted to ignore me, I would be forced into new found antics that I could dial up to ever increasing levels, until he finally communicated again.

Von nodded to both Charlie and Moby, completely avoided answering and ducked into Mr. Benedict's room for American History.

Moby stood at the door, pointing at Von. "You can run but you cannot hide. We will invade your head too."

Yea! Company! I hollered. *The unexpected arrival of like-minded fiends. Let the blood sport commence. Unless of course one MIGHT WANT TO RESPOND.* I felt Von's nerves tense but he stubbornly remained silent. I had to give him credit for putting such energy into his little silence experiment.

Moby knocked his knuckles on the door frame, waved and left for his class. Von sat in his usual place in class just as Mr. Benedict announced that the class would watch the first part of a movie showing the Pearl Harbor attack. Meanwhile, two girls across the row from Von chatted, one of them describing a dream she had last night.

On a lark, I decided to throw myself into my flip-wrist imitation of how girls speak. *Oh honey. You want dreams.* I ranted, *I had a doozy of a dream last night. Some silver thread thing and then two huge floating clocks, one of them weird and then this compass thing. I had dreams, girl.*

Whoa. Wait a minute, D.G., Von suddenly answered me. *I had those dreams too.*

Oooh. Little mister socialite conversationalist suddenly wakes. Guess that marks the failure of silence experiment number one. Interestingly, my taunting had failed but the mention of the dreams brought him right around to talking with me.

Ok. Ok. Uncle already, Von relented. *I didn't know you'd turn yourself into an obnoxious clown. But listen. Those dreams. I had the same dreams.*

The same? No, I told Von.

Yeah. The same.

Ok Von, let's see. Describe each dream with all the detail you can remember.

He started with the thread dream, silver, connecting to something in him and went from there, just as Mr. Benedict's film showed a huge swarm of Jap Zero fighter planes taking off from aircraft carriers in the middle of the Pacific. His description of the opening clock that turned to two clocks, one running backwards, was exact. Then came the giant compass. His descriptions were so accurate, the realization of it exploded in me just as the first Jap Zero's bombs landed on an American battle ship. We did have the same dream. No doubt about it.

Ok Von. Apparently, one dream occurred but we both experienced it.

But D.G. How did we do that? Von asked as the battleship Arizona exploded.

You think I know? I have no idea how any of this is happening. Oh. And the Ph.D. degree on the wall in the psychiatrist's office. Did you see it rewrite itself?

No. I remember you said you saw something like that, but I didn't see that. What did it say?

It said J___ somebody had a Ph.D. in astrophysics from MIT, Massachusetts Institute of Technology. And I think this is another memory image. It clearly showed for a few seconds.

Maybe you're the Ph.D. astrophysics guy from MIT, Von guessed. *Maybe you're 'J.'*

His statement struck me into silence, though the silence was quickly shattered by a rapid-fire machine gun mounted on an American destroyer. Possible, I thought. I felt really comfortable in that Biology lab equipment closet, all those beakers, test tubes, glass tubes and Bunsen burners, that is until little Ms. Jourst gave us her breast massage.

You seem to be going further and further into me, Von said. *First you access my memories. Now you're seeing my dreams.*

Strictly speaking, Von, you might have it backwards. You may have witnessed my dreams. The whole dream thing puzzled me. *And I wonder where that thread went off to?*

And the clock that ran backwards, Von said. *It had three hours left, from 3:00 to midnight. Three hours until what?*

We both quietly pondered the questions we had about the dreams. Bit by bit, the bombing of Pearl Harbor took over our attention. The first half of the film used up the whole period and before long the bell rang signaling fourth hour P.E.

Von made his way to the boy's dressing room and got ready for exercising. He joined one of the basketball teams and threw himself full force into a game. I decided not to bother him while he needed all his attention on quick response skills. Once the game ended, he showered and headed to the cafeteria with the next bell.

Von and Moby arrived at their favorite picnic table at the same time, lunch bags in hand. Charlie, Derrick, Vivian, Nick and others were arriving at the same time.

"Hey mental, how's tricks?" someone called from a table next to theirs.

Von took a big bite of his sandwich and refused to answer. Just then Julia walked up and sat on the opposite side of the picnic table facing away from Von. He just continued chewing and glanced now and then over his shoulder at Julia. She slowly chewed part of her sandwich while gazing at the ground.

"Well you're the one that got this whole voice in the head shebang going," Vivian sneered. "Now you're just gonna clam up? Answer us."

Von chewed.

Denying them an answer may intensify their attacks, Von. But he didn't answer me either.

Vivian simply turned away and began typing something into her Twitter account. Von stood and walked around to Julia's side of the picnic table. He sat next to her not taking his eyes off her.

"Are you in trouble from yesterday?" Julia asked, turning to look at him. Their eyes met for a long moment.

"I'm probably in trouble with you," Von muttered.

"Just as I left campus yesterday," Julia went on. "I heard your name over the loudspeaker. Then they said your parents were there too. That you should hurry to a meeting. Were you in trouble?"

"Your folks came to school? What happened?" Charlie asked.

"It wasn't what you might be thinking, Julia," Von responded. "It wasn't about . . . ahh . . . you coming back for your notebook and all that."

Moby and Charlie looked at each other and then back at Von, questioning looks on their faces.

Von launched to a full report of the meeting with the counselors, his parents and a psychiatrist. His friends asked if he would attend the meeting with Dr. Kalchavic and he told them he already had. They enquired about that too and he revealed all he could. Then, Von told them about the upcoming exorcism.

"You're kidding me. A freaking exorcism?" Charlie joined in. Julia stood with her jaw hanging. Then slowly, Charlie and Moby began to chuckle and then laugh. Julia simply stared at Von. She sat down as Von launched into an explanation of how his mother had arranged the whole thing.

Moby stood, pulled his hair upward away from his head and marched back and forth, laughing. "An exorcism? A freakin' exorcism."

I thought they'd react like this, I told Von.

Charlie nodded. "Ok. Now I get why you wouldn't talk with Vivian and the others."

Julia leaned in a bit closer. "Von. Is this voice, like, hurting you? Scaring you? Messing with your mind?"

"Naw. I mean we argue a bit," Von said. "But it's mainly an inconvenience. D.G. wants to figure out what put him in my consciousness. That's all. He's not mean. Pretty civilized, overall."

Well halleluiah. Thank you, Von.

"Yesterday, Derrick credited you for saving us from that eighteen-wheeler. Was it you or D.G.?" Charlie asked.

"I didn't see it coming. D.G. warned me. Or we'd all be dead."

Finally. Credit where credit is due.

"Huh. Maybe we should take D.G.'s side in this," Julia mumbled.

Oh Von. I love that little woman. Yeah.

"Oouuh. Now there's an idea," Moby whispered. "Hey. What about an exorcism party? We want to be there too, Von. Heck, I want to cheer for Director Guy," Moby said, giving Von and Charlie high fives.

"Would you want to make a thing of it, Von?" Charlie asked. "All we have to do is tell Vivian, she'd put it on Twitter and Facebook and then others would probably show up. How big do you want this, Von?"

"I guess the question is, do I really want that many people

thinking I'm nuts, or that I have some evil spirit inside me?" Von said.

"Why not?" Charlie blurted. He stood up, spread his huge arms and began spinning around. "Why not make fun of this screwed up society that's so caught up in being judgmental. They want to be that judgmental, then why not make fun of what they believe? Screw them if they can't take a joke. We just turn the whole thing upside down, Von. You might end up being the leader of a movement or something."

"My mom arranged it without even telling me," Von grumbled. "Came at me with that "Mister" crap. I hate that."

Ok, D.G. Should I do what they're suggesting? Von asked.

Why not stir things up? I responded. *I'm sure there'll be teasing. If you have a thick enough skin, go for it. But this has to be your call, Von. I won't decide it for you.*

Von became very silent inside. He sat slightly nodding, thinking it over. I watched Julia, Charlie and Moby stand there, big-eyed, staring at him. He slowly looked up at Moby and Charlie.

"Tell Vivian. Von's exorcism. Friday night at midnight. Perpetual Peace church."

Huge grins appeared on his friends faces. Just then the bell rang. Everyone touched fists and took off for class. "Vivian and I have fifth hour together," Moby said as he grabbed his backpack and hustled off with Charlie at his side.

Julia stood, cradled her books in her arms and turned to leave but Von grabbed her hand.

"Julia, we have to talk. I'm terribly sorry. I apologize. I got myself into that situation with Jourst and I was a stupid ass. I realize I disappointed you and I could kick myself. I . . . I . . . ."

Julia stood listening to Von, watching him. "Jourst has a reputation, Von. Some of the kids have a real rumor mill going about her. I guess you didn't know that."

"Yeah. I think I figured that out," Von quickly added. "I'm sorry. I care about your feelings."

Slowly, a slight smile came upon Julia's face and she nodded. She reached up and placed her hand on his chest.

"Walk me to class?" she said.

Von snatched up his backpack and the two of them walked toward Building Two. I thought of congratulating him, of lending my encouragement to his nice apology, but decided I'd just be a buttinsky. Von's mood lifted higher as Julia's smile continued. At the end of the east hallway, they'd have to separate, Von going upstairs to Art and Julia turning left toward her English class. Again he squeezed her fingers. She smiled and winked at him. With that he bounded up the stairs.

Wow. An exorcism party, I told Von. *A newly contrived idea for little ole me? I feel honored, Von. How thoughtful. Thank you.* I was beginning to get a feel for teasing Von. It seemed to relieve the stress of my still not knowing how I'd ended up in his head.

Cherry, already seated at their table in Art class, peered deeply into her unzipped backpack, reading her Twitter account. She looked up at Von with an inquisitive look.

"An exorcism party? At the church? You serious?" she asked. Von nodded and smiled. Cherry tapped Nick on the shoulder and whispered. Nick leaned forward, looked at Von and gave a thumbs up.

"Can we go?" Nick asked.

Von again smiled and nodded. Nick and Cherry looked at each

other like they didn't know if they should take this seriously or not.

Mrs. Wrathe's class passed quickly. Von and Cherry spent much of the class peeking at all the responses to Vivian's Twitter announcement of Von's exorcism.

As Von made his way down the hall to last hour class, many more students stopped to look at him. He smiled but kept walking. Once inside Ms. Jourst's class, he found her leaning against her podium. She asked everyone to get quiet and quickly announced that Von had decided not to continue with the inventory job and that the job was again open for applications. As four students took application forms from her lecture table, Julia turned in her seat and threw Von a wink in response. Charley, Cherry, Sammy Daxtal and Nick nodded their approval and smiled at Von. Ms. Jourst's lecture on plant and animal reproduction processes was rather uneventful. Soon, the bell rang ending the school day.

Ms. Jourst waited till most of the students had left and then Von noticed her coming toward him, a small note card in her hand. She said nothing but slipped him the card as she passed him. He scanned the card, realized it was her address and phone number. He pulled his backpack over one shoulder and walked to the doorway. There, he turned and looked back at Jourst. She watched as Von shredded the note card and dumped its many pieces into the trash can. He turned and left without a word.

That evening, it became obvious Von wanted to avoid his parents, especially his mother. Harper and Oma checked in on him once and had more questions about exorcism. Oma had looked it up on Google.

"It said you might get tied down," she announced.

I was surprised to hear Oma's pronouncement. Von laughed too, until Oma showed us where Catholiconline.com actually said that.

"What? Well, at least I found out ahead of time," Von proclaimed. Once they went back to their rooms, Von did a lot of Internet research on exorcism. He even found topics like exorcism rituals and the liturgy of exorcism. But, stopping suddenly, he shut his laptop.

I really don't want to know, he said to me. *Just let 'em do whatever.* So using his cell phone, he checked his Facebook page, his Twitter account and his email. There were too many messages to read. Texts built up on his phone, so much so that he just did a mass delete.

I could tell it made him nervous. He didn't sleep well. He tossed and turned, waking me often. He even woke in the middle of the night and studied science notes to get his mind off things. The glow of the clock radio flashed something past two a.m. when he finally allowed us both to drift off.

Friday, May 8th

Von's mother hollered from downstairs and Von bolted straight up in bed, jolted awake. He dressed, ate and grabbed his books. Charlie, Julia, Vivian and Moby were already on the sidewalk. They wanted to talk about all the Twitter traffic they had, all of it concerning me, the ever more famous voice occupying Von's head. Here I was, unable to prove I existed yet I had become popular.

"Director Guy got anything new for us today?" Moby asked.

He's funny, I told Von.

Von's steps came to an abrupt halt. *Wow, I've worried so much about the ritual tonight that I hadn't even spoken with you this morning.*

Not to worry, Von. I'm right here. And no, I don't have anything particularly interesting for Moby.

"Nope," Von said out loud. Moby nodded and everyone kept walking.

Von and his crew made it to school on time. First and second hours passed uneventfully. Both teachers handed out lists of items that might be on their particular final exam. I assisted Von with two math equations and we talked about the interpretation of a Shakespearean sonnet.

In third hour, Mr. Benedict gave lecture notes on conditions that lead to the bombing of Pearl Harbor and had his students copy a list of the topics that would be on his final.

I had actually become bored with that list, so I got to rummaging around in Von's mental space again. Something new developed. It wasn't an image like any I'd seen before. It looked like a structure composed of thousands of strands of slightly translucent filament, loose and separate at one end but all bundled together at the other end. When I concentrated upon it, something jerked. Some involuntary muscle twitched. Just considering it made it move again, only more forcefully.

Von stopped taking notes and looked down. His foot kicked sideways, its toes twisting over to the left. Once it hit the table leg and made an abrupt noise. He jerked his foot back, stretched it in different directions and put it back down.

Sorry Von.

Sorry Von? D.G. did you do that?

I think I did. I was unaware it might move something. Sorry.

You moved my foot! No. No. You can't do that. I don't want you moving . . . controlling anything.

Von, I interrupted, *yesterday, when I found some of your memories, you said that if I found other new things, to let you know. This is me letting you know.*

Stress built up throughout Von's entire being at an alarming speed. I realized, too late, that my controlling a part of his body ran through him like an electric shock.

No! Don't try to avoid this, Von stormed. *Don't move my body. Don't control . . . This is all I have, damn it. This is me. You're taking over, aren't you? You're sneaking around in my mind, lighting up all those little spaces and finding the controls to every part of me. YOU ARE A DISEASE! DAMN YOU! And you've only been here since Tuesday night. You're like an invading army.*

Von, I promise you, that's not what I'm about. I don't want . . .

He quickly rose and pointed toward the door. Mr. Benedict noticed him, knew he needed the bathroom, nodded and waved him on. Von stomped down the hall, threw open the bathroom door and entered. Luckily, no one else occupied the bathroom.

"What were you thinking! Damn it. It's my body!" he growled.

I don't want to control you at all, I said as calmly as I could. *I came upon something and didn't know what it did. I moved it just to find out. I promise. Von. Calm down.*

He threw himself into a fury and took on a silence even more severe than before. Now I had really gotten his attention. He threw some water onto his face, toweled off and went back to class, all of it in a huff aimed at me.

Damn it D.G. Damn it. Let's see how your funny little sense of

91

humor will work on me now, he fumed.

I had upset him so much he couldn't take notes even when he tried to. His anger pumped like a turbine. Elaina sat in the next row and he let her know he'd need her notes. She nodded. Before long the bell rang and he took off for P.E.

Four times on the way to P.E., I apologized and tried to get Von to respond. No deal. He ignored me except to rant, *Silence experiment number two is officially on.* He joined another basketball game and played like a mad man, his team winning by nineteen points.

On the way to lunch, I tried to talk to him two more times. I did not get an answer. He and Moby were about to reserve their usual picnic table when Moby grabbed Von's sleeve and pulled him toward building two.

"Von. Derrick and I have a total solution," Moby said. Von stared at him, waiting. "Look," Moby went on. "Derrick and I got to talking with his older brother, Jonathon. He's back from college. They let out before us. He brought blotter acid with him. Jonathon's a psychology major."

No Von. I jumped in almost panicked. *That kind of thinking is delusional. Drugs aren't the answer. We need memories to . . .*

"Tell me more," he told Moby. Just then, Derrick trotted up.

"Von. Moby. Did you tell him?" Derrick asked. Moby nodded. "Von, this stuff is powerful," Derrick went on. "I tried some. It would completely clean your head out, man. My brother said they're experimenting with LSD on schizophrenics. Why not try it?"

Just then, Elaina walked up and handed Von her notes from Mr. Benedict's class. "Have you guys told him yet?" she asked.

"Yeah. Just did. Can we use your place?" Moby asked.

"Sure," Elaina responded. "My mom works all day Saturday. Come over around nine. We'll have the place to ourselves. But, I get to trip too, right? I've done it a few times and I love tripping."

I felt Von's smile come across his face. This was just the kind of plan Moby and Derrick would conspire on.

Von, I protest. This is dangerous, I pleaded. *Research on LSD is miniscule. Scientific studies give no assurance about LSD's actual effects on the mind. There's just too many unknowns. Do not do this.*

"I'm in." Von announced. "So, we meet at Elaina's apartment, nine o'clock, tomorrow morning."

All four of them nodded and tapped fists.

"Don't tell Charlie or Julia," Derrick said. "You know they'll try to talk us out of it."

They quickly decided to eat in the cafeteria because all their friends avoided lunch in there.

As Von calmly chewed his fish sticks, I tried to explain the dangers of LSD. He never once recognized that I'd said anything. For now, his psychic doors were closed to me.

The exorcism tonight didn't worry me at all. That might actually be fun. But the ingestion of lysergic acid diethylamide presented untold dubious possibilities. I didn't know why I feared LSD. But that fear came across quite powerfully and served to stir something deep inside.

Abruptly, another memory hit me and this time I easily sensed it came from my life, not from Von's. I remembered being asleep in a large grass field. Music played, a single flute giving rise to a beautiful warbling call, waking me to a morning sunrise. I caught sight of a man, asleep on the ground, curled in a fetal position. An overwhelming familiarity told me that I now looked down upon myself from twenty feet up in the air. I could feel it was me. I had done this. I'd taken LSD at a rock concert. I had projected out of my body, an out of body experience that only the LSD could have brought on. As I hung in the air above my body, I remembered moving my attention to the flutist, a tall long-haired woman alone on stage, the sun breaking over the horizon behind her. Her soft alluring music wove through me as I again looked down upon my twenty-five-year-old body, such a wonderful body, such a wonderful machine that had carried me effortlessly through life with such grace. An enormous appreciation, even love of this body glowed within me. How fortunate that I inherited a basic natural health. I slowly sunk lower, closer and closer to my body and found myself flowing into it. My eyes opened. I had awakened, within my body; the out of body experience had ended. But the same music was there. I sat up, saw the same flutist, the same sunrise, just as I had witnessed while out of my body. Quietly, the memory faded.

Von, I just had another memory. From my twenty-fifth year, in college, at a rock concert. Von . . . But all he did was chew another fish stick.

I couldn't remember what form of LSD I'd taken then. But if this LSD separated me from Von's body, would I be washed out of him all together? Now that he cut off communication between us, I had little chance of talking him out of participation in Derrick and Moby's plan.

Chapter Eight

{ *You need to be the demented fiend, a real example of Satan, . . . not some unrehearsed wimp.* }

Perpetual Peace church stood a few blocks down from my high school, a big block building that tried to copy some famous church in France, I forget which one. I stood near the street, straight-jacketed into a new suit my mom had gotten while I was at school, again not telling me I'd have to wear this monkey suit. I felt like an orangutan stuffed into a sausage tube. The church's steeple stuck straight up into angry clouds, rising so high above me that I just knew any lightning within twenty miles would end up hitting the pointy church lightning rods and blasting the cement below my feet into sand. I wanted to strangle my mother.

"Stop playing with your tie, for goodness sakes," my Mom jabbed at me with her buzzing voice. She elbow-crooked her purse, straightened my tie even tighter and then smoothed her own dress, checking and rechecking that we looked just so.

"Yeah, see. If I'm dead from strangulation, they won't be able to get the demon out, so maybe this is too tight?" I fussed. Oma stood next to Mom in her pink frilly dress and black patent leather shoes, her dead pan stare working full force on me.

She is such an interesting kid, D.G. said, trying again to get me to answer him, which didn't work.

"It's odd that we're dressed up like this, as though it's a wedding or a funeral," I said. "I'd think a potato sack would work better for the possessed to wear, you know, so the priest could beat him with sticks or set him on fire."

Is that your scheme to purge yourself of me, Von? Self immolation?

I ignored him. One corner of Oma's mouth curled upward, the best reaction I could cull from her, so I winked at her. Mom remained stoned faced, turned away and watched for Dad and Harper, busy parking the car. We heard Dad just before they strode around the corner of the church, both dressed in black suits, black tie, white starched shirts. Why would people dress up to have a demon yanked out of them? I just couldn't understand that. It seemed to me they should wear work clothes. Dirty work clothes at that. Then, after they're sure the demon has left, the possessed person could take a shower and then dress up in really nice clean clothes. But what did I know. Basically, I was an admitted heathen. I checked my cell phone. It was 11:40 p.m. We walked up the church steps and heaved open the gigantic door.

Goodness. Someone neglected to pay the electricity bill, D.G. muttered.

The dim lighting just inside the entrance of the giant stone church surprised me. People entering this church usually needed sunglasses. But tonight, the only lighting in the entire church was hundreds of candles, all of them near or on the altar. The church stood empty, except for the tall silhouette of Father Winnlyn, blazing candles behind him, standing with his bible in his crossed arms against his chest. We slowly wandered down the main isle toward the glowing altar, Oma clinging to Mom's dress, Harper staying close to Dad. It felt like entering a cave lit by a campfire. The candles' yellow glow reached out into the church only so far, and beyond that was darkness. As we moved from dark into the light, Father

Winnlyn raised a hand.

"Ah. I thought I heard the squeak of hinges on that heavy door. Please come up to the front."

A second figure over to the left stood and turned toward us. I recognized Sister Gill right away, all five feet of her. How was it that I had once feared this nun?

This is all so strange, D.G. mumbled. *I must have been raised in some other religion.*

Father Winnlyn stepped down from the altar sanctuary and shook my father's hand.

"George. Martha. And Von," he said shaking my hand too. "So, a voice, hey? Well, let me get you all situated and we can begin right away. I've encountered possessions before and I can assure you, we can certainly remedy this."

"Good. Just us. I'm glad this is private." My mother pointed at the empty church. "People start rumors and such. I'd like to avoid all the talk, people sticking their noses where they shouldn't. Thank you, Father, for these arrangements."

"Actually Martha, exorcisms are generally public events. But, I thought a Friday midnight schedule wouldn't draw a crowd. We didn't announce this event to anyone," Father Winnlyn said shrugging. "You made clear your need for privacy."

You know Von, this priest has established quite a mood here, all these hot candle flames ready to exterminate the maladies and afflictions from your head, D.G. said. I tried to ignore D.G. but he seemed surprised by the surroundings. If only Father Winnlyn knew the noise bouncing off the walls of my head right now. I only grinned at him.

"Oh Von. Good to see you again, though I wish different circumstances," Sister Gill said walking up with outstretched arms. I turned toward the nun as she floated across the floor, her long penguin habit concealing her feet.

Oh yes. Is this the nun your friends mocked at the railroad tracks? D.G. mumbled.

"I'm so sorry," Sister Gills went on. "Perhaps you have forgotten the angelic army prayer I taught you and your class. It would protect you from such voices. You need to strengthen your faith, my boy," she said patting my hand. "Oh Martha, I'm praying nightly for your family." She gave Mom a hug, put her hand on Oma's head, touched Harper's shoulder. "But you're in the best of hands. Father Winnlyn is certified by the International Association of Exorcists of Rome. Certified."

This is building up to be entirely the event, Von. This certified priest knows how to do a bit of advertising I'd say. Quite the affect.

"Hello, Sister." Dad extended a hand to Sister Gills. "We have confidence in Father."

"These young people these days," Sister Gills went on. "They gather up such power and habits that are so strange to me. Things you and I never had growing up, and it leads to all kinds of devious ends. Lord, help us."

"Oh goodness. You're so right, Sister," my mom said. "Von has completely changed since the days back in your class. A changed person. I question a lot of it. Less respectful. Does what he wants. Big bad bear attitude. Lord, let us survive adolescence."

I think your mother subscribes to this angelic army. D.G. said. *These two could easily form an allegiance against you, Von.* I nodded in agreement but didn't answer him.

"Yeah. It's obvious that I'm right here, having to listen to all this," I said expecting it to make no difference at all.

"Hang in there, Von," Father Winnlyn chuckled, putting his hand on my shoulder. "We should get started now, everyone. If the family would just have a seat right here," he said pointing to the very first pew.

As my family sat, the squeak of hinges caught my attention. Far out there in the darkness at the front of the church, I detected movement. Strolling slowly into the light came Julia, Charlie, Moby, Derrick, Vivian, Nick and Cherry, all with big grins.

Oh, my cheering section. Familiar faces. Halleluiah, D.G. sang.

"Well." Father Winnlyn's surprise showed. "Welcome. I suppose we'll have other witnesses to the mysterious workings of the Lord. Moby, Charlie, Julia, everyone, please be seated. We were about to begin." Julia and Moby waved. I nodded back. I felt some of the tension in my back relax, now that friends had shown up.

My mother, however, turned and gawked at the group approaching. She spun around to look at me but I anticipated her motion and turned away. I didn't want to start this thing off with an argument.

Father Winnlyn beckoned me to a chair next to the altar. There were four tall candles on golden stands surrounding the chair. He had me remove my coat and tie. So, the orangutan gets free of the sausage tube. I celebrated by thanking Father profusely. Then I spotted the leather straps on the chair. I froze. I had only thought about it for a few seconds when Oma had warned me about being tied, but now with those straps in front of me, in the midst of a dimly lit, haunted church, the hair on the back of my neck became prickly. I forced myself to take a breath, touched one of the straps and looked at Father.

"I'll explain those in a moment," Father whispered.

It suddenly stuck me that I could outrun anyone in the church and I thought about bolting, but then the squeaky hinge sounded again. I peered into the darkness, wondering who else might join us. The sound of heels clicking across the marble floor grew louder. Father Winnlyn, hearing it too, turned and moved to the front of the altar. I estimated a crowd of about thirty people walking into the candle light, all students from school. They whispered as they approached, their eyes bulging at the peculiar lighting in the church. Now it would be too late because some of those guys coming in could outrun me.

"Well, welcome everyone. Please come forward and take a seat on either side of the isle. We're just getting started," Father Winnlyn said with a big wave and a side glance of curiosity at my mother.

My mother stood and looked back, her head swiveling from one side of the church to the other. She slowly turned and scowled at me. Oma looked back at the new arrivals, turned back to the front, her poker face expression still in place. I imitated Oma's look back to Mom. My dad reached out, touched Mom's arm and motioned for her to sit.

As the crowd got situated, the big door squeaked again. Sister Gill stood and went to the back of the church, assisted in seating people and waved for Father to begin the ritual. Father Winnlyn's look went from curious to concerned, more and more ridges appearing on his forehead.

It seems, Von, Vivian has had her effect. The audience and the plot thickens.

The door's squeaking now sounded like some tiny harmonica playing a tune. I counted at least a hundred and fifty people so far, but the squeaking continued and the crowd kept growing. I saw graduating seniors, a lot of juniors I recognized from my class, quite a few sophomores and even one or two freshmen. Vivian turned in her seat, smiled at the crowd and turned back with a look of triumph. Father Winnlyn kept welcoming students, left the altar and walked out into the crowd to personally shake hands. The crowd now filled the first third of the pews.

"I must express my surprise at this attendance. This is overwhelming." Father's chest seemed to stick out just a bit more. "This is more people than we get during Sunday services." The door kept squeaking. The church filled to more than half, a crowd I estimated around four hundred people. Finally, the un-oiled hinge grew quieter.

Again, Mom stood and brooded over the crowd, her hands on her hips. She turned to me, a very angry look on her face. I held onto the blank look. She stepped forward, and whispered.

"Did you tell all these kids to show up?"

I tried to freeze my facial muscles but finally I burst into a giggle and smiled. Her jaw hung down and she fumed. Her shoulders fell and her hands came off her hips. Dad tapped her on the arm and again coaxed her back to the pew.

Father walked from the middle of the church back to the altar, turned and began. "Exorcism is an ancient ritual. The casting out of evil is needed now and then and the Church considers such rites a necessary tool in the fight against Satan. Two things. First, you'll notice that Von will be tied to the chair. This is to protect himself from himself and to protect others around him. Demons leaving the body can sometimes become violent."[3]

Oooh? Perhaps I am a really virulent demon? D. G. said. *No common run of the mill succubus for you, Von.*

"Secondly, this ritual, once it begins, must be completed," Father Winnlyn continued. "For it to stop before the demon is cast out could make things even worse for the penitent and give the evil spirit renewed strength. [4] When I begin a prayer, please pray along with us."

He motioned for me to sit. I hesitated but Father put his hand on my shoulder. Reluctantly, I eased into the chair and watched as he tied my left and then right leg to the lower legs of the solid steel chair. He then tied my right and left hands to the back braces of the chair. I looked up feeling nervous and found surprise on my friends faces too. This whole event seemed to be taking off in a scary direction. A few giggles came from somewhere.

Father Winnlyn stood at a side table where he put on purple vestments. He then stood next to me and traced his hand across the top of my head and I guessed he made the sign of the cross. Julia got a big grin on her face and I figured that my neatly combed hair now stood on end, probably spiking upwards, demon like. An altar boy passed a fancy silver bucket by its fancy handle to Father who then sprinkled holy water right into my face and eyes[5], as he mumbled through some ritual prayer I'd never heard before. I shook my head trying to get the water off. When that didn't work, I tried wiping my face against my shoulders. When I looked up at Father Winnlyn, his eyes seemed to glow. He stared at me,

---

[3] Rite of Exorcism, Catholic Online at http://www.catholic.org/prayers/prayer.php?p=683

[4] The Roman Ritual, translated by Philip T. Weller, S.T.D., Part XIII Exorcism, Chapter I: General Rules Concerning Exorcism, Rule 17, www.ewtn.com/library/prayer/roman2.txt

[5] Catholic Online: Rite of Exorcism, http://www.catholic.org/prayers/prayer.php?p=683 as of 12/15/2016. (Note: Incomplete version of this ritual used for the sake of brevity).

taken by some thought in his head. He reached down and tested the leather straps binding my hands. Everything secure, he went on. Water still dripped off my nose.

Humph. Certified huh? This water treatment seems weak at best. I rolled my eyes just letting D.G. blabber away.

Next, Father Winnlyn stepped down near the pews and began sprinkling holy water over my family, friends and fellow students. A few of the non-Catholic kids ducked. A giggle or two came from the crowd. Sister Gill walked down the aisle and shushed someone. Father turned back to the altar, knelt at the front of it and began to loudly recite the name of every saint in the Catholic religion. He then begged these saints to keep us safe from lightning, lewdness, scourge, plague, famine, war, anger, hatred, all ill will, sudden and un-provoked death, everlasting death, two other types of death I can't remember, and a whole lot of other bad stuff.[6]

In the middle of all that recitation, Moby brought his hands up over his head stretching his fingers in all directions, stuck his tongue out to one side of his mouth, crossed his eyes and silently began flapping his head from side to side. I muffled a laugh and had to struggle against a big smile fighting to take over my face. I began to chuckle and looked down at my knees to avoid seeing Moby. But when I looked again, Derrick jutted his lower jaw forward, bulldog style and stretched his ears outward from his head. I simply couldn't hold in my laugh but just as it began to burst from me, another splash of holy water slapped me in the face. Father scowled at me and whispered, "Take it serious." Charlie doubled over, a huge smile on his mug. Julia shook her head and covered her face.

---

[6] Ibid.

Derrick sat silently laughing. Lots of whispers came from all over.

Ok. I'm bored. Naming saints? Surely, he has more ammo in his bag of tricks than this. This ritual was only making D.G. hyperactive.

The altar boy returned with a large silver incense burner on a chain and handed it to Father Winnlyn. He announced and began reciting Psalm fifty-three[7] as he swayed the incense burner back and forth. He walked around me spreading smoke all over me. I coughed. The smell was sweet, reminding me of Margarita Paris' Voodoo shop. I coughed again. My mother made big angry eyes at me. I gave back my most innocent expression. Father Winnlyn stepped toward the audience and sent smoke over them. He placed the incense smoker on the floor, threw his hands in the air and raised his voice to a loud holler.

"Holy Lord, almighty Father, everlasting God and Father of our Lord, Jesus Christ, who sent that fallen and apostate tyrant to the flames of hell, who will crush that noonday devil. Fill your servants with courage to fight manfully against that reprobate dragon, Satan himself. Let your mighty hand cast him out of your servant, Von, so he may no longer hold captive this person whom it pleased you to make in your image, and to redeem through your Son; who lives and reigns with you, in the unity of the Holy Spirit, God, forever and ever."[8]

"Amen," the students answered, a few of them punching their fist in the air.

Well, at least he's louder. Can't he just open the heavens and let the lightning bolts rain forth? Something's missing. This needs more, D.G.

---

[7] Ibid.

[8] Rite of Exorcism (This is the Official Rite for expelling demons from people certified as being possessed by authorized Catholic priests), http://www.catholicdoors.com/prayers/english/p01975b.htm as of 12/15/2016. (Note: Incomplete version of this ritual used for the sake of brevity).

grumbled.

Sister Gill moved from pew to pew handing out sheets of paper, probably some prayer, I figured. Father retrieved the incense smoker and began circling me as he swung the incense and called out.

"I command you, unclean spirit, whoever you are, along with all your minions now attacking this servant of God, that you tell me by some sign your name, and the day and hour of your departure. I command you, moreover, to obey me to the letter, I who am a minister of God despite my unworthiness; nor shall you be emboldened to harm in any way this creature of God, or the bystanders, or any of their possessions."[9]

Well now, I presume he's addressing me, the demon, directly. Finally, a little overdue recognition. D.G. perked up a bit.

Father Winnlyn stopped circling me, laid his hands on my head and shouted so that his voice echoed throughout the huge church.

"And this, the Exorcism. I cast you out, unclean spirit, along with every Satanic power of the enemy, every specter from hell, and all your fell companions; in the name of our Lord Jesus Christ. Be gone and stay far from this creature of God. For it is He who commands you, Satan, you enemy of the faith, you foe of the human race, you begetter of death, you robber of life, you corrupter of justice, you root of all evil and vice; seducer of men, betrayer of the nations, instigator of envy, font of avarice, fomenter of discord, author of pain and sorrow. Why, then, do you stand and resist, knowing as you must that Christ the Lord brings your plans to nothing? Fear Him, who in Isaac was offered in sacrifice, in Joseph sold into bondage, slain as the paschal lamb, crucified as man, yet triumphed over the powers of hell."[10]

---

[9] Ibid.

I felt Father trace three signs of the cross on my forehead. He then slapped me hard across the side of my head. I couldn't believe he'd hit me. It hurt. A dull "ouhh" rose up from the crowd.

Oh, a strike! Action, at last. Finally, real meat to sink my teeth into, D.G. all but hollered. *Perhaps a challenge, hey priest?*

I ignored him. Well, for a moment I did. But then a clanging sound from the chair I sat in grabbed my attention. Looking down, I found my left foot twisting hard to the left, banging against the metal leg of the chair.

Oh no. NO D.G.! I begged. *Not my foot again. Not now! You'll make me look like an idiot. Stop!*

Stop? Oh come, Von. Killjoy. The fun's just starting. You know. Mwaahhaahhaahaa and all that.

The clanging sped up and got much louder. I strained to get control of my foot, tensing every ankle muscle I had. For a second, it stopped. But then it suddenly started again. I panicked. Father Winnlyn stepped back and watched my foot hammering away on the chair. The edges of his mouth turned downward, his bottom lip protruded a bit and he slowly nodded as he seemed to analyze the situation. Then his mouth slowly turned to an evil grin.

"Be gone then demon!" Father continued, raising his hands far above his head. "Give place to the Holy Spirit by this sign of the holy cross of our Lord Jesus Christ, who lives and reigns with the Father and the Holy Spirit, God, forever and ever." [11]

"Amen," the crowd answered, more raised fists pumping the air.

---

[10] Ibid.
[11] Ibid.

I saw my mother slowly stand and step forward with a look of horror on her face. Her eyes were on my slamming foot. Harper stood next to her clinging to her hand, my foot holding his attention too. Dad leaned forward, concern written across his face. Oma sat relaxed in the pew, dangling her legs back and forth, her arms across her chest, while she gave me a smug look of total boredom.

"It's nothing, Mom. I'm fine," I called.

Behind her Moby, Derrick and Charlie slowly stood up craning their necks for better view of my banging foot, surprised looks on their faces. Julia sat, her eyes squinting as she looked from my face to my foot, back and forth. A few of the students sitting next to the main isle got up and walked closer to watch, disbelief on their faces.

I looked down at my drumming foot, striking the chair's leg even faster. I struggled to control it. For a second it came to a complete stop.

We having fun yet, Von?

D.G., please. I'm begging you man. Let my foot stop.

Oh, come now, Von. If it's worth doing, it's worth doing right! D.G. stated. *Do it full force. You need to be the demented fiend, a real example of Satan with all the bells and whistles, not some unrehearsed wimp.*

Again, the altar boy arrived next to the priest handing him a large gold crucifix. Father Winnlyn held the cross aloft and shouted.

"I adjure you, ancient serpent, by the judge of the living and the dead, by your Creator, who has the power to consign you to hell, to depart forthwith in fear, along with your savage minions, from this servant of God, Von, who seeks refuge in the folds of the Church." [12]

Father Winnlyn swung the gold cross zooming down and

---

[12] Ibid.

slammed it flat against my chest, nearly knocking the wind out of me. I heard a few people in the audience "oooh." My foot went back to knocking the chair leg. The altar boy stood a few feet away, smoking me with incense.

The priest again looked me over, made his estimate and raised the cross high above his head.

"I adjure you again, not by my weakness but by the might of the Holy Spirit, to depart from this servant of God, Von, whom almighty God has made in His image. Yield, therefore!"[13]

His hand and that gold cross came down upon my head. That hurt. Another moan rose from the audience.

Yes! Now we're talking, Von. The Demon of all demons! D.G.'s excitement scared me; I wanted him bored again. My foot continued clanging away.

"Yield, I say! Tremble before that mighty arm that broke asunder the dark prison walls and led souls forth to light."[14]

I felt the cross leave the top of my head, saw Father swing it high in the air and again slapped it flat against my chest. I managed to tense my chest muscles just before it struck.

"Make no resistance nor delay in departing from this man, for it has pleased Christ to dwell in man." [15]

D.G., D.G. Come on man. Give me a break here. I'll let you stay. Get your memories. Figure it out. Just let my foot stop, please.

Oh. Ooooh. What? What's happening? I can't see out your eyes. What's going on? Von, open your eyes, please.

[13] Ibid.
[14] Ibid.
[15] Ibid.

My eyes are wide open. What are you talking about?

I can't feel. It's like I'm floating, coming unglued or something. What is that? What is that?

D.G. Don't play around man. What's going on? Come on D.G.

Something's grabbing at me. I can't . . . It won't leave me . . . leave me . . .

I'd never heard D.G. sound that way before, like he was desperate. Suddenly, everything inside me got silent.

D.G. Stop clowning. Just let my foot stop. Please.

There was no answer. Father's booming voice shook me again.

"Depart, then, impious one, depart, accursed one, depart with all your deceits. Begone, now! Begone, seducer! Your place is in solitude; your abode is in the nest of serpents; get down and crawl with them. God you cannot mock. It is He who casts you out, from whose sight nothing is hidden. It is He who repels you, to whose might all things are subject. It is He who expels you."[16]

"Amen," the congregation answered. Almost everyone's fists rose in the air.

D.G.? Director Guy? Come on man. Where are you? The quietness inside shocked me. I looked down and found my foot still, the banging against the chair ceased. Could this priest actually do this?

Father Winnlyn signaled Sister Gill. She stood before the congregation and spoke.

"Everyone please stand. The page I handed out earlier is a prayer I taught to Von and his classmates years ago. Please recite it together now,

---

[16] Ibid.

loudly and clearly."

There was the sound of hundreds of people standing, of people rustling paper and then it got quiet. Sister began the reading and the voices of the masses joined her.

"Christ, guard me today against every poison, burning, drowning or fatal wounding. Please have your angelic army bind up Satan, his demons, all forms of witchcraft, of divination, of sorcery, the Ouija board, astrology, horoscopes, fortune telling, palm readings, and anything else associated with the occult of Satan and baptize us, your disciples, on the day of Pentecost."[17] [18]

I sat quietly listening to the prayer. I listened for D.G. He seemed gone. Was it possible? But, where would he go? If he didn't have me to keep him alive, then what? Had I harmed him, by going along with this?

D.G.? Say something, dog gone you. There was no answer.

Father Winnlyn stepped back and took a long look at me. I must have looked a wreck, but a huge grin broke across his face. He reached down and untied my feet and hands. Then he turned to the congregation and raised his hands high in the air.

"Please. Everyone, come forward and celebrate. For it is done. This demon has been cast out. Please welcome Von, safely back within the fold of the forgiven."

Applause filled the big church. Mom climbed the steps and hugged me as I stood up. Harper shook my hand. Dad patted me on the shoulder. Oma stood by Dad looking me over, almost suspicious. Father

---

[17] St. Patrick's Breastplate (Long version), http://spiritofthesword.net/?page_id=508, 11/11/2016. (Note: Incomplete version of this ritual used for the sake of brevity).
[18] The Catholic Warrior, Spiritual Warfare Prayers, Denouncing the Occult, https://www.catholicwarriors.com/pages/warfare_prayers.htm, 11/11/2016. (Note: Incomplete version of this ritual used for the sake of brevity).

Winnlyn pressed me forward, into the crowd where bunches of students, some I knew, some I didn't, crowded in close and congratulated me. I tried to smile, amazed at the number of them, surprised at their involvement and their enthusiasm. Julia slowly managed to squeeze through the horde and walked up to me. Her hand found my shoulder and she hugged me.

"How do you feel?"

I shrugged. "Not much different. Bruised where he hit me with that metal cross."

"Yeah. That looked like it hurt. Just tell me you're ok, ok?"

I smiled. "Yeah. I'm alright."

Then Moby, Charlie, Derrick, and Vivian crowded around me, tapped fists and patted me on the back. They even congratulated me.

Over the next twenty minutes or so, the service became a big social event and Father Winnlyn and Sister Gill joined right in. But because it was so late, the crowd began to slowly squeak their way out through the massive wooden front door. After a while, Father Winnlyn, Sister Gill and a small group of students were the last ones remaining. My family started edging toward the big front door as they traded final words with some of the congregation. But I found myself sitting in the second pew, wondering about Director Guy.

Julia saw me and sat beside me, put her hand on my knee. "What is it, Von?"

"If some voice decides to occupy someone's head, that voice then takes its own risks. It's not their head. Right?" I reasoned.

"I guess," Julia nodded.

"He was determined to figure it all out," I went on. "How it

111

happened and how to fix it and all that. Something about him just stood out, can't put my finger on it. But in the end, it's my life. It's my life. Right?"

Julia smiled. She squeezed my knee. "Who else's life could it be? I just want to know that you're alright."

I nodded. "After the holy water flood, smoke inhalation and cross slapping, I think I just need rest."

We stood. I noticed Charlie nearer to the rear of the church, waiting. "He said he'd give me a ride home," Julia said, leaning forward and giving me a peck on the cheek. I watched her walk away as I swung my coat back on. It dawned on me that she'd just kissed me. I buttoned my coat and smiled. D.G. might be gone but if I had more kisses like that in my future, I'd be fine.

I told Father Winnlyn thanks, told Sister Gill goodnight and began walking for the big entrance door. It happened just as I got to the edge of the candlelit area.

Salutations, Von, from the hell of a teenager's brain. Yours! A fate worse than death itself.

Aww D.G. God damn you.

Excuse me? You can't be using the name of the Lord, your God, in vain, especially after you've just been through an exorcism. You're in church after all.

I thought . . . I thought you were cast out, done for. Dead. Or something like that.

Look Von. Seriously. I refuse to be your local demon. I'm not schizophrenia, nor depression, not bipolar affective disorder or any of those second-rate amateurish maladies. I realize I can't define myself as

112

well as I'd like to, but I am certain about what I'm not. I am not going to harm you and the only way, the only way, we will ever reach an acceptable solution to all this is if we work together. That means communicating and cooperating. There should be no more silly silence experiments and I fully expect your help in figuring all this out.

I slowly turned back toward the candlelit altar. The altar boy was slowly going around extinguishing candles. Father Winnlyn took off his vestments. Sister Gill carried the incense burner and holy water bucket back into the storage room behind the altar. I shook my head and chuckled. Then I laughed.

Yeah, ok. I'll talk to you and be my usual irritable self. What a night. I'm not doing this again. I laughed again. *I'm tired and I'm going home.*

Good. Get some rest, Von. But you should be informed that other events occurred tonight.

Chapter Nine

{ Interpreting dreams can be tricky, Von. But in this case, I think it's a warning. }

Outside Perpetual Peace church the usual family argument developed. Martha wanted Von to ride in the car with the family. Von wanted to walk, reminding her it was only four blocks. Martha became angry that Von no longer took part in anything family. Von turned and started walking, his mother barking at his back as he faded into the night. I started to comment about his relationship with his mother, thought better of it and brought up a different topic.

Since we're just walking, Von, I need to tell you about the two memories I had tonight while your exorcism occurred.

This seemed to get his attention for he slowed a bit. *Two memories? Alright, fill me in.*

Well, as the priest tethered you to that chair, I remembered being strapped into a test pilot's seat on a high G-force centrifuge. Some technician strapped me in with a very heavy-duty harness, checked on the connections and then closed the cockpit over me. The whole cockpit began to speed up, spinning me around and around at the end of a long arm, with ever increasing speed. They use these centrifuges to test pilots and astronauts to see how much G-force their bodies can take. For some reason, I went through that kind of test. I don't know why though. I just remembered being tested in a centrifuge. The clarity of the memory surprised me, as though I was there living through it again.

Von stopped walking, put his hands on his hips and thought for a moment. *So, you must be some kind of pilot? Maybe we could look up current events in the news dealing with pilots?*

Perhaps. The memory might have lasted longer but then your priest friend started hollering, cuffing you with the crucifix and interrupted.

Von nodded and began walking faster. *But you said you had two memories. What's the other one?*

When you were walking in, I saw the altar illuminated by those hundreds of candles and I got a memory of being in a marriage ceremony. A beautiful woman stood next to me, shoulder to shoulder with me but I couldn't see my bride's face. We stood before an altar sort of like that one. The priest wore vestments of a different color but otherwise similar. That memory didn't last long, just a quick glimpse of her from the side, her shoulder, arm, her incredible dress and the layout of the big church we were in. I wanted to see her face.

So you're a married pilot, Von said. *At least, you have a little more to add to the puzzle. Maybe you crashed and died and your spirit isn't ready to go into the hereafter.*

Except that if I were a spirit, that exorcism might have driven me right out of you, Von. I'm not a spirit. That's why it didn't succeed. Somehow, I feel solid.

Von paced along Esplanade Avenue. But then he spoke to me as he walked.

Exorcism. I just went through a freaking exorcism. Like some vacuum cleaner being run over me trying to suck out all the dirt.

He turned onto Bell Street and moments later, made his way into the back door of his house. Everyone else wore pajamas and was turning in for the night. Von showered and went to bed, obviously tired. Within moments he was sound asleep.

I too felt drowsy and could feel sleep coming on quickly. I don't know how long we slept before the dream began, but once again, the gigantic clocks were back. Within the dream Von and I both stood there observing these two clocks, one running forward, one running backwards. For no reason I could determine, the backwards clock went from its vertical position to horizontal. Von and I were immediately transported to its surface and had to jump over the second hand every time it came around. A tiny cockpit with two pilots' seats appeared at the tip end of the second hand. Von and I began to shrink. Suddenly, we were both strapped into the two pilots' seats that faced each other. The second hand began to move faster and faster and as it sped up, we both felt more G-force crushing down upon our bodies. Between us was a digital display telling the time on the big clock we rode on. It too counted down. Everything else outside the cockpit blurred. We went so fast that all we could see was each other. As we sped up faster and faster, our feet began to merge into each other's feet. Von and I recognized what was happening to us and tried to resist, but the straps holding us and the extra gravity force pressing down rendered us helpless. I felt my feet and Von's feet become one. It scared me. I got the feeling that the merged feet didn't belong to me and didn't belong to Von either. Curiosity registered on his face. He wasn't enjoying this, but it didn't alarm him the way I experienced it. The digital readout between us read two hours and thirty-four minutes left to go.

The whole clock began to speed up. We spun faster and faster and as we did, our ankles and lower calves began to merge. My screaming surprised Von completely. The digital readout now read two hours and nineteen minutes. I screamed again and then I woke up.

Though I felt the sheets and mattress below, Von's eyes were shut, so I couldn't see anything. I presumed the sun wasn't up yet or he'd probably have woken up. I went back to sleep but before I knew it, the big clocks were back. The backwards clock again went horizontal and I found myself standing on its face. The face changed right before my eyes, morphing into a compass. I stood on the big 'E', east. This time, the compass dial gave off a soft glow that radiated upward a short distance. Everything else, the surrounding area off the dial, was black as night, so there was nothing else I could look at except the dial of the big compass. All the usual marks showed—north, south, east, west. The calibrated lines in between, all three hundred and sixty of them, ran the entire circle. Then, I noticed a bit of silver thread. It contrasted with the big 'W' at the west position. I picked up the thread and as I touched it, one end of it started growing, straight away, reaching out into the night, out into the darkness, it's end quickly going out of sight. I stood looking down at the big 'W' below me. The silver thread almost beckoning me to follow its trail. What was out there?

Saturday, May 9th

The next thing I knew, it was morning and I surmised we didn't have school that day. Martha appeared at the side of the bed, pulling the curtain aside, letting sunshine stream in upon Von. He awoke and sat up, stretching. He tapped his cell phone, got the time, found a text message to meet at Elaina's at ten a.m. instead of nine. I noted the frown his mother gave him, her hands on her hips, looking down at him.

"So. Do you feel any different? Is the voice gone?" Martha demanded.

"I feel fine, Mom. And yeah. The voice is gone."

Unmoved, she demanded more. "And would you tell me if it were still there?"

"I'd think about it." Von said, climbing out of bed and dressing.

His mother huffed, turned and walked away. She could be heard waking the younger children.

Ok. So D.G., I had a dream about spinning at the end of a second hand, you and me facing each other. You had that dream too?

Good morning. And yes, I experienced that same scenario. Our feet got pressed into one set of feet.

And the time kept ticking down, running out, getting closer to zero. Right?

Right. I saw all that, I answered. *Our feet merged and then our ankles.*

Yeah, Von said in a monotone. *I couldn't feel them anymore or have any control over them. That's weird. What does that mean? And why did you scream?*

I screamed because it scared me. I was losing myself. Scary stuff. Interpreting dreams can be tricky, Von. But in this case, I think it's a warning. The more time passes, the more you and I become one. I hadn't considered that until I had that dream. And that's the second occurrence where the countdown clock showed itself with less minutes left on it than before, which insinuates time is running out.

Yeah. It does run backwards, Von said. *So, I'm absorbing you, feet first. It's like I'm gonna have you for dessert. Not sure I like that. I never had dreams like this before.*

The second dream had something to do with west, I said. *I'm not sure what.*

That one didn't impress me much, Von answered. *I don't see any use for that dream. The first one caught my attention more.*

Von punched his cell phone and dialed Derrick, who answered almost immediately. "So it's at ten, right?" Von asked. "We're still on?"

"Yep. Everything's arranged," Derrick said. "Be there, OK?"

"Oh, I'm coming." Von pocketed his cell phone and headed downstairs for breakfast.

Von, LSD is not predictable. You have no idea what the results of Derrick's experiment will be. Don't go. Don't do this. I waited for his response, but he simply kept scooping scrambled eggs onto his plate. He seemed to be ignoring me again. *Von. You promised to communicate. Look. At least go look up LSD on Wikipedia or something. Get some information. You don't have to believe me. Find other sources. I'm certain of what I'm saying. This is not good. It could . . .* I stopped because he wasn't listening. He shoveled scrambled egg into his mouth quicker than anyone I'd ever seen eat. He took time to chew everything and then answered.

You invade my life, take up residence in my head, more or less put me through an exorcism and a psychiatrist and now we've got just so much time before I absorb you. Complain all you want, Von huffed. *But I'm determined here. You are digging around in my memories. You're controlling my foot. Hey. I'm gonna do what I gotta do.*

With that, he dumped his dish into the sink and took off out the back door. Within fifteen minutes, he knocked on a third-floor door of an apartment building just off Esplanade Avenue.

Chapter Ten

{ *Oh, so now, right in the middle of a volatile LSD experience, you suddenly get the existential angst?* }

"Lick paper?" I asked. Holding the page up to the light, I examined the whole thing and could barely make out small outlined rectangles on the sheet. "You want me to lick paper."

"It's blotter acid, Von," Derrick explained. "They soak each little square with LSD. You cut out the number of squares you want and soak it in your mouth. Don't swallow the paper. Just swallow your spit. You'll love it. Hey Elaina. Tell him."

She stood at a wall mirror adjusting her hair. "That's kid's stuff, Von. Can't hurt you. A lot of colors." Elaina turned and joined us at the kitchen table. "Trust me, you'll like it."

Von, please. Get out of here, now. These kids don't know what they're . . .

"I've never done acid, so what's a normal dose?" I asked. "How many squares?"

"Oh, start out with ten or fifteen. You can add more later if you want," Elaina said popping a strip of paper into her mouth.

"Here, try this," Derrick said using a scissors to cut a long strip from the white sheet. He stuffed a strip into his own mouth and began swirling it around.

I shrugged and swished the strip of paper around under my tongue. "Where's Moby? He wanted to trip too, right?" I asked trying to talk past the lump of paper. Derrick and Elaina looked at each other. Then Elaina gave an apologetic shrug.

"He called me an hour ago," Elaina said as though divulging a secret. "His dad came home drunk again and they had a big run in. He sounded confused, nervous. I think one of them hit the other one, but I couldn't tell which. I expect maybe he'll show up later."

After five minutes of soaking paper in our mouths, Elaina spit her paper into her hand. "That should do it." She stood, threw the paper in the trash can and slowly strolled away.

I found myself watching her wonderful hips move, happy that she'd decided to wear short shorts and a tank top that showed off her skinny waistline. Her long black hair reached her waist and danced across her back as she moved. She stopped at the doorway to her bedroom, looked back at Derrick, and then disappeared into the room. Derrick moved to his feet, then across the kitchen and disappeared like a summoned ghost into her room. "Scuse me," was all I heard from him. A second later, the door to her room closed.

Well. Guess I know what they're up to, I told D.G.

Von. Now, when nobody's looking. Into the bathroom, quick. Use your finger to gag. Make yourself regurgitate. Hurry, before it's absorbed into your blood . . .

I laughed. *Ahh, no. I don't think so. Barfing's never been my favorite sport. Besides, I'm not even feeling anything. I mean nothing at all and . . . ahh . . . at all . . . .*

Just then, my body began to register some strange sensations. It began like a mild floating feeling. Like gravity went away a bit. It was kind of nice. If this was all there was to it, I might try some more paper squares.

Oh oh, D.G. mumbled. *I felt that. The body absorbs its own saliva very quickly, Von. This version of LSD might enter the blood . . . the blood stream . . . fast. Oh Von.*

I began to feel like a balloon being overinflated. My neck and arms seemed to double their diameters and then immediately shrunk back to normal size. I checked my hands and arms. Then, an overbearing tidal wave of blood entered my head. I leaned forward, dropping my skull onto the wooden table and ignoring the loud 'thump' against the surface.

Vvvoooooonnnn, D.G. called. *Ooohhh Vvoooonnn iitttt mmaaaaayy beeee tooooo llaattttee.* There could only be one reason D.G.'s voice sounded like that. Game on.

The LSD came on so strong, I couldn't pick my head up. An ocean sound filled my ears so that I imagined the room filling up with surf-like waves. The rushing ocean flooded through my brain, cutting me off at the knees. My shoulders and arms collapsed, and I was just stuck there on the table. I think I passed out for some time.

When I could again open my eyes, I found that the refrigerator, the kitchen sink, in fact the entire room looked back at me, sideways. Colorful electric bolts outlining every object in the room. My head hurt from lying on the wooden table and the grinding air brakes of the garbage truck in the alley next door made me flinch. I forced myself to sit up, wiped slobber from my cheek and looked around.

As I lifted away from the table top, an overwhelming feeling that I wasn't alone in the room seeped into me. Because moans came from Elaina's bedroom, I thought maybe it was just those two going at it. But then the electric blues and reds that lined the kitchen sink, the toaster and the microwave oven distracted me.

Wwoooww, D.G. Are you getting this? I asked. I managed to sit up straighter. Then I tried to stand. It took me forever to get to my feet, but I got there. *Deee Geeee. Calling Deeee Geeee. You there, head voice?* I found myself swaying like a sailing ship on rough seas. *Saaay something man.*

I remember doing this before, D.G. finally said. *A college rock concert I attended. And then again for some military experimental project. I ingested LSD. Capsules I think. A military guy handed them to me. And that woman . . . the woman from the marriage ceremony, the one I married, she watched me ingest LSD with the most beautiful smile on her face. Her face. Yeah, she is beautiful. She recorded notes on a clipboard. She writes fast. Why would I marry someone that writes that fast? Why would my wife watch me consume LSD? For goodness sakes Von. This stuff is strong.*

I nodded my agreement but then the feeling returned that someone else was there, in the kitchen. I tried to look around, but the electric border visuals interfered and I couldn't focus well enough. I sat down hard and rested my head down onto my forearm.

Elaina had left her Apple iPad on the table. I pulled it closer and tried to look up blotter acid. A Wikipedia page came up, but all the letters of text splintered into little bitty parts and rose up off the screen. I pushed back just in time to avoid the black letter crumbs morphing into expanding blackbirds, the entire flock surging past my head. The swoosh of beating wings filled my right ear. As the whole flock circled above the kitchen table, I heard Director Guy call out.

For real? Birds? Hitchcock? Oh god, Hitchcock. RUN!

I struggled to speak but the flying vocabulary flock filled the room, the drumming of wings echoing all around me. Their wingtips dusted against my shirt and skin. In a few seconds, the entire flock shrank itself back down onto the iPad page into a perfectly formed lysergic acid diethylamide article.

Von, you took LSD, Director Guy muttered. *And you took a lllooooottt.*

Though the Wikipedia article went from blue to yellow to red, stretched, shrunk and wiggled, I managed to understand the words psychedelic drug, psychological effects, closed and opened-eye visuals, altered sense of time, delusions and a few other concepts that melted into meaningless mush. The last thing I understood was water soluble and that vitamin C helped to counteract symptoms.

Goodness Von. Don't take this stuff again. Uuufff. Dodge Derrick's damn delusions, dimwit.

Wow, all those 'd' words. That Shakespeare? I asked and pushed the iPad away because reading made my head wobble too much. The blotter acid twisted the venetian blinds around the window into a bow tie, the light streaming in around the edges of the blinds glowed a brilliant blue. The window frame went lemon yellow and my body began demanding more air. Candy apple red lines bloomed where the room's walls met ceiling or floor and then all those red-lines slowly expanded and contracted to match my breathing. Either the room was panting, or I was caught in my own lungs. My nerves screamed.

What the hell. Are you getting all this? I moaned, my head again down on the kitchen table.

Getting it? It owns me. Over-fucking-whelming, D. G. mumbled back.

Ok. At least you're there. I could not handle this alone. You seeing these memory flashes? That's when I first met you D. G., at the railroad spur.

Oh yeah. I see it, he answered.

I slowly raised my head off the table and again felt there was another person in the room. I barely managed to stand. The electric colors were still around all the furnishings, but if I turned slowly enough and took deep breaths, I could gaze around the room in focus. One of the table chairs stood by the bathroom entrance and there sat a guy I'd never seen before. An adult with a well-trimmed beard, maybe thirty-five or so, lanky, a little over six feet tall with a full head of dirty blond and slightly curly hair, just sat there. He had thick shoulders and looked strong. He wobbled when he stood, got his balance and stepped closer to me. He had the face of some Greek statue with a perfectly chiseled nose, strong cheek bones, sturdy jaw line. A blazing concentration from his deep set eyes at first scared me. But then I realized he was trying to recognize me.

"Who are you?" I asked.

Yeah, you have psychedelic borders too but try to look past that. It's me, Von.

His mouth hadn't moved. His words came to me in thoughts. I'd never seen him before, but that voice was definitely his.

D. G.? I've never . . . you've never . . . appeared. You've jumped out of my head and . . . landed? But how, D.G.?

No, Von. Don't ask the how questions. Neither of us has any idea. But, welcome to acid world. I told you so. Very unpredictable. What were you thinking? Neither of us controls this situation now.

Control? Are we ever in control of our lives? I asked him with my mind taking off in some unknown direction. *Half of the time I think control comes down to luck.* I had no idea why that just blurted out of my mouth, like I hadn't said what I'd meant, or maybe like I'd accidently said exactly what I meant, so I tried to correct it by going on. *And then an extra voice shows up and everything gets even more iffy.*

Oh, so now, right in the middle of a volatile LSD experience, you suddenly feel the existential angst?

The existen . . . the what? I had no idea what he'd said.

Teenagers. Existentialism man. The big questions. What's the meaning of life? Who am I? Why am I alive? How'd we get here? Where is civilization headed? You know. The big stuff.

I stood just staring at his electric blue face. I thought maybe my jaw hung open. Mouth breathers really creep me out.

You know D.G. I'm young. Ok? Screw the big stuff. We never get that stuff right anyway.

Yeah. You're right, Von. We're in the middle of this now. We'll just have to make our way through it. Though D.G. wobbled, straining to stand, he looked a little miffed.

I strained to understand that Director Guy had solidified and stood right there in front of me, never mind all his fringed electric glory.

So this is what you look like? Not what I expected. I reached out and pressed against his chest. I was astounded that he felt solid, moved a bit when I pushed.

Perhaps we should consider more relevant expectations than looks, D.G. said, his speech slurred a bit.

I expected you to look like . . . that guy that works the counter at the coffee shop. He strikes me as weird. Like he might actually enjoy getting into someone's head, you know.

D.G. just stood there looking into my eyes. He looked at the bedroom door as a new set of moans came through. Then he looked back at me, a questioning look on his face. For an instant, his whole face and chest turned brilliant yellow, electrified to red and came back into focus. I turned and leaned on the table, catching myself. He wobbled backward and sought the safety of the chair again. As I sat down, I thought about my smartphone. I fished it out of my pocket, tapped the camera app and aimed the thing at D.G. If he was solid now, I wanted proof that he'd been there. I tapped the red button and the flash went off. When I looked at the picture, D.G. wasn't there. The chair he sat in showed, as well as the refrigerator on the left half of the picture, but he wasn't visible at all.

I break your camera? D.G. asked.

Wow. You really are stuck in me. Exorcism. Now LSD. You can't be photographed. People only know about you because I tell them. I can't really prove you exist. But how to get you out of me? I mean, I like you and all but . . .

If I could get up and leave, I would. You're correct. I'm stuck. But at least we could get out of here. This place is drab and depressing.

No more sounds sprang from the bedroom. I figured Derrick and Elaina were exhausted, asleep or tripping. I steadied myself on my feet, unlatched the hallway door and started down the stairs. Stepping out onto the street, my body celebrated having more breathing room. The gray overcast clouds slid sideways across the sky, churning as they went. I sat down on the stoop and was joined seconds later by Director Guy. The traffic on the street seemed about average but each car moved in jerky fits and starts, colorful trails outlining and trailing each vehicle, the blotter acid still having its way with my vision. The park across the street displayed the greenest trees I'd ever seen with yellow outlines around all the trunks and branches. The black wrought iron fence had turned to battleship gray. Each bird's chirp sounded as though it were addressing me personally. A blaring car horn nearly knocked me off the stoop. I had to catch my breath.

Maybe a walk, I suggested standing.

People strolled about, mostly shoppers running errands, carrying bags of all sorts, checking their smartphones. A bike rider nodded at me and I wondered at how his feet cranked through blue and red spirals so slowly yet the bike flew by so fast. The photography supply store next to Elaina's apartment complex was closed. Perpetual Peace church next door to it had its doors wide open. I started walking past the church and realized D.G. was following. It felt strange. He'd always been a voice that I could turn off and on as needed. Now, he tagged along, right there, as unstable on his feet as I felt.

We walked past the church, past the flower shop, the instant check cashing business and came upon Julia's mother's business, Madam Paris' Voodoo shop. 'Traiteur, Palm & Tarot Card Reader, Healing Arts,' it said on the sign. Sister Margarita Paris herself sat in a wicker chair under her awning that shaded the front porch entrance. A colorful shawl wrapped around her shoulders and dress. She watched us wobbling along on the tree root cracked sidewalk, taking hits off her cigarette as she watched.

I knew Margarita Paris well, Julia, and I having gone to the same school since second grade. My mom actually paid this woman money for palm readings and for advice in general. She considered Margarita Paris her backup religion. Julia, Moby and I had grown up playing hide and seek in the Paris store and outside patio, hiding among the charm necklaces, the black polished leather capes, posters, candles, incense, woven garlic and untold magic items her shop held.

I realized D.G. was absent and turned, looking back down the wide sidewalk. D.G. stood, still in front of Perpetual Peace church, gazing up at the tall steeple that pointed upward to the clouds. He turned, saw I was ahead of him and meandered my way until he caught up.

Religion. Completely unsubstantiated suppositions. But, the exorcism turned out to be great fun, huh? D.G. said, wobbling along.

You totally freaked me out grabbing control of my foot, I told him. *Nothing scared me like that.*

You mean, like this? My left foot turned unexpectedly outward and then inward. I tripped and nearly fell. Though I knew he meant it as a joke, I hollered at him, out loud.

"Damn it D.G. I told you I don't like that. Cut it out!"

Margarita Paris immediately came out of her chair. She blocked my way, moved close to me staring straight into my eyes.

"Mais Von, whoo you talk'n to?" she demanded. She glanced to my right and back at me. For an instant I thought she saw D.G., but then that would be ridiculous. "Whoo you see der? Somebody der." She leaned in really close to my face, focusing in on my eyes.

Julia's mom, right? D.G. muttered trying to stabilize himself. *The one that does Voodoo?*

"Beeg eyes. Uh huh. I see you eyes. All bloodshoot. You stoned," she jabbered at me in her Haitian accent, pointing at my chest. She grabbed my wrists and turned them up examining my forearms. "Horse man? Cocaine? You shoot up shit?"

"Naw, Sister Paris. I took some acid. LSD. Lots of visuals, you know. And I was just talking to myself. Probably the acid's effect on me," I said hoping it would calm her down.

"No play me, boy. I see dis before. You talk at somebody. Den you hear answer. So, dat somebody talk back. I see dis before. Whoo's der? Tell me, Von. Don't play."

Von. Can we just sidestep this Gris Gris woman and keep going? Her insistence and LSD are an ill combination. Let's go.

I glanced sideways at D.G. "Why man? I know this lady. She's cool." I realized too late I'd said it out loud again. Margarita Paris' eyes got even larger.

"Freend? You got maginary freend? Huh Von?" she insisted.

"Did your beautiful daughter tell you about the voice I've had in my head a few days now?" I asked. "I wouldn't mind if she told you cause she's just so beautiful and I'm a gutless bastard 'cause I can't even admit I'm in love with her and of course you're so outstandingly cool . . . '

Von, keep your wits about you! If she drags us into that shop . . .

" . . . and this voice is . . . is . . . like I don't know . . . like interesting, bothersome and perplexing all wrapped into one, you know? And I gave him the name . . . Director Guy . . . well D.G. most of the time." There didn't seem to be any brakes on my talking.

Margarita grabbed my arm steadying me. "You com eenside. You trippin'."

Von. Von. No. Please. Von, D.G. protested as I was led inside.

131

"Can I marry your beautiful daughter?" I thought it an earnest question, but Margarita only nodded quickly.

"Julia want cleen man. Sober. Ok? You com eenside. You com. We get to bottom quik quik." For a skinny mulatto woman she had a steel worker's grip. She tugged me along with little resistance.

Aw Von, really. A palm reader? You want superstitious quackery while on acid? D. G. protested.

I didn't even bother to answer him. There was no resisting Julia's mom. Her shop was dimly lit. I bumped a table she led me up to. Every little gris gris doll on the shelf seemed to stare at me, little color lines surrounding each of them. She pulled out a deck of cards that were twice the size of any I'd ever seen. She placed the entire deck face down on the table and with one quick multicolor motion spread them fan-like across the table. Each card pulsed with color.

"Peeck card to tell of D. G. Guy. You chooze. Chooze wone," she ordered.

Temporarily drawn to the flexing muscles of her halo-lined face as she spoke, I managed to break the trance and look at the cards again. I picked the sixth card from the left.

"Uh huh. Mais. Wat I say?" she said after I handed her the card. She turned it toward me showing a man wrapped in a long, hooded, black robe standing next to a river. He stood alone, unmoving, perhaps sad, crying or at least lonely. There were clearly no electric outlines around this card, though everything else still showed the effects of LSD.

That does not accurately represent me, Von. I'm bored and tripping, not depressed. Can we go now?

I looked over at D.G. and chuckled. Marguarita caught the look right away.

"Der huh? D.G. Guy right der?" Her left hand flashed out, leaving a blue red trail through the space between us. She grasped at the air. To my total shock, her hand caught Director Guy's arm and dragged him toward her.

Hey! D.G. protested trying to yank back against her.

"You leeve Guy here. Yeah. I keep leetle while," Marguarita commanded.

Tell her let go! Get her off me! D.G. struggled to free himself but her grip held him. He panicked, his face cringing.

How in the world? I asked.

Who cares how. I feel it. It's taking energy. It's taking something. Get her off. D.G. struggled but couldn't free himself.

"Clock dreem," Marguarita muttered. Her eyes drooped, almost closing, but her left hand kept its grip on D.G. "Clock go backward? LSD looze clock time? Waste time." Suddenly, her eyes popped open and she looked hard at me, each line in her aging face outlined with a rainbow of colors. "Wat dis clock dreem?"

How in the hell did she know about that? I asked. D.G. looked stunned.

Don't know. Her grip is sucking me dry. I . . . I . . . Get her off! D.G.'s panic grew more severe.

"Mama Paris," I begged, "you have to let him go. Please. You're hurting him."

Her eyes drooped again. Her grip remained but then she mumbled, "No, you go eenside, find medicine cabinet. You go now," she said with flicking fingers shooing me out the door, red and green waves flashing off her fingernails. "Get vitimin C. Shewable."

D.G. again struggled to release her grip, but she didn't even seem to notice his effort. I tried to focus to get the colors to go away.

"What? Vitamin C? In your bathroom?"

"Vitimin C. Stop LSD. I have herbs but Vitimin C more fast. You go. You go." Again she pressed me toward the door, still holding onto D. G.

I stepped toward the door stunned at how she controlled us. Had she reached into my head? I stood bewildered, electric outlines all over the place, amplified sounds coming from the street again. She motioned at me to get going, so I turned further into her shop, my eyes trying to accommodate the dimmer environment.

Electric outlines began to surround objects as my eyes adjusted. I walked through a display room showing off shelves full of her merchandise. The skulls on the top shelves made eye contact, their broken tooth smiles animated in orange. I swear one of them spoke to me, but I had to find the bathroom, so I went on. The beaded curtain separated their living quarters from the shop and as I eased through the clattering jewels strung there, they sounded like snare drums in my ears. Their wavy movement caused oceans of visuals as I stepped through.

"Hey Von," came Julia's cheery voice. "You feeling ok after last night?" She put her book down as she came up from lying on the couch. Her feet touched the floor and her expression got serious, her eyes concentrating harder. "Von?" she said standing. She crossed the room at a superhuman speed until she stood before me. She focused on my face. "What the hell? Are you on something?"

"Your mom sent me to get vitamin C. The medicine cabinet."

She glanced over my shoulder and back at me. "Where's Mom?"

"In the front room. She got hold of D.G. Won't let him go. I think she's hurting him."

"D.G.? Is he still around? I thought the exorcism . . . "

"Yeah. That exorcism didn't work. She said get vitamin C."

"Von," she asked touching my chest. "What are you on?"

"LSD. Derrick and Moby's idea. They thought it might . . . "

"Oh, Von," she said frowning, closing her eyes, making waves of yellow vibrate into the air around her head. She turned and marched into their bathroom. I thought I heard a car wreck but then realized she'd slammed the medicine cabinet. She came back, handed me a bottle of vitamin C, spun me around as if I were the middle of a tornado and pressed me through the cymbal-crashing bead curtain. Her hands upon my shoulders, she drove me back into the front room.

Marguarita Paris stood stone still, her left hand holding onto D.G., her fingers like talons closed around his arm, her eyes drooping, trancelike. Julia parked me in front of her mother and then stood there looking over her mother's posture.

"Mom. What are you doing?"

"Hold D.G. guy. Voice guy jump in Von head," her mother answered from her deep trance.

D.G. seemed weakened. His knees were about to give out. He leaned against Margarita's grip, his head beginning to droop forward.

"I'm sure she's hurting him. He looks weak," I told Julia.

Julia's head snapped toward me, again throwing yellow vibrations out around her. "Looks? Wait. You mean, now you can see him?"

"Yeah," I nodded. "It started after I took the LSD. He followed me here. How can she grab him like that?"

135

Julia turned back and placed her hand against her mother's cheek. "Mom, I want you to let go. Turn loose of Director Guy. Now."

Slowly, her mother's eyes opened completely. She gazed into Julia's eyes. To see these two lock eyes was like watching a slow motion lightning strike. The two haloes that surrounded them became one.

"You feel too, yes? You have power eenside you dear child. You get my powers. Inherit, yes. You . . . "

"Mom. I'm going to college. To study psychology. We've talked about this. Please let D.G. go. Mom."

"Dreem clock. You feel? Very important for Von. You feel through me, I know. Very important see Von again. You must help."

"Ok. Fine. We'll help him," Julia reassured her mother. "Now turn D.G. loose."

Slowly, Margarita's grip relaxed, her fingers spreading wide. D.G. stumbled backwards and went to his knees on the floorboards. Smokey gray outlines wavered around his form. He sat on his heels, his hands upon his knees bracing himself up. He took deep breaths, turned and looked up at me and nodded.

Von, we have to get away. No choice. We have to. Damn this LSD stuff. And whatever powers she has. We have to go.

Julia stepped closer to Margarita embracing her. As she held her mother with one arm, she turned toward me, took the vitamin C bottle from my grasp and held it one-handed in front of me. I marveled as she held the bottle with her ring and little fingers, unscrewed the top with her first finger and thumb, carefully poured three one-thousand milligram tablets from the bottle into my hand, and then re-screwed the top back onto the bottle. Julia, goddess of my life, had pulled off another miracle.

How could she do that? For a moment we just stood there staring at each other.

"Von. Put them in your mouth. Chew them up. Ok?" Julia fussed.

I suddenly realized that my hand still held the three tablets. I did as she instructed.

"Can you walk home?" she asked, her arm still around her mother.

I nodded.

"Get your butt home and go to sleep. Get rest. Take this with you." She pressed the bottle of vitamin C back into my grip. "I'll see you Monday at school. Sober up." She leaned forward and pressed her forehead to mine, her hand on the back of my neck. It felt really good, her forehead, her warm hand. I watched her walk with her mother back through the hanging bead curtain.

D.G. stood. *Rest sounds really great.*

I stood in a trance watching Julia and her Mom retreating toward their living quarters.

Let's go to your house, D.G. said.

Are you ok? I asked D.G. but watching Julia and her mom disappear behind the beaded curtain.

Weak. I feel so weak. And I'm worried about what Margarita said about wasting time on the clock. Let's get out of here.

Chapter Eleven

{ Doc, you know good and well you can't force me to do anything. }

Von got us home, showered and asleep in short order. Luckily, by the time he arrived at his back door, the LSD was beginning to wear off. He knew all the tricks to moving through the house so as to avoid his mother, father and siblings. I resided within him in a totally exhausted state, barely alert and retreated as far into Von as I could go. I didn't want to talk at all. I felt the warm shower and relaxed a bit and once he pulled the sheet over us, I slept almost immediately. I sensed a dull passage of time, maybe a few hours, during which I slept hard. But after a while the dreams arrived with such a bold vibrant presence I thought LSD still persisted in his bloodstream.

The clock presented itself horizontally right at the beginning. I stepped up upon its face and walked around noting the positions of the hour and minute hands. Still counting down, I discovered that the clock now read 2:07. Had Margarita been right? Had we wasted twelve symbolic minutes on this dream clock? What did these minutes mean? How many of these minutes equaled one day in Von's life? How many days would two hours allow? I stepped over the hour hand and wandered around the big clock's face, hopped over the sweeping second hand as it came around and then I realized I was dreaming, yet I still occupied the dream.

The realization of dreaming I assumed would wake me, but

remarkably, it didn't. Somehow, I was cognizant of being in a dream and awake, all at the same time. How could this be? Suddenly, another memory hit me. I had had these kinds of dreams before, in whatever life I'd come from, I had once done this. There came a brief apprehension, but I managed to quickly adapt and the fear vanished. Then I recalled having some control within the dreams I'd had and even remembered that such trances are known as lucid dreams. I wished the second hand away so I wouldn't have to keep leaping over it and instantly, it disappeared. I wished the clock to reverse its direction so as to give Von and I more time before reaching zero, but that didn't work. Apparently my desire for more time antagonized the 'rules' of this dream and wouldn't be allowed. Instead, the clock face transformed to the compass face. Again, I stood close to the large black 'E' on the east side of the huge dial. North and South were written in the same large black letters, but a bright red 'W' occupied the West position. That seemed odd. I approached the W and as I did, it turned yellow. I stopped, backed away from it, wondering if it would return to red. Instead, it turned blue. I moved over the 'W' and while staring straight down at it, it turned red again.

The entire compass floated in complete blackness, but just touching the dial near the W, was the thread. I remembered it being silver before, but now its color matched whatever color the W took on. The thread reached far out into the darkness, its end still out of sight. Without warning, the clock face and its hour, minute and second hands were back.

I thought of Von and willed him to be here, with me. Instantly, he stood next to me.

Von, look.

Wow. We're back here, huh?

It switched to the compass, emphasizing west . . .

Yeah. Like before, right? What is all this trying to tell us?

We both hopped over the second hand as it swept past. As it did, I willed us into the centrifuge. Both Von and I were immediately strapped into the two pilot seats, facing each other, the long arm of the centrifuge beginning to accelerate. The increasing G-force pressed upon us and the digital indicator between us showed two hours and five minutes remaining. Von yelled, "Naw, not that again." Our feet, ankles, shins and knees were now merging into one being. It scared me into silence and I felt the muscles of Von's jaw grind his teeth together.

I willed us onto the compass face again and right away, we were there.

I can see you D.G., just like with the LSD. Are we still tripping?

No. It's a lucid dream. I think it's telling us to go west, Von. Some kind of answer lies to the west and we don't have a whole lot of time.

Suddenly, the clock face reappeared below us but for some reason we slid off of it into the darkness and then, I was completely awake. The dream ended.

Von sat up, turned on his table lamp and looked around the room. He stood, made his way down the hall to the bathroom and peed into the toilet.

I presume you got that entire dream? I asked.

He nodded. *Uh huh*, he said as he washed his hands and looked into the mirror. *I must not be tripping anymore 'cause I can't see you.*

That was the most powerful dream yet, Von. It's telling us something. We're merging more. Time is running out. We have to go west. I feel sure of it. We have to.

Von nodded and walked back to his bedroom. He took a deep breath. *I can't go west now. We have final exams. I may not like school, but I'll be damned if I want to fail junior year and have to repeat it all over again. Especially with all my friends going on to be Seniors. Hell no. I'm not going anywhere, D.G.*

Von. If we merge, you may not be around to experience junior or senior year. Some new guy might replace you. Better to redo junior year as yourself rather than lose yourself and get replaced by we-don't-know-what.

He turned out the light, lay down and pulled the sheet over himself, but remained silent.

Von. I have to figure this out. For me to get the hell out of your head, we must go west.

Yeah, but see, I got to thinking about the merging thing. I figure I'll just absorb you. That's all. I get full control again and problem solved. Let me sleep. He turned over and shut his eyes with such finality that I knew he wouldn't talk any more. I didn't want to force him into ignoring me, so I left him alone. In fact, I still felt tired and fell asleep not long after that.

Von slept late and so did I. The Sunday morning sun filled the window, hanging above the next door neighbor's elm tree. His mother and siblings were gone. He said they usually made Sunday morning church services. Obviously, Von didn't and scrambled eggs for his father and himself instead. They ate breakfast together and traded interesting comments about the exorcism. His father even admitted he hadn't expected the exorcism to actually accomplish much. After that Von stayed in his pajamas and closed himself off in his room and the hours passed as a laid back low key day.

I was about to confront Von again about proceeding west when Martha broke into Von's room having heard a 'horrible rumor' from her husband. When Von confirmed that the exorcism had only bruised his chest and top of his head and that otherwise it failed, Martha grew angry. She accused him of manipulating his parents, the school counselors and Father Winnlyn. Von responded by opening an English book and saying he had to study for finals. She stormed out of the room. And I happily avoided that argument, but it messed up my chance to again speak with Von about going west.

Soon, Harper and Oma asked if he wanted to play checkers. He agreed and played one game with each of them. Harper asked if the demon had hurt.

"He never had a demon," Oma fussed. "He had a voice. You said it was a voice, right?"

Von nodded and made his next move.

"So what's the difference between a voice and a demon, huh?" Harper insisted. "They're both in your head, bothering you."

Von suddenly rose from sitting cross legged on the floor up onto his knees. "It's like having a little brother or sister. You can trust them sometimes but sometimes, YOU WANT TO KILL 'EM." With that, Von dove toward Harper sending all the checkers and board flying. Oma rolled away just in time so that Von fell upon Harper covering him almost completely. Harper giggled and squirmed trying to escape. Oma quickly regained her footing and dove onto the pile of brothers, flopping down on Von's back.

She managed to wrap her arms around Von's head covering his eyes, which Von allowed. He flailed his arms forward trying to grope for Harper. The three of them wrestled and rolled around on the floor for a while squealing and laughing. Suddenly, both younger siblings broke for the door, giggling as they ran. Von feigned a clawed monster roaring pursuit which made them squeal louder and run faster but once he reached the door, he simply closed it as they thundered away down the hall.

After the two of them left, he actually began reading material in his English book. From there, he asked for a little help with math problems and I got that he secretly worried about passing his finals more than I'd previously anticipated.

I attempted to speak to him about the ticking clock, that time slowly slid by, that merging may not mean he remains the same. He immediately froze me out, slicing at me with his sword of silence. Sunday turned into a muted demilitarized zone with no real communication allowed. He studied or napped, both of us still feeling the exhaustion from tripping on LSD. We got to bed early that night.

Monday, May 11th

The day arrived and the morning began with his mother hollering everyone awake. She reminded him that he had another appointment with Dr. Raoul Kalchavic. After breakfast, Martha and George drove Von to Dr. Kalchavic's office. They agreed he'd take the city bus to school afterwards.

Dr. Kalchavic's demeanor seemed uplifted today, with a big smile and energetic handshake. "Well Von," he began, "I've looked over my notes and you have such an interesting case that I've decided we'll try hypnotism. I think we need to, as they say, shake things up."

"But I don't know how to do hypnotism," Von answered.

"Not to worry. Your part is only to relax. I take care of the rest. And we record the session with this video camera. Very valuable data we will gain, oh yes."

Von nodded, shrugged. It was all still a mystery to him. But, Dr. Kalchavic gave very precise instructions, explaining what to expect and that Von would simply feel sleepy. "I for the most part want to talk to Director Guy. Hypnotism can be very handy tool to draw out an extra interior voice."

"You think he'll talk to you?"

"Oh yes. I can almost guarantee. He will respond."

His confidence proceeds him. Talks like an expert alright, I told Von.

The good doctor had Von sit in a big overstuffed chair, lean back, relax and concentrate on the sound of the doctor's voice. I must say I thought the doctor very proficient in his technique of lulling Von to sleep.

"You will remain asleep Von. You will be completely relaxed. I want you to bring Director Guy before me. I would speak with him." Von gave the slightest of nods. "Is Director Guy there?"

I'm not sure how the hypnotism accomplished it, but I abruptly discovered that I could control Von's voice. "I'm here doctor," I said aloud.

"Ah, very good Director Guy. Now let me say one more thing to Von. Von, you will now drop into such a deep sleep that you will not be able to hear the conversation between Director Guy and myself. Do you understand?"

Von nodded. I could feel his heart slow to very few beats per minute. He barely breathed. The boy was out of it. Interestingly, I remained alert. It was like being home alone.

"And so, Director Guy, I will need you to actually identify yourself. Who are you?"

I found it odd speaking through Von's mouth, the voice protruding from him didn't sound like Von at all. In fact, after just a few words, I got another memory. I remembered my voice, from my past life, so I went ahead and explained that to the good doctor. I then began at the beginning, explaining the first night I occupied Von's head at the abandoned railroad spur. I told of the near wreck, of helping Von through math and English classes and went on and on about how our relationship developed. Often, the doctor interrupted and asked questions. I apologized, because much of the time, I didn't know the answer. I explained that I had no memory at first, that I only had emotional reactions that insinuated things I'd learned in some past life. I began to tell him memories that had come up lately. I told him of the lucid dream, the clock and compass dreams and gave him all the background I could remember.

"This is very unique case. I don't sense any psychosis or neurosis in your responses. This is so very odd. So, you interpret these dreams. You think you and Von merge when countdown clock ends. Yes?"

"Correct doctor," I responded. "The best thing you can do for Von is assist us in determining how all this occurred. You should recommend he travel west. The sooner, the better."

"This is an indication that you want to take control at this point. I cannot allow such a thing. No. No, instead you will no longer have the ability to speak with Von. You will now be completely silent. Forever. You will never contact Von again. I command you to be silent. Starting now. Silent forever."

"Sorry doc. I can't comply with that one."

"I order you, I direct you to comply. Be silent. You now lose your voice. You lose the ability to . . . "

"Doc, let's not waste time. The clock is ticking. Be honest. You know good and well you can't force me to do anything. All the psychology texts say that a hypnotist can never make their subject submit to anything against their will. I refuse this silence you propose."

"You don't understand," Dr. Kalchavic answered forcefully. "That statement applies to the patient. You are just a figment of his imagination. You are not the patient, and so you are bound to follow my command. I demand it."

"No doc. Afraid not. You have mis-defined me. Basically, you've mis-diagnosed this case. What you don't get is that I am not a figment of his imagination. I'm not his disease, or his psychosis, or his schizophrenia. I am in fact, a completely self-sufficient, free-willed consciousness. I just happened to have ended up inside Von, I don't know how. If we can determine how that happened, if we can possibly reverse it, we will learn the answers to all these questions. So, I do have free will. And I will not submit to your directive. I do realize my refusal may bruise your professional self confidence and believe me, I don't mean to insult, but Von's need and my need are more important than your hurt feelings. Sorry."

I could tell my statement gave him pause. He was quiet. So, I continued.

"But doc, what I can do is stop talking to you. I assure you, Von and I will communicate. Bye."

"What! No. No you must answer me. Now. Right now. Answer. Answer I say!" Von's eyes were still closed, so I couldn't see the good doctor's reactions, but I could tell by the sounds I heard that his breathing had increased. He grabbed Von by the shoulders and shook him. Von slept through it, undisturbed. Then the doctor began to mutter, somewhat panicked.

"Impossible. This has never happened." I heard him move around the room, open books, read passages half out loud, slap the books shut. His frustration grew to new heights. Then he noticed Von beginning to stir. Slowly, Von rotated his neck, rubbed the back of his neck and opened his eyes.

"Wow. I don't think I've slept that hard in months," Von moaned as he stretched. "Phew. That was an incredible rest. I feel really good. Thanks doc."

The doctor leaned forward, frowning and flustered. "No. You must not wake up yet. I have not given commands for you to wake."

"Oh," Von looked surprised. "Sorry doc. Director Guy told me you wanted me to wake up. I guess he got it wrong, huh?"

Hearing that, Dr. Kalchavic flopped backward onto his psychiatric couch frowning at Von. He shook his head, went to his desk and began furiously typing on his laptop. After a few minutes, he took a deep breath, stood and shook Von's hand.

"Never in my experience have I seen a case so perplexing. Very interesting. I must call Dr. Donovitch and confer with him about this.

Incredibly interesting. Unfortunately, our time is up and this session is over Von. I will carefully review my notes and the video. We meet again here in a week."

They shook hands again and as Von exited the office, he turned back. "Wow, I like hypnosis. That was easy. I mean really easy and it felt great. Thanks, Doc."

Von virtually skipped to the trolley car stop on St. Charles Street. Once seated in one of the wooden seats, he asked me my opinion about the hypnosis.

What did you and Doctor Kalchavic talk about?

I gave Von a rather complete rundown of what we'd exchanged. The history, the dreams, the merging, the exorcism and the LSD trip.

But when I suggested that we should go west, he thought that indicated an attempt to take over your life. He tried to silence me. Ordered me to never speak to you again. He told me I would lose my voice right then and there. I, of course, refused.

Refused? Surprise ran through Von. *Wow. That means I would have never heard from you again.*

Right. That's why I refused. But I hadn't anticipated Von's reaction.

Damn it D.G. Why couldn't you just do it? I would have been alone again, just me in here. Finally back to normal. You think I like this screwed up situation?

Von. I thought we'd agreed. No more silence experiments. That we must communicate in order to reason our way through this. There's no choice but to talk to each other and to cooperate. You promised, remember?

148

Damn it. Didn't he hypnotize you?

Von, try to understand. I'm not going to be silent, period. I have to find out how all this happened to me and somehow, undo it. I'm not quitting.

Von smoldered. He went silent with a vengeance. Once the trolley reached Broad Street, he transferred to the Broad street transit bus. At Esplanade Street, he got out and walked to school.

Chapter Twelve

{ She has no idea how awkward it is to endure, her and her big Voodoo mouth . . . }

It was different walking to school without the regular crew of friends. D.G. didn't appreciate my not talking but I didn't care. I was pissed.

Von. I simply cannot retreat into some mental cavern and go silent.

"Yeah," I huffed but just kept walking. I didn't care. I checked in at the office, arrived late in first hour math to find my class reviewing for our final exam, scheduled for three days from now on Thursday. In second hour, Mrs. Keife took us through a list of things to expect on the English final exam, also coming up Thursday. I kept my head down, avoided participating in class discussion and didn't ask questions. My anger at D.G. hung on. I gathered up Mrs. Keife's handouts and stuffed them in my backpack. In the hallway, D.G. piped up.

Von. Silence guarantees mutually assured destruction. We only survive through communication and cooperation. Talk to me. Nothing else has brought any progress.

Oh, you call this progress, D.G.? The shrink had me hypnotized. If you'd have just done what he asked, I'd be free of this whole damned situation. But no. You have to be stubborn. Oh, you do piss me off.

Von. It was tantamount to him asking me to destroy myself. If instructed to go shoot yourself, would you comply?

Shut up. Just shut up.

Mr. Benedict reviewed for his American History final, coming up on Friday. Again handouts. I reread Lincoln's Gettysburg Address just to get my mind off D.G. Soon it was on to P.E. We'd have a skill drill final exam today and tomorrow. No way to study for those, thank goodness. I didn't find the final exam difficult at all in P.E. I completed the first day skill drills in twenty minutes and was sitting in the bleachers with Moby when the lunch bell rang. Moby and I ran like hell to beat the lunch line crowd but Charlie stood at the cafeteria door holding four sandwich bags.

"I got out of class early and one of the cafeteria ladies is a friend of my mom," he said as he handed us our lunch. "We need to talk. Julia is over by the band room waiting for us."

Hmmm. No doubt she'll have some questions about your LSD trip.

Leave me alone. I'd rather be with my real friends.

We crept around the administration building and found Julia, sitting on the tall cement steps of the music building. I hadn't seen these three since the Friday night exorcism. I hoped one of them might have a good idea of what I could try next. Everyone settled in, got a few bites of their sandwiches and the questions started.

"Von, Saturday at my house, you said the exorcism didn't work. So during that ceremony why were you shaking your foot so hard, banging it against the leg of the chair?" Julia asked.

"That was D.G., not me. He's figured out a way to move my foot. He got to clowning around, acting like he was a poltergeist or something," I answered.

"Wait," Charlie demanded. "You're telling me that D.G. controls your left foot?"

"At times," I said. "I can struggle against it, but he's figured out how

151

to wiggle my foot from side to side. He kept banging that chair. I fought to stop it. We struggled against each other."

"That's a really bad sign," Moby said. "If he's starting to take over your body, what's next?"

Von. I'm not some nefarious monster possessing you, ok? D.G. protested.

Un huh, I answered and went on.

Next, I told the group about the clock dreams and what D.G. thought they meant. They grew quiet and listened intently.

"Those dreams sound really detailed," Charlie said.

"Yeah, it was like I was actually there."

Of course, Julia and Moby wanted to know about the LSD trip. I described the visual effects of the LSD, along with being able to see D.G. and then told them how Margarita Paris had grabbed D.G.

"Yes. Whatever got into you deciding to use LSD?" Julia barked. "I don't like seeing you messed up like that, Von."

"Yeah. Ahhh. That was my idea," Moby said quickly. "Derrick and I planned it out. But when my dad came home drunk, I couldn't go to Elaina's apartment. Otherwise, I might have been there to keep an eye on Von."

Julia glared at Moby. "You came up with this lamebrain idea? You, on LSD, would have kept an eye on Von, also on LSD?" She rolled her eyes and shook her head. "You looked really strange Saturday afternoon when my mom confronted you," Julia said. "That whole thing scared me, Von. Didn't it scare you?"

I nodded. "You're right. Not my best idea. I doubt I'll do that again. Don't blame Moby. I could have said no to their plan. I agreed to take

LSD. The weirdness of it all got way out of control. And how the hell could your mom do that? Grab D.G. and hold onto him. That really freaked me out. She had him. He was getting weak."

Oh really. These exaggerations threaten to raise sea levels. She brought on a slight agitation at most. I was fine.

You were fine. You were weak as a kitten. I was there. Shut up.

"I have no idea, Von. Over the years, I've seen Mom do some undoubtedly . . . strange things."

I quickly changed the topic to the hypnosis session this morning. They asked plenty of questions and I answered them as best I could. Then I told them about the argument we'd had about going west and how the countdown clock made D.G. think time is running out.

They mulled over what I'd told them and before long their greatest concerns oozed right out of them.

Julia shook her head. "Boy, this is all coming up at a bad time. You have finals. And on top of that, you have to handle dreams and an extra voice that wants to run away? Yuck." She was right and they all looked as worried as I felt.

"I can't fail Junior year," I told them.

"That makes two of us," Moby said.

"Well Von," Julia went on, "My mom said she wants you to come by and talk with her. She's certain she can help you with this extra spirit, as she calls it. She wants you to promise to come by."

Oh hell no! D.G. exploded. *That's a negative, Von. I will not have that woman touching me again. Tell her no right now.*

Wait a minute, D.G. When she grabbed you she made a statement about the countdown clock. How could she know that? I never told her about that and I know you didn't. D.G. went completely silent. *Come on. We have to talk, remember. How did she know that?*

I don't have an answer for that, Von. A very curious occurrence, no doubt. But Von. I detest her grabbing me.

I knew that Margarita Paris was the only person that had been able to do anything at all that had a direct effect on Director Guy.

"Yeah," I perked up. "Yeah, I'll meet with her."

No Von! I swear, I don't want to go to war with you, but I'll fight to stay away from . . . "

Ok. Ok. Simmer down, D.G. Let me make some arrangements.

"But, your mom has to promise, no grabbing D.G., ok?" I told Julia. "She really freaks him out."

That woman won't concede that, D.G. raged. *She'll strategize some trap for me.*

Julia shrugged. "Sure. I can get her to agree to that. She listens to me."

"Maybe we should all go," Charlie said.

"Wow. Good idea. I love going to your mom's place," Moby said smiling.

"After school?" I asked.

Julia nodded. "Yep. I'll call her, let her know we're coming. And I'll get her to promise not to harass D.G. Ok?" We all tapped knuckles just as the bell rang.

Art and Science classes went quickly, those teachers also giving out review material for final exams. Again, I avoided eye contact with the teachers and didn't participate. When school let out, I found Julia, Charlie and Moby waiting near the front of school.

The walk to the Paris Voodoo shop passed quickly, us talking mostly of questions that might come up on various final exams. Reaching Margarita's Paris' Voodoo parlor, Julia grabbed the front door and waved us in past her.

Damn it, Von. Must we be here! I'm nervous as a cat. I do not trust this.

She really has your number, huh D.G.?

I swear. You're being vile, loathsome, foul, malicious; I could go on, D.G. growled.

Yep. Big ole vocabulary. Must have had dictionaries for parents. Maybe you're really a book.

Julia escorted us through the hanging bead curtain, back into their living quarters. Margarita stood next to her large round séance table, big smile on her face. The room was mostly dark, lit with twelve candles set away from the table on high shelves around the room.

"Good you com, Von," Margarita said with her ever ready smile. "We have beeg talk. Charlie. Moby. Good freends you bring." She and Julia kissed cheeks. Margarita hugged me as D.G. growled. She hugged Charlie and Moby and then assigned us each a particular place to sit.

"Not to worry, Von. Julia say I don touch D.G. I promise, ok?"

"You grabbed him and held onto him Saturday," I asked. "Could you pull him completely out of me?"

Julia, Charlie and Moby looked totally surprised, sat up straighter and leaned in. "Whoa. I didn't see that coming," Moby muttered.

VON! What! You've been scheming against me? YOU concocted this as a trap.

Slowly, everyone turned toward Margarita. She smiled. "Tear
155

spirit out? Yes, possible but make beeg domage. Do no good. Better to get whole story. So. First, you tell story. All about D.G. guy. From start."

Von! You traitor. A Benedict Arnold, D.G fumed.

I could tell D.G. was madder than I'd ever seen.

Why, I'm . . . I . . . At least the Voodoo witch demonstrates restraint. She hasn't tried to grab me. At least she can keep a promise.

I ignored D.G. and began to explain the entire experience to Margarita. I started with the night at the railroad spur and went from there. I covered everything. When it seemed I'd left something out, Julia, Charlie or Moby jumped in to remind me. After an hour, I finished with how Dr. Raoul Kalchavic failed to silence D.G. this morning. D.G. said not a word to me the whole time.

Once I finished, Margarita sat back in her chair, thinking, her arms crossed, her eyes moving over the surface of the table. "Tell wonce more time. Compass and thread. Just dis small part." I repeated the dream to her after which she reached across the table to me. "Geeve hands, Von." I held her hands. She closed her eyes, concentrating, completely still. After a few minutes she let go.

Moby and Charlie's eyes were wide with amazement. Julia observed carefully, her eyes moving between her mom and me. Finally, Margarita nodded and began to speak in a voice an entire register lower. Something in her rumbled the words out, like a voice for a three hundred pound man. It surprised us all.

"Most important eez trread. Spirit trread tie spirit to body. Find end of trread, all questions answered. Next, compass. West. Yes, you must go. I don know where. D.G. must lead. You follow."

Ha! You might recall my interpretation, Von. That we must go west. Me thinks this traiteur proves she's worth her salt after all.

"Next, dreem clock," the deep voice went on. "Time running out. You must to find eend of trread before time gone. Must. Merge very bad sign."

Again, my theories were applied accurately. Do you see, Von? You should listen to me, D.G. ranted.

She hesitated, closed her eyes for a minute, then opened them and spoke again in the same deep voice. "More cloze you com to eend of trread, D.G. will remember more. Memory get more strong, get more power."

Oh. Once again I'm vindicated. I told you the memories would prove crucial, Von.

"D.G. must remember every ting of his past to finish," Margarita continued. "Memory open door at eend of trread. At eend of trread, big challenge waits, I cannot see. Now, very important. Eef you fail, you must com back to me before clock run out. Den, I tear D.G. out. Not let merge happen."

Tear me out! Absolutely not. After we go west, I'll either resolve this to its completion or I'll be dead. I doubt I'll be returning here. But, we have to go West, Von. She's right about how serious this is. The sooner the better. Now would be best. Let's go now.

Margarita's eyes closed and her head lowered. Her chin touched her chest. She remained like that only a moment, then her eyes opened and her natural voice returned.

"So," she said. "You go, Von. Very important. Leave now." She flicked the back of her fingers toward her door, motioning me to respond.

Yes. She's right, Von. Let's go.

"But, I can't go now," I protested.

"Mom. We have final exams this week," Julia interrupted. "Von has to take those or he'll fail his Junior year."

"Yeah. I'm willing to go with Von too," Charlie said. "Seems like a great adventure. Find the end of the thread before some clock in Von's head runs out, a great adventure. And I'm worried about him. But I have finals too. We all do. We can't leave now. And there's another problem. Go how? None of us have a car. What do we do? Take a train or bus? That seems awkward. We don't have any way to go."

Hey Charlie's right, I told *D.G. I don't have transportation. How would we go? And suppose this chase west leads us to some place a bus or train doesn't go? Then what?*

Margarita listened to Julia and Charlie's comments but her eyes were riveted to me. "Eef you wait, you take beeg chance, Von. Tell me. When you see dreem clock first time, how much time clock say?"

I thought for a moment. "It said 3:00 and it started counting down backwards to 12:00 midnight. So I think it had three hours left to go."

"Ok. Wat eez first day you dreem of clock?" she asked.

"Wednesday a week ago," I said.

"So that's seven days," Julia said. "When's the last time you saw that clock and how much time was left?"

"I dreamt of it last night and it said two o'clock, so I have two hours left." I could see us all calculating out the remaining time in our heads.

"Ok. Seven days took up an hour," Julia reckoned. "So, you have fourteen days left before time runs out. That's if the ratio of clock hours

158

to days remains consistent. If that ratio changes, the amount of days left is anybody's guess."

"Finals start Wednesday," Moby reminded us. "And end at noon Friday."

"So final exams takes up two and a half of those fourteen days," Charlie said, "which leaves eleven and a half days to find . . . to find whatever."

That's inaccurate, Von. We lack adequate information of distance we'll need to traverse. We lack knowing how many days this task requires. It would be best to leave now. Don't you wish me gone?

But Charlie's right, D.G. I have no wheels and I have to take finals. Eleven days is longer than you've been in my head. It'll have to do, man.

The room became quiet, each of us digging into our own thoughts. Moby glanced at Charlie, tapped him on the shoulder and motioned with his thumb toward the door. Charlie nodded his agreement. They stood, swung their backpacks on and began wishing everyone goodbye.

"Don't forget finals guys," Julia said as she gave hugs to each of them.

Charlie and Moby hugged Margarita Paris goodbye and were out the door. Julia, her mother and I sat silently for a few moments. Margarita rubbed her thumb back and forth across a shiny black knot in the table's wood grain. Then Julia perked up.

"Mom, I want to go with Von too when he goes west. You know how long I've known him and we're good friends and . . . "

Oh, sweet girl, D.G. chimed in.

But Margarita's fingers halted. Her eyes met Julia's so that it stopped her mid statement. There was a silence between them that struck me as familiar between them. "Why you travel with Von?" Another silence, Margarita's stare intensified, her fingers frozen still. "Julia?" Margarita said. "No sex wid two spirit man. You Von long time freends, yes. But no sex wid two spirit . . . "

"Mom! Stop that! How embarrassing. I never said sex. He's my friend. I believe him and his situation and I simply want to . . . "

"Sex wid two spirit man make beeg mess. No way to predict. Beeg trouble," Margarita plowed on. "Wonce Von extra spirit gone, well then, be sure you on the peel, no problem. Den you want sex. Fine."

D.G started laughing uncontrollably. *Incredible. This woman is unstoppable.*

My jaw hung open in shock.

I watched Julia squirm with her mouth wide open, her surprise obvious. Though I strained to control my face muscles, I broke into a great grin. My shoulders began to shake and I couldn't hold back a laugh. Julia's face suddenly went red. She huffed a deep breath, brought both closed fists down upon the table's surface and tried to continue.

"Mom! You're embarrassing me. God sakes. I never said sex. I simply believe Von and . . . oh shit. Von, I'm so sorry. Oh how embarrassing. She does this to me all the time. Can't predict what comes out of the woman's mouth."

I sat with my hands over my mouth, fighting to hold back laughter.

A mother willing to expose her real concerns, no doubt, D.G. laughed. *How refreshing.*

"Ok you go west wid Von. Yes," Margarita ranted on. "You drive careful. But no sex wid two spirit man. Eez simple."

"Oh! I swear," Julia stood, her knees sending her chair skidding backwards, looking like she would come out of her skin. "You're going," she said pointing at me. "Get your backpack, Von, right now. Out. I don't want you hearing any more of this."

I stood, my effort to hide my stupid grin failing completely. I broke out laughing as I reached for my backpack.

Margarita stood and hugged me, completely composed as if nothing unusual had occurred. "You com back before dreem clock run out. Very serious, Von."

I nodded, giggles still seeping out of me. Julia grabbed my arm, pulled me toward the beaded doorway and pressed me through. Once in the store, I burst out laughing. When I looked at Julia, her face went as red as I've ever seen. Finally she rolled her eyes.

"She's done that to me . . . she can be so embarrassing. Oohh! The woman has no limits, none at all," Julia ranted with a hand on each side of her head.

"Are you kidding?" I managed between laughs. "You mom is so much more fun than my mom. I love it." I said wiping my face with a tissue from a box on the counter. "Hey well anyway, at least she's ok with you coming along."

"And she doesn't even see it. Has no idea how awkward it is to endure, her and her big Voodoo mouth . . . oh. I'm sorry. She can really be infuriating." Julia stood, her arms folded across her chest, taking deep breaths. Finally, she glanced at me and smiled, shook her head, dropped her arms.

I stepped close to her, touched my forehead against hers. "You ok?" I asked.   She nodded. "Ok, then there is something I need you to remember," I added.

"Remember? Remember what?" Julia looked confused.

"No sex with two spirit . . . "

"Oh stop, goofball. No. Don't you dare. Don't you dare take her side," she cried, pushing me toward the front door. "Don't you dare tell anyone at school either, especially Vivian."

"I'll see you tomorrow," I said stepping onto the sidewalk, still giggling.

She waved. "Don't forget to study. Finals, remember," she said, flipping the store's 'open' sign over to 'closed.'

Oh Von. Julia is such an alluring beauty. Don't tell me you haven't at least considered . . . D.G. couldn't stop himself so I did.

Oh gross. You think I'd have sex with you there watching? There could be no bigger turnoff than that. Yuck. Might as well have my mother watching.

The more serious topic we need to discuss, Von, is leaving. Going west now.

I wasn't going to leave. So, I just started walking, didn't answer, and D.G. remained quiet. Hopefully, he'd just get it.

Chapter Thirteen

{ "You're fighting with that voice in your head, aren't you?" }

As Von stepped into the back door entrance mud room, he spotted his mother standing at the stove using a spatula to shovel sautéed vegetables around in her cast iron skillet. Her interest in hearing the evening news kept the little kitchen TV blaring at a level that allowed Von to quietly tiptoe past. He was up the stairs in a flash, undetected. Once safely in his room upstairs, he dropped his backpack on the floor and flopped onto his bed.

I, on the other hand, had been thinking things over, considering the meeting with Margarita Paris and Von's friends. The notion of remaining in New Orleans, of not immediately going west, grated severely upon my nerves. I didn't want to assail Von with my insistence of leaving right away, but my very existence might be at stake.

Von. We could hitch-hike. We could leave tonight. Like Margarita said, I'll lead and you just go that direction. I'm sure we'll find . . .

Hitch-hike? Are you out of your mind? Do you have any idea what Louisiana cops do to hitch-hikers? You and me, all alone, out on the open highways? NO. Damn sure not that. And I love the idea that Charlie, Moby and Julia want to come with me. They're just the kind of back up I need for such a completely insane situation. If you get too much control of my body, Charlie is strong enough to hold me down and Julia and Moby are smart enough to talk me down, until I get control again. I'm sure as hell not going out there alone.

Von, you observed Margarita. She cautioned about the seriousness of all this. She said leave now.

Look D.G. I take finals. It leaves us almost a week to go west and seek whatever. If I can get some transportation. I don't even have a bike.

I considered his tone, his demeanor, his teenager stubbornness. But living inside an obstinate teenager has its limits and my nerves were wearing thin.

Oh yeah? I said belligerently. *Well, let's just see about that.* I yanked hard on his right arm, sending his hand straight up as far as he could reach. He looked in amazement at his arm as though it belonged to someone else.

Oh, you bastard, he fussed. *Fiddling with the controls again, huh.*

He yanked the arm back down but I immediately sent it right back up. He yanked down and again I forced it up. As we fought against each other for control of the arm, I decided to again use the left foot twitch to complicate his struggle. Now he had to deal with both. He reacted by wrapping his right calf and ankle around his left, entwining the left leg to stifle its movement. Because that failed to stop it completely, he rolled over onto his left side thereby gaining more control of the left foot by laying on it. However, I noticed that this maneuver got him very close to the edge of the bed. So, I yanked his arm up again. He tried a new tactic, grabbing his right wrist with his left hand, yanking down with both arms. I strained to force the arm upwards and it threw him off balance and toppled him off the bed. He crashed onto the floor and was forced to wrestle with himself for control.

Fond of this, my young adolescent?

164

Screw you, you bastard. Gimme my arm back.

I twitched the foot hard to the outside and it rolled him over, his knees and then his elbows knocking hard against the floorboards.

"Ow, you rat!" He hollered out loud.

I sent the right arm out to the side, tearing it out of the grip of his left hand, and used it to flip him over again the other way.

"Damn you," he hollered again.

I say we leave at midnight, young one.

"Screw you brain invader!"

The noise of our struggle grew louder. Suddenly, the door to Von's room sprung open and there stood Harper and Oma, both of them with enormous grins.

"Yeah!" Harper yelled, jumping onto Von and starting to wrestle with him. Oma was only a second behind wrapping her arms around Von's neck.

Assistance has arrived, I yelled. It was just the advantage I needed. I flipped us back and forth on the floor using both foot and arm. Though we rolled over Harper once, I managed to avoid both children each time I pressed us over with the right arm. Oma hung onto Von's neck giggling wildly. Harper had wrapped his legs around Von's middle and clung to his left arm. Frustrated, Von hollered.

"Damn you, D.G. You'll never control me."

It took Oma only a second to realize what she'd heard. She turned loose, slid back from Von and stood, a focused frown on her brow.

"You're fighting with that voice in your head, aren't you?"

Harper turned loose and quickly stood by Oma. "What? Is it taking over your body?" Both of them looked worried.

Damn you D.G. You're scaring them.

Oh wretch. If they go to your parents with this, I told Von, *we'll never get out of here.*

I got this. Let me go, Von said.

I immediately relaxed and let him sit up and face them.

He swung his feet under his thighs and sat Indian style.

"Ok, so do we still have our bank?" Von asked big eyed.

Both Oma and Harper nodded, their eyes as large as his.

"And what's the bank really for? Why did we invent it?" he asked.

"It's our private place where we hide our secrets," Harper piped up.

"Things we don't tell Mom and Dad," Oma added.

Oh Von, you sly manipulator of children.

"That's right," Von nodded. "Very good. Now, you remember about two months ago you two had locked your bikes together and the next day when you tried to unlock them, you accidently knocked over the gas can in the shed, caused a spark and caught your back tires on fire? Remember that?"

Harper and Oma stood just a bit straighter, their expressions sober as they quickly glanced at each other.

"And you remember that I fixed both your back tires and we never told Mom or Dad, right?"

They both gave somber nods.

"Ok. Well, I need for this little wrestling match to also go into our bank. We don't tell, ok?" Von watched them carefully waiting for the nod. After a moment, both their heads bobbed up and down.

166

"But is the voice still there?" Oma asked.

Von nodded. "Yeah. But not to worry. I got this. Ok?"

"But you were fighting with it," Harper protested.

"Well, we were wrestling, but we're not angry. We're just deciding something. Ahh, something important." Von grinned.

Both Oma and Harper just stared blankly back at him.

"Just a friendly little wrestling match. That's all. I promise," Von added.

Still the blank stares.

"So, this is in the bank, right?" Von regarded his siblings cautiously.

Harper and Oma glanced at each other and then both nodded. "Yeah, ok. In the bank," Harper added.

Von immediately held out his fists, one before each child. They each placed their right fist on top of Von's and their left fist below. They then brought their fists against his, tapping his fist twice. "Chick-a-lock," they recited together.

"Right on. You guys are the best," Von told them.

Still, they just stood there, blank expressions. "What?" Von asked.

"So what will you do with that voice?" Harper asked.

"Not to worry babes. I have a plan and all will be taken care of. I'm fine. I promise. The voice won't be with me much longer. Ok?"

"Ok," Harper mumbled. He turned and left.

Oma stood, suspiciously considering Von. "We might be little but we're not easy to fool," she grumbled. Slowly, she turned and left too.

What is the probability they divulge that secret? I asked Von.

Naw. You'd have to beat it out of them.

If they don't inform on us, we could disappear tonight.

How D.G.? You want to walk? Buses and trolleys shut down at night. I'm not hitch-hiking.

I do not relish making threats Von, but if you do not proceed west within ensuing hours, I will refuse to assist on your final exams. The prospect of a second year as a junior looms.

So that's the card you're playing, huh D.G.? Well, here's my bid. If you don't help on my finals, I'm not going west at all, ever. Those tests are all on computer, graded digitally. We usually find out our grades within five minutes. Cause me to fail and we go nowhere. Now top that, sucker.

He might have been a failing junior in high school, but his negotiating skills were every bit as innovative as mine. I had no rebuttal and though I labored to fabricate one, I remained silent.

After a while, I felt that sneaky little smile of his creeping across his face. That grin grated my nerves and I didn't know how to control his facial muscles. I was certainly intellectually superior to the spoiled little brat, yet, I couldn't convince him to leave. Though I could make him wrestle with himself, I didn't control enough of him to make an escape.

Teenagers! Twerps. What good are teenagers? They whine about the unfairness of living, don't care about politics unless it involves their Facebook page, build their egos on toothpick stilts, have no notion of where money or value comes from and work ethic, well, you could just forget work ethic. Whoever the hell invented teenagers should be condemned to teaching high school classes of at least four hundred students for months on end.

For a while, I wanted to stomp. To throw things. Oh, to possess arms and legs able to express how pissed off I felt. I was had, by a teenager, a teenager that didn't even study. Which should be illegal. It got to me so much I felt I was becoming a pouting teenager myself.

And the more frustrated I felt, the lighter Von's mood became. He danced around the room, took a shower singing some ridiculous tune from some obscure group I'd never experienced, a close approximation of salt in the wounds. Then he dried off, climbed into his pajamas and hit the sack. He was asleep in moments. I however grumbled away for at least two hours trying to think of some maneuver, some tactic I could use to force the situation to my advantage. I finally tired of the effort and fell asleep.

Tuesday, May 12:

In the morning, Von bounded out of bed like an athlete. He was downstairs before his mother, cooked his own eggs, ate and was washing his dishes when George and Martha entered the kitchen. His parents were taken aback. They asked if he were ok. His friendly attitude toward them was obnoxiously sticky sweet. I wanted to slap him.

He left with his backpack, found his friends on the sidewalk and delighted in their company. He hadn't acknowledged me since last night and I still felt too bruised to speak first.

Of all the rotten luck. Stuck in a teenager, in this teenager. What had happened to cause all this? I wasn't any closer to answering that question and if I discovered such an answer, I might still have no way to get out of Von. I abhorred the possibility of living out my existence in his head, a fate worse than death itself.

My complaining did no good. I would have to relent. I would have to assist with his final exams or just wait for this merging thing to absorb or consolidate both of us. And if he didn't go west at all, stayed around here and the clock began to run out, he'd obviously approach Margarita Paris so she could tear me out of him, a fate that would equate to death itself. Grrrr.

My emotions steamed ahead of my thinking, breaking my concentration often. I gave no effort to attend to the various teacher's final exam reviews. Interestingly, I did witness Von taking notes, of all things. Brilliant. He waits till the last possible moment to absorb freely presented knowledge. Math and English classes whizzed by. American History seemed to forget all the wasted turf wars in foreign lands and crooked politicians that got us there. Finally, PE presented the second half of his final exam skill drills, making Von huff and puff through huge numbers of pull-ups, push-ups and sit-ups. But, the teacher gave him a C+ for the year. So, for the next few days, Von would sit the bleachers and hopefully study for other finals. One class down, five classes to go.

Von continued the day ignoring me. I reciprocated. I was forced into allowing him to gloat over his victory, at least till finals were over. The reviews bored me anyway. To think I had at one time been at this level of learning. I did wish I could drag up some memory image of it.

His art teacher's final would be a performance test, an application of past learning. She would hand each student a pencil and sketch pad, put a model on her lecture table and they'd have to hand draw it. That was it. Art felt foreign to me. I doubted I could handle a straight line without a straight edge to press against. I thought about asking if Von felt confident about accomplishing such a task, but my mood hung on and I didn't. Even if he failed art, the other courses would get him into senior year.

Science class would require study, but would also be a performance exam graphically presented on the computer. The test would feature a virtual science lab. Seven unlabeled digital test tubes containing unknown liquid compounds would be presented to each student. They would then have to run tests on the contents of each test tube in order to identify each compound. Fortunately, Von liked science and managed to maintain a C average without studying.

After school that day, he walked home with Vivian and Nick. He and I maintained our mutual silence. He visited with his brother and sister, beat his father at a game of chess, ate supper without getting in an argument, showered and looked over some of his math review material. I waited for him to ask for help, but he never did. Before long, his eyes grew heavy and he fell asleep for the night, math book still open on the floor.

Chapter Fourteen

{ I'd never seen a woman give birth before. }

Wednesday, May 13:

The next morning, I awoke and discovered my math book on the floor where it must have fallen from the bed, still opened to the last page I'd studied. Moments later, Mom hollered up at us to get up. I thought about D.G., but he'd remained silent since just after our wrestling match. Well good. I just didn't feel like arguing with him. I dressed, got downstairs for breakfast, told everyone good morning and before long left for school.

I was early meeting the gang gathering on the sidewalk. We got to school on time and before long were drowning in final exam reviews. Finals started tomorrow. I tried my best to pay attention and only fell asleep once in American History.

In PE, Moby and I sat in the bleachers talking. "You know Von, I might know where we could come up with a car. I'd have to check with Derrick, but his older brother, Jonathon, the one that got us the blotter acid, used to drive an old Ford Focus in high school. He and his friends really dogged it, about ran the wheels off the thing. Jonathon left it on blocks back in that bamboo grove behind their parent's big garage. The tires are probably dry rotten and airless. Derrick and I fiddled with it once, thinking it could be Derrick's ride, but then his parents bought that new Mini Cooper for him, so we dropped the plan. I'm pretty sure it's still back there. It sure needs work though."

Von! D.G. suddenly blared. *Transportation! For venturing west.*

I nodded. *Thought you had died,* I told D.G.

"When the bell rings, we have to reserve the picnic table, fast," I told Moby. "Derrick always shows up there." Moby nodded. We grabbed our backpacks and made our way to the gym exit. The bell rang just as we got there. Moby and I ran like hell, but we were in luck because once again, Charlie, having gotten out of class early, stood grinning in the cafeteria doorway holding extra bags of sandwiches. The picnic table was ours. As the three of us sat there, Moby explained to Charlie his idea and I smiled watching Charlie's face light up with realization that it might be a good plan.

Derrick came out of Building Two talking to some girls, but instantly, Moby and Charlie were tugging at him. I watched from the picnic bench as they took him aside and quickly explained the plan. Derrick nodded a few times, bobbed his head from side to side considering and then shrugged. His palms came up and he nodded. All I actually heard him say was "Sure. But, I don't know if it runs."

They walked to the table and we quickly made arrangements to meet at Derrick's house after school. Julia stood watching, suspicion on her face that something had just transpired. We quickly filled her in.

Art class was a practice session for the final exam and science class finished our review of analytic work in the lab. When the last bell of the day rang, we met at the picnic table and walked together to Derrick's house. Everyone dropped their backpacks on Derrick's back porch and stood before their gigantic four car garage. Behind the garage a large grove of timber bamboo covered an area equal the size of the garage itself. The old car was there alright.

Timber bamboo grows huge, its stalks getting up to six inches in diameter and reaching heights of fifty feet. Stalks punched out of the ground six to ten inches apart so we were barely able to squeeze through between the forest of trunks. In some places, even Moby's skinny frame couldn't get between those huge plants. Once next to the car, we could look inside, but opening the doors proved impossible. The little car sat trapped by a jail of bamboo stalks that had grown there three years or more.

I surveyed the area around the car. It didn't look encouraging.

Moby informed us that it had been almost nineteen months since he and Derrick had last started the car. Derrick however was certain the battery had died since then. And indeed, the tires were ruined and would need to be replaced.

So, lots of forestry work, obtaining a battery, replacement tires, D.G. calculated. *And there could be problems from aging and not being run during all that time. I have my doubts, Von.*

Charlie estimated we'd have to remove a swath of bamboo ten feet wide and eighty feet long to drive the car around the back corner of the garage. But immediately Derrick saved us lots of work by pointing to a back alley that bordered the rear of their property. Only twenty-five feet of bamboo stood in the way of that route.

Charlie asked if Derrick had any machetes or cane knives.

"No Charlie. That would be too much work. I don't know if you noticed the woodpiles alongside the driveway but we own two chain saws."

Charlie's eyes lit up and within minutes, the screaming engines of the chainsaws were sending woodchips in all directions as Charlie and

174

Moby sliced down a bamboo stalk every twenty seconds. Julia and I dragged the cut timbers into a pile where Derrick said they could just stay until they rotted. Within forty-five minutes, we were all dripping sweat but a five-foot cleared area now surrounded the car on all sides and a passable runway ran all the way to the alley. Derrick's mother showed up with a tray of lemonade, treated us very politely, but gave Derrick an angry look. She waved her head sideways and Derrick followed her around to the front of the garage. We quickly silenced the chainsaws and waited till he returned.

"Yeah. Don't worry. I got this," Derrick told us. "Mom's just a bit pissed that I didn't ask her or Dad first." Without a second thought, Derrick whipped out his cell phone and spoke with his father. After two minutes, he turned toward us as he closed his phone. Then he smiled. "It's yours. Believe me, they can afford it." We all slapped high fives celebrating Derrick's quick maneuvering and our muscle-powered handy work.

Finally, we could get our hands on the little Focus, open the doors, crank down the windows and get under the hood. Three rats scurried out of the trunk when Moby opened it, causing Julia to squeal like a girl. Within an hour, we determined that the oil in the engine looked dirty and had to be replaced and the gas smelled funny so we'd have to replace that too.

The sun dimmed in the sky and everyone began to drag their backpacks onto their backs. I stood before the old car gazing across the hood at the windshield.

Von. Don't move. Don't move, D.G. insisted.

Why? What's up?

D.G. remained silent for a while and I sensed something had overtaken him, but I had no idea what. I stood, just looking at the car. Julia had walked off with Derrick and Moby talking about final exams and Charlie busied himself putting the chainsaws back in the garage.

I saw her. In the car, behind the windshield, looking up at me. D.G. muttered sounding all emotional.

You ok, D.G.? Her who?

Do you recall the marriage ceremony memory I had, the one I saw before our exorcism? It's the woman that stood next to me in that marriage ceremony. The one with the clipboard when I was given LSD by the military. When you looked at the car windshield, a memory struck me hard. She fixed me with her gaze, relying on me, depending on me. We had stalled on the side of a highway. She sat there, both her hands on her big pregnant belly, looked through the windshield and pleaded, "Can you get it running again? My water just broke. It won't be long now." Von, she knew me. Not just knew me but appreciated and understood me through and through. And somehow, I knew I would die for her. That face. Her face. D.G.'s talking dropped off suddenly.

His tone grabbed my attention. I could tell this memory had carved deeply into him. But he remained silent and I sensed he didn't want to be disturbed. I grabbed my backpack and joined the others.

Just before we parted, we agreed to meet again tomorrow after school. We walked home leaving Moby at Derrick's huge two-story home. Charlie turned off toward his house; I walked Julia to her mom's shop and went on to my house.

Mom had kept my plate warm and she and Dad asked where I'd been. I told them about the car but gave away nothing about going west. I didn't need to fight that battle right now. Maybe I'd tell them later.

After supper, I checked on Oma and Harper, showered and then climbed into bed with my science book. Tomorrow finals would start. But even that couldn't keep my eyes from getting heavy. Before long, I turned off my table lamp and went to sleep.

I'd probably slept for a few hours before the dream came. I seemed to be floating around in the wide hallways of a well-lit building. Two nurses pushed a gurney through double swinging doors into some operating room with a very pregnant woman aboard. The man walking along beside the gurney, holding the patient's hand, I suddenly recognized as D.G. He looked only slightly younger than the man I'd seen when I'd done LSD. It was him, no doubt. He followed them into the operating room, a surgical mask across his face. I drifted through the door right behind him and floated near the ceiling, looking down upon the quick preparations being made as more nurses came through the doors followed by a doctor.

That's her. That's her, on the gurney. The woman in the car, D.G. said.

D.G., you're seeing this? I asked.

Oh goodness, am I, D.G. answered. Standing next to the gurney, he glanced up toward the ceiling at me. *I'm re-experiencing it and dreaming it all at once.*

"Well, you guys ready to meet your baby?" The doctor's tone made the whole event seem like a fraternity party. "You brought beer, right?" He poked at D.G., big smile bursting from his face. "Yeah, relax Dad. Believe me, we got this. We do thousands of these each year. Lots of practice. Right girls?"

The nurse staff hesitated only a moment from hooking monitors to the mother, checking vital signs and giving encouragement. D.G. held his woman's hand, his other arm around the back of her shoulders. They clung to each other as she perspired, her breathing picking up its pace.

The doctor and head nurse conferred beneath a sheet draped over the woman's bent knees and called out that she was nine centimeters dilated. "Yep, just in time. We wouldn't have it any other way." The doctor came out from under the sheet, big smile on his face. "This looks by the book. Honey, you can start pushing anytime you're ready."

D.G. clung to the woman, whispered into her ear. She gasped and suddenly locked down her breathing and gave a great heave. Two nurses stood between her knees and gave approving nods. They called out instructions about when to breathe and when to hold her breath. Long minutes passed as I observed an experienced medical team anticipate every need, every vital sign change, every drop of sweat from the soon-to-be mother's brow.

"We've got crowning," one of the nurses said. Another suggested the woman push as hard as she could and with one massive churn of breath the woman D.G. clung to gave everything she had, her face flushing, her blood pressure count rising, her pulse swirling and from her came a yelled growl scream that I would never have imagined could come from this woman. The baby's cry brought smiles to the entire room, especially the woman on the birthing table. The nurses drew back the sheet and placed a trembling baby boy upon the mother's chest, her arms embracing him instantly. D.G. held her, the child and cried as much as the new born babe.

"Classic," the doctor called out. "Yep. We do good work. Looks like you guys did good work too. Ten fingers, ten toes. Good heart beat. All pinked up from breathing. Hell yeah. Good job, Mom."

All pinked up. I remember that, D.G. hollered. *What an incredible child. What a beautiful . . .* D.G.'s voice trembled and broke, his tears mixing with his thoughts. *I remember that. Ohhh, I remember it. And now I see it again . . . Ohh I need to return to them. I have to get back. I must discover what's occurred. What happened to take me away from them?*

I'd never seen a woman give birth before. It hit me hard, right in the heart, startling me. Something had slammed me down to earth. Somehow, a lot of questions had been answered, so many questions that I knew I couldn't name them all. And then knowing she was D.G.'s wife and this crying newborn was his child crashed the whole scene into my head even harder. It was almost as though I was the woman's husband and my child had been born right before my eyes. Like it or not, I was woven into all of it. And D.G. couldn't get to the end of the silver thread without my help.

Then the ceiling of my room appeared above me and I woke up. My eyes were wet and I found myself brushing tears away. I sat up and looked out the window into the dark back yard, the quarter moon high above the trees. I closed my eyes and could almost reach out and touch that mother and child. The feeling increased in weight, a heaviness bearing down on me. I felt shame. D.G. was real. All this time, I'd seen him as some ghost, some wandering spirit with an unknown purpose. I'd taken his arrival personally, like an insult or huge annoyance. But no, he was real. Or had been real, with real feelings and real involvements. I'd only thought about my own inconvenience. I'd been put out by it all and hadn't considered beyond that.

You there? I asked flopping onto my back, still watching the moon. Though he didn't answer, I sensed him nodding. *That was powerful,* I told him. Again, he nodded. *Look. I'm sorry we can't leave right away. But we'll get the car running and then . . .*

I absolutely need rest, Von, was all he said.

I could tell he was sad. He didn't want to talk so I left him alone.

My clock radio read 2:37 a.m. Before long, I again slept, for a while, restfully. But then I again stood shoulder to shoulder with D.G. on the big clock face. We both overstepped the long second hand as it swept past, running backwards. Both D.G. and I scanned the face and found one hour and twenty minutes left on the clock. The darkness surrounding the big clock face remained unchanged. "Still west," D. G. mumbled. The clock face had changed to the compass again and again, the 'W' pulsed red. From there the silver thread floated out in a westerly direction, floating off into unseen space. Both D.G. and I stood at that edge of the compass, again attempting unsuccessfully to see the thread's destination.

I opened my eyes briefly, just long enough to realize the clock dream was finished. Though I thought about it briefly, sleep again overtook me. I hoped there would be no more dreams tonight.

Chapter Fifteen

{ "This is gonna be wild. Chasing dreams and spiritual threads. Who'd a thunk." }

Thursday, May 14:

Wake up, Von. I tried not to be harsh about it but as he sat up and shook his head awake, he quickly sensed that it wasn't his mother shouting up the stairs.

D. G.? It's early man. The sun's barely up, Von complained as he stretched.

But, finals commence today and you are in need of auxiliary cramming. Math is your first exam. I will be unable to divulge how to accomplish a correct answer for every single problem while the test is going on, since that would hinder your progress. You'd never finish. The more problems you complete without my support, the quicker you complete the test. I'll collaborate only when you require assistance. That should speed things up. So, get up. I calculate two and a half hours to rehearse various problems before the test.

Von nodded, yawned, stretched and fumbled his way into the bathroom. Once he splashed water onto his face, he came fully awake. His gaze into the mirror struck me as different, as though he'd changed in some way.

Look D.G. That birth dream last night. I kind of realized a bit more.

Not to worry, Von. Some vague portion of you has been annexed and you are justified to feel invaded. But, our being irate with each other

181

or my being downcast simply does no good. Defeating these exams is our
next step. Let's go.

Von nodded, dressed, ate a quick bowl of granola and was out the
back door in ten minutes. He walked much quicker to school than his
usual languid pace. The janitor taking a smoke break out on the front
steps nodded to Von as he approached. "You much earlier than usual."

Von nodded, "Hey Mr. James. What time did you get here?"

"Me? Five-thirty for me, 'specially with these finals coming up
today. Library's open already, if ya need."

And so began the final exams. We spent two hours going over
math and English, the first two exams Von had. Though we'd anticipated
using every second of the test period, that's not what happened. Von
required five hints at the middle of the computerized test and longer
explanations toward the end. But, he completed the exam with twenty
minutes left in the two-hour extended period. Mrs. Dillman, noted his
finished test arrive on her computer and nodded. After a moment, she
wiggled her finger at Von. He leaned over next to her as she pointed to
his final exam grade, a ninety-six percent. She ran her finger across to the
right edge of the screen where his final yearly grade showed. He nodded.
A 'C-' wasn't great, but he didn't argue. He'd passed. Two tests down,
four to go.

English class proved surprisingly challenging. I had not read all the
short stories Mrs. Keife assigned throughout the year, so I provided little
help there. Luckily, she asked many questions about Shakespeare and I
filled in any unknowns Von needed. Surprisingly, she also required a short
written essay asking the student's opinion on the constitutional rights of
intelligent robots. Von wrote well and I only tossed out a few opinions he

might consider. He completed the test five minutes early, learned his final exam grade was a ninety-four percent and his yearly average came to a 'C'. Three down, three to go.

At lunch, Von's usual gang gathered. They quickly exchanged information about what kind of questions were on various teacher's tests.

That afternoon, I struggled with my mounting impatience and frustration but was able to assist Von significantly on his American History and Art II final exams. Both teachers were shocked that he'd done as well as he had. With final passing grades of 'D' in American History and a 'B' in Art II, Von felt encouraged. After school ended the group gathered and made the usual pilgrimage to the bamboo forest.

As they walked along, I retreated further into Von and tried to deal with my own developing anguish. I had seen my wife give birth, seen my child born, seen myself clutching to them both and relived the whole experience. Having to wait for these teenagers felt like someone had set me on fire. I did not want to wait. I would have to maintain a heavy guard on my emotions, for I wanted to scream obscenities to the high heavens. Best I just remained silent.

"Why don't we call it the Bamboo car," Charlie suggested plopping his backpack on the roof of the little car. "It's green."

Julia shrugged. "Fine by me."

"Bamboo car it is," Von said.

Moby lifted a car jack out of the trunk, used the lug wrench to loosen the wheel nuts, cranked the wheels higher and removed each tire. Von and Charlie opened the hood and looked over the dusty motor.

"We should split up," Charlie announced and I began to see some tiny developing flame of leadership in Charlie. "Von and Julia, you get fresh gasoline and oil. Moby and I will hunt up used tires and a battery. Back here before sundown. OK?"

Though I continued silently pouting within Von, the kids easily bore the needed organizational energy for their tasks. The work on the car seemed to speed up. Within an hour, all four of them were back with gas, oil, a battery and four used tires. They changed out the tires, changed the oil, drained the gas tank completely, replacing it with one gallon of fresh gasoline, mounted the new battery, and hit the starter switch. It took a full minute of cranking, but Bamboo car wheezed, huffed smoke out the exhaust and chugged until the engine finally idled. "It still runs!" Moby screamed, Julia clapped, Von and Charlie hooked arms and danced a jig, and I felt a small bit of my impatience relax. At least we'd have transportation. Moby revved the engine a few times and then let it idle. They watched the gauges and finally decided the motor wouldn't be a major problem. Moby pumped the brakes and got good resistance.

"Brakes might work but we'll have to get it rolling to really tell," Moby said.

With the used tires mounted, Charlie and Moby used the jack to remove the blocks that held the car off the ground. Its springs creaked as the car began to bear its own weight. Moby hopped inside, started the engine and tried reverse. The car began to roll slowly backwards and with Von and Julia signaling, Moby nudged the car safely onto the asphalt back alley. Moby tested the brakes a few times by getting up to ten miles per hour and stomping down hard on the pedal. Each time, the tires skidded on the pavement.

"We got brakes. Who's for a ride?" Moby yelled stepping out of the driver's seat so someone could enter the two door coup. Julia bounded by him into the back seat, Von slid through on the other side and Charlie took the front passenger's seat.

Turning right out of the alley, they entered Esplanade Avenue and drove toward the French Quarter. The afternoon was fresh and sunny and everyone smiled at their newly discovered freedom. I enjoyed seeing young enthusiasm encouraged by their successful effort but I still cringed inside. I was like a race horse ready to bolt. My frustration at having to remain anchored within Von's life and his daily environment, while time whittled away, bore down hard upon me.

Moby played loud music on the radio and everyone sung along. He tried the windshield wipers and a great 'yea' burst from everyone. They waved and yelled to friends they saw walking or biking nearby. But, he noticed the gas gauge, with only one gallon in the tank, looked very low and the sun neared the horizon again, so they drove back to the alleyway and parked the car amongst its accustomed bamboo forest. They stood admiring their accomplishment, an imaginary space ship ready to take them to the stars and free them of all that had ever held them back. Freedom beckoned.

Julia suggested that early tomorrow morning, they store extra clothes and money in their backpacks because finals ended at noon. They could be on the road by one o'clock.

Finally, I said, somewhat relieved. I felt Von smile and nod.

Hang in there D.G. Tomorrow we go west.

But images of my wife kept fluttering through my consciousness. Sometimes she held our child. I wanted their names. Why couldn't I get a name to come up? I wanted to hold them. I wanted the warmth of their skin against mine, even if it was just Von's skin. I retreated back into silence.

As Von walked along with Charlie and Julia, they talked about preparations they'd each make for tomorrow's road trip. But, as they chatted, it suddenly hit me that in a way, I'd been lucky I had not remembered everything about my past. If I knew it all, the frustration I would feel would be overwhelming. I would be screaming mad wanting to return to my former life, to my wife, child and all the others I might love. Perhaps I was fortunate in that this well-paced unfolding of memories kept me from going stark raving insane. Maybe I received memories as I could endure them. It was a nice realization, but I still yearned to go.

That night, sleep didn't result in much actual rest for me. The countdown clock showed up again in my dreams and this time, it registered fifty-five minutes left and at that moment, it struck me that a lot of time on the clock had passed in only one day. Julia had been right. If the ratio between clock time and days passing in reality changed, the allotted time left in real days before the clock ran out of time would not be predictable. This changed everything. We now had fewer real days left to find the end of the thread and to figure out what had put me in Von's head.

I immediately wished Von next to me and he appeared. *Do you see the time left?* I asked him.

Yeah. It's changed a lot, Von muttered. *It's moving faster. That means . . .*

Yeah. Von, if we get to the Bamboo car right now, we could . . .

Nooo D.G. I'm not leaving without Julia, Charlie and Moby. Today's the last day of finals. We leave at noon. As planned.

The frustration pulsed within me. I just didn't know what to say to

186

the boy.

Suddenly, the face of the clock converted to the compass. The silver thread floated off into the western darkness, its destination unknown. It only added to my mounting exasperation.

Friday, May 16:

The next morning I woke Von early.

I reckon I can count on you being the alarm clock from now on, D.G., Von mumbled as he rolled out of bed. *At least the sun's up this time.*

His grogginess lasted only until the lavatory water splashed his face. He looked up into the mirror again and if he hadn't thought it to me, I would have been able to know by his look.

How many more days of having you in my head?

We only learn the answer to that once we journey west, Von. You saw the dream last night. Fifty-five minutes left. That doesn't equate to ten and a half days, like we had thought. We might have four to four and a half days left before we merge. I'm nervous.

He nodded and dressed in less than two minutes. As he packed changes of clothes, his toiletry supplies and extra money into his backpack, he found his father standing in the doorway.

"Dad?"

"You seem in a hurry, Von."

"Yeah. Ahh, we have finals today. Guess I'm nervous."

His father slowly walked into the room, his hands stuffed into his jean pockets. "Derrick's father called late last night. Seems he asked Derrick what you kids were doing with Jonathon's old car. Something about a trip to figure out the voice in your head? That about right?"

I felt Von's muscles freeze and his breathing lock up.

"Yeah. That's right. I've been having these dreams and . . . they point at how to solve this thing with this voice."

His father nodded and sat on his bed. "You trust these dreams, do you?"

Von nodded. His father nodded. They were both quiet.

"I have to do this Dad. It's the inside of my head. Nobody else can do this, not even the shrink. I have to." His father nodded. "We're heading west. Not exactly sure where but . . . "

"The thing is," his father said, "that car needs insurance. It's registered in Derrick's father's name, he don't mind you using it, but there's no insurance."

Von stood, paced the room. I wanted to say something, to offer some wise advice, but before I could, Von wheeled around and faced his father.

"Could you help me out? I have to do this. I know Mom will hate me for it. I have to do it anyway. I'll pay you back, I promise."

"Relax. Your Mom doesn't hate you. She's just the nervous type. Panics a bit. Worries about her kids. I'm gonna front you the insurance. I'll pay one month's worth of insurance on that car. You have to be back in thirty days. And you have to promise me to drive safely."

Von's breathing returned and I felt his eyes tear up. The relief he felt made him bend over and brace his hands against his knees. He took another breath and stood.

"Thanks Dad. We'll be careful, I promise."

His father stood. "That ole clunker runs ok?"

Von nodded. "Yeah, amazingly. Brakes work, motor runs,

everything seems to be functioning ok."

"I just want my son back in one piece. That's one piece. Ok?"

"Thanks Dad," Von repeated and the two men hugged.

His father nodded. "Leave your Mom to me. I'll talk with her." With that, he turned and left the room.

Von was at his backpack in an instant, finished packing it and headed downstairs. There, he gulped down a bowl of cereal, dumped his bowl in the sink, and flew out the back door moving fast and headed for school.

First period students filed into the science room fanning out, seeking seats at one of the computers. Von got in early and sat near the door. Charlie, Julia, Nick and Sammy Daxton took turns nodding at him, wishing him luck. Luck wasn't as necessary on this exam, science being Von's favorite subject, probably because he actually read articles in Discover magazine, Popular Science, Astronomy magazine and watched Neil deGrasse Tyson videos on YouTube. He had watched every episode of MacGyver and Star Trek available to him.

Once the computers were unlocked by Ms. Jourst, Von logged onto his account within the virtual science lab and got down to business. He was able to figure out the biological process occurring within the first three test tubes without my assistance. He and I discussed two different issues involving the fourth test tube and another two for the sixth. He managed to think his way through the questions I posed for those problems.

Things went fairly well for him. He maintained his concentration with vigor, that is until Ms. Jourst ambled up next to Von and laid her hand upon the back of his neck. Von's hands immediately came off the keyboard. He bolted straight up, stood and faced her. As he did, he pressed her arm away from him. Her hand slid off his back. He stood glaring at her. His jaw muscles clinched and I hadn't known a face could generate so much heat. He didn't speak but I felt the anger she had kindled in him. Von's shoulder, back and arm muscles began to tense and I feared he would strike.

Oh Von. Please don't hit her, I whispered.

Von didn't answer me but held his stance. The sound of a chair screeched across the floor and Von and I both realized Charlie also stood, looking fixedly at Ms Jourst. Two more chairs slid back as Julia and Sammy Dalton stood, frowning at their sexy teacher. Next, Nick, Cherry and Moneen stood and stared. Every other student in the room now watched the silent drama unfolding, ignoring their test.

As each new student rose, Ms. Jourst looked more and more confused. She took a step back, her eyes moving from one standing student to another. She finally spoke.

"Ahh . . . please continue with your exam. There should be no interruptions allowed in an exam period."

"Yes Ms. Jourst," Julia responded. "No interruptions . . . caused by anyone."

Jourst seemed nervous, stepped past Von and walked to her lectern. As she moved away from Von, the students slowly sat down. Within seconds, their attention went back to their computers.

Oh. Well good, I whispered to Von.

It took Von a minute to stop smoldering and the incident probably caused him to make a mistake on the seventh test tube. I thought I would just let him get that one wrong. He'd pass the test anyhow. But, at the last minute, he caught his own mistake and corrected it. I congratulated him.

He finished the exam with eighteen minutes left in the period. When Ms Jourst signaled for Von to approach her computer, Julia, Cherry and Moneen also stood and accompanied him. They stood close by, observing. Jourst took on a distanced professional attitude, unusually cool for her low-cut short-skirt style.

Von found out he'd made an 'A' on the final exam and had a 'B' in the course. His final exams were finished and most importantly, he would pass Junior year. The bell rang ending the first testing period causing Von and the crew to head for the gymnasium. Everyone exchanged high-fives in the hallway, congratulating themselves that they'd united to stand up against their science teacher without any help from the office or any other adults.

OK. Now D.G. You did what you promised, Von told me. *I can't leave campus till the next bell, but that's when we leave. Hang in there.*

You're finished with finals, Von. Can't we leave?

We can't leave campus until noon. Lots of students have one more test to take. Moby's gonna sneak out and come back with the car. We leave from here then.

I bit my non-existent tongue, but found my frustration under control. As the three of them headed for the gym bleachers to wait out the last testing period, Julia pulled out her smartphone and with Von and Charlie looking over her shoulders, they explored a map of the local highways. The simplest route west was Interstate 10 and each of them had traveled that before. They looked through their backpacks checking supplies they'd each packed.

"Has D.G. had much to say to you lately?" Charlie asked.

"He's been quieter than before, very impatient and really frustrated," Von said. "He just wants to get moving." At that, Von described the latest dreams we'd both had.

"So you know what his wife and child looks like?" Julia asked.

"If the dreams are accurate, yeah," Von said.

Then Von told them about the latest clock setting. They discussed it for a while and both Julia and Charlie realized there was less time available for the hunt.

Charlie came up with a huge grin. "But, we're Seniors. And this is summer time. This is gonna be wild. Chasing dreams and spiritual threads. Who'd a thunk."

Suddenly the bell rang and a great cheer rose up from every student in the gymnasium, a clear indication of the end of another school year. Von, Julia and Charlie made their way to the front of school and there sat Moby in the Bamboo car, motor idling. But as they got closer, I saw that Moby's lip was bleeding and his face was bruised. Charlie opened the driver-side door and drew Moby out. Julia reached out and wiped a tear from Moby's cheek.

"I can't go guys," Moby choked on his words.

"Your old man drunk again?" Charlie asked, his big hand on Moby's shoulder.

Moby nodded. "He came home and hit her again. I told him to stop and he slugged me. I called the cops but they can be slow in coming. I gotta go home and handle this. You guys go. I gotta make sure Mom's ok."

They drew around Moby and took turns hugging him. Nobody knew the right words to say so they were mostly quiet. I instructed Von to tell Moby that it had been a pleasure knowing him and I wished him luck dealing with his father's problem. Von told him and Moby put his hand on Von's shoulder. "Tell D.G. I've never met a finer voice in anybody's head. And I hope you guys figure this craziness out." He turned and walked back toward his house. Von and I watched him go.

Uuff. Laboring under the influence of an alcoholic father. I can't imagine, I told Von.

Yeah. His dad's been a drunk for years. My dad has tried to talk to the man but he doesn't listen.

How unfortunate. Moby assisted so much on the Bamboo car. And we could have probably used his skills.

Well, he'll have to deal with the police, Von said. *Moby knows the drill. He's had to have his father arrested twice before.*

Chapter Sixteen

{ *What? We're done with west, D.G.? Heck, I thought we'd go to California or at least Texas.* }

"I'll drive first," Julia declared. "Take the back, Von."

I climbed into the back seat and Charlie took front passenger seat. Noon day traffic flowed well as we entered the I-10 highway. We traded our regrets that Moby wouldn't be here and reminisced about times Moby's father had scared each of us as children. Slowly the conversation quieted and by the time Lake Pontchartrain glided by on the right, smiles were beginning to break on our faces again.

"How's this gonna work with D.G.?" Charlie called above the wind rushing through the car.

"By the time we passed the airport he told me he felt a lot less stress," I hollered back. "Just keep going west. Says he can feel this is the right way. He'll let us know if we need to change course."

Julia nodded that she understood, both her hands gripping the steering wheel. Though the Bamboo car hustled along, I noticed almost all the other highway traffic passed us as though we were dragging an anchor. When I asked Julia about it, she told me she had the accelerator floored. The car barely made sixty-five miles per hour. It shimmied and rocked from side to side, its older shock absorbers almost completely used up.

"Well, it's an old motor, right?" Julia called.

"This thing's a piece of junk," Charlie laughed. "We could end up walking."

"Well, right now it's our piece of junk," I answered, "and we're heading west. It'll have to do."

How do you feel about that, D.G.?

I feel much better, thank you Von. We're finally accomplishing some kind of progress. My concern now is with the countdown clock and how much time remains to accomplish this vague unknown.

I nodded my agreement. I might have passed my junior year but now I would be chasing shadows. After an hour of driving we began to see the outskirts of Baton Rouge. Traffic on the eight-lane Interstate began to thicken and Julia drove a little slower. Without warning, D.G. howled as though going mad.

No more west, he hollered. *We must go south. That sign for Dalrymple, right there, take that next exit.*

What? He'd caught me off guard. *We're done with west, D.G.? Heck, I thought we'd go to California or at least Texas.*

I leaned forward and told Julia and Charlie of the change and she adjusted through lanes to take the next exit. Once off the interstate, we traveled through the slower Dalrymple street traffic. We soon came upon the LSU campus. Each of us had been there before, though not often.

We're getting close to something, D.G. nervously exclaimed. *I'm feeling drawn to this place. Try a left.*

Julia crossed Highland Road, meandered along slowly next to an open area park. The sign said Parade Grounds.

Circle around this park a bit, D.G. instructed. *I'm close to something, real close.*

I passed D.G.'s instructions on and Julia dutifully circled the parade grounds until we came to Tower Drive. There was a small sign that read Student Union and D.G wanted us to park here. Julia parked, killed the engine and we exited the car, everyone scanning these new surroundings in the middle of the LSU campus. I detected D.G.'s anxiousness from deep inside me.

You're picking up something. I can feel it too. What's up, D.G.?

Over there, Von. Across the street.

"He says this way, guys," I said pointing to the beige three-story building across Tower Drive.

We crossed the street and stood before the large building beneath two very old live oak trees. Carved into the building in large block letters were the words Physics and Astronomy. D.G. wanted to walk around the building, so we turned right and started down a side street. That street led us to a central quadrangle, a long grassy area populated along its outer perimeter by lines of gigantic, moss-draped Evangeline Oak trees. At the opposite end of the physics building, we came upon a triple archway entrance with James W. Nicholson Hall written over the arches. An emblazoned fresco under the center arch showed the sun, moon, stars, planets and comets contained within a large circle. Beneath that were eight symbols that I thought might be Greek letters.

"Wonder what those mean?" Charlie asked.

Tell Charlie it's Mercury, over there on the left, and then Venus, Earth, Mars, Jupiter, Saturn, Uranus and finally, Neptune over on the right, D.G. said.

After I told them, Julia asked, "D.G. knew all that?"

I nodded. "Yeah. He and I are both feeling a lot of vibes around here. Let's walk through the building."

Entering, we found long, well lit halls. We stopped along the way to read bulletin boards and peek into classrooms. A clock hanging from the ceiling read 2:15 and it seemed strange that I'd been taking final exam tests just a few hours before. A student came walking down the hallway, a large book under one arm, backpack over his shoulder.

I taught that guy. His name's Robert, I think. Von, ask him about me. Say something.

"Hey there. Ahh, have you taken any courses from a teacher that got his PhD degree from MIT? I forget the guy's name but it began with a J."

"Oh, you must mean James. James Howlynd," the young man answered as he quietly glanced at Julia and then back at me.

Ouuhh, D. G. started suddenly. *James. James. James. That feels like it really fits. James Howlynd. That could be me, Von.*

"His office is upstairs," the young man went on. "I haven't seen him around for a couple of weeks. I heard they had to get a substitute to take his class. I'm not sure what's going on with him but the secretary's in the office. Maybe she can put you in contact with him." He smiled at each of us, nodded and stuck his hand out. "I'm Robert. You guys considering LSU? It's a good department here."

"Coming to LSU would be super," Julia said quickly.

Robert nodded at her flashing a big smile, then suddenly glanced at his watch. "Oops. Class coming up. I gotta run. You guys take care. Hope to see you on campus." With that he turned and marched off.

"D.G. said that James Howlynd might be his real name. Said it felt right."

"So, D. G.'s name might be James? And he taught here? I'm

impressed," Charlie said.

We turned and kept walking down the long hallway. When we came upon an elevator, Julia stepped into it saying, "Let's look for his office." She punched the second floor button and up we went.

Dr. James Howlynd's office door featured a large window right above his nameplate. The office was dark and the door locked, but on a shelf close by stood a picture of a square, very plain building with no windows. It seemed to be one big block and I wondered why anyone would bother to photograph such an uninspiring structure. But D.G. recognized it right away.

That photo, right there, on that shelf. That building. North! We have to go north of here. Von, it's imperative we find that building. I've worked there. I'm sure I've worked there. I'm getting new memories, lots of them, but they're coming so fast. Do you see that picture Von?

Yeah, I see it.

But Von, do you see the silver thread attached to it?

His words stood me up straighter. *No. No, I don't see any thread.*

Oh, don't worry about it. Leave, Von. Let's get out of here. That building is the next thing we have to locate. And I think I know where it is.

I told Julia and Charlie about the building in the picture and that we should go. We were back in the elevator in a flash and as the elevator doors opened on the first floor, we stepped out and started down the hallway toward the Tower Drive entrance. We came upon an office with an extra wide doorway to our left. Julia, without warning, stepped ahead of us and turned into the office. There, an older gray-haired woman stood before a file cabinet putting papers into folders. She noticed us entering.

"Hello. May I help you?" Her desk nameplate said Emily Clauss.

"We're trying to contact James Howlynd," Julia said smiling back.

The smile slowly melted from the woman's face and she began to look us over from top to bottom.

"May I ask what business you have with Dr. Howlynd?"

"We're interested in studying here and he said he could show us around," Julia said turning on the charm.

"Well dear, Dr. Howlynd is very busy these days." She turned and for a moment, seemed to ignore us as she placed more pages into slots in the file cabinet. She turned back, looked as though she was surprised we were still there and then forced a smile. "Let me get your names and contact info. Dr. Howlynd can contact you the first chance he gets," she said, handing us a pen and small note pad.

Charlie's hand intercepted the pen and pad and handed it back. "No thanks. We'll check back later when he's available. But thank you for your help." When Julia and I looked at Charlie, he motioned with his head toward the Tower Street entrance.

"She wasn't happy we asked about Dr. James Howlynd. Her whole mood changed when you said his name," Charlie said. "I didn't want to give her our names after that."

"She did change right away," Julia agreed. "I got the feeling there's something she didn't want us to know about him."

She is irrelevant, D.G. said. *We must proceed north.*

As we walked back to the car, I explained D.G.'s new directive. Once in the car, Julia and Charlie looked over Julia's smartphone map of Baton Rouge. "Are we going into Mississippi? How far north?" Charlie asked.

Oh. No. Tell them we'll stay in Baton Rouge, D.G. said.

Chapter Seventeen

{ "Oh, I'm sure it is very hard, since you are a bald-faced liar. Is this a god-damned joke or something? }

Memories flashed through my mind faster than I could interpret them. I knew I'd been in Nicholson Hall many times. The fresco above the old entrance had started an avalanche of recollections. The secretary's look of suspicion struck me as somehow appropriate. She wasn't supposed to give away information about ... well, about something, but I wasn't sure just what that something was as yet. And the name, James Howlynd kept eating at me. Was that my name? Somehow, it felt like a very comfortable old shirt, perhaps my favorite.

I directed Von north on a familiar looking street that turned out to be Highland Road and we went past the point where it doglegged into St. Ferdinand. At the corner of Government Street I felt strongly drawn toward the river and then north again past government buildings, past the Louisiana State Capitol, the Mississippi River sliding past on our left. Though I didn't realize at first that the scenery around us on S. River Road slowly changed to a warehouse district, still, I felt pulled, as if by some magnet. Storage buildings, an unused repository and an old granary slipped past us. But then on the left came a massive three story gray cinder block building with no windows.

The big building on the left, Von. That's it. Have Julia drive slowly past it so we can get a good look. Then circle back and park in front of it.

"That's weird," Charlie looked confused. "There's nothing written on that building, not even its street address. No windows. Just one big front door. Wonder what they do there?"

As Julia crept us past the building, images of the silver thread snaking across the big grass lawn right up to the front door spontaneously appeared.

Von, we absolutely must gain entrance to that building.

Ok D.G. Relax. Let her turn around.

Julia made a circle in a large driveway, approached the building from the other direction and drew to a stop at the curb where the sidewalk from the front door met the street. Von told the others of my wanting to enter, so they all piled out and stood looking at the building.

"Well, it's the one in that picture alright," Julia said.

"Yep. I guess we try the door," Charlie suggested and started walking up the sidewalk.

Just then, the front door of the building opened and three men dressed in dark suits stepped out. All three of them were Charlie's size; they stood shoulder to shoulder blocking any advance to the door. Their faces were stern. The one on the left muttered, "Find out why they're here and what they want." All three marched in step aggressively toward Von and the group.

Von, greet them. We must gain entrance to that facility. I'm feeling a major attraction to this place and . . .

"Those three are not friendly," Julia blurted. "We should go. As in RUN." She turned and bolted for the driver's door. Charlie, taking his cue from Julia, grabbed Von and stuffed him into the car ahead of himself.

No. Wait. Von, make them stop. The end of the thread is here. The end of the thread . . . Von. Go back.

The engine roared to life and the Bamboo car took off just as the men reached the street. Von watched as one man pulled a cell phone from his coat and took a picture of the car.

Von. You'll need more courage than that if you ever want to rid yourself of me. I ranted. *I'm telling you, that building is crucial to . . . That silver thread went right through the wall to somewhere inside.*

"Wow. They seemed pretty severe," Julia called out as she managed to get the Bamboo car above the forty mph speed limit. "Are they following us?"

"No. It's just regular traffic behind us, I think," Von answered. "But D.G.'s freaked out about our leaving. He says the thread ends at that building and that we have to get in."

"Yeah, well tell him to get out here and take on those three," Charlie chuckled.

"I didn't anticipate this kind of resistance." Julia peered into the rearview mirror again as she spoke. "That secretary's look didn't set well and now this. It's scary. Even that building seems to be hiding something."

"Heavy security for such a plain building," Charlie pointed out. "We weren't there for a full minute before they came out. They had to have seen us pull up to react that fast, which means they're very active in guarding the place."

Von. I'm sorry if I scare you, but that silver thread ends in that building. That's the place we're looking for. I mustered a composed voice, trying to sound reasonable and collected but I began to see that a teenager's inexperience and general fear of the world might well be problematic. *So how do we get in there, Von?*

203

"So how do we get in there?" Von asked the others.

"No windows. There were no side entrances so I doubt there's a back door," Charlie estimated. "It would be just as guarded if there were. Those three were probably armed. Got a handy helicopter?"

Ok D.G. Even if we went back and tried to talk with those guys, how am I supposed to explain to them that I have this little voice in my head. I'd be in a straight jacket in the first five minutes. So now what?

I had to admit that Von had a point. And those three men were every bit as large as Charlie. I could feel the energy of the group receding. Julia drove aimlessly, everyone silent, pondering the dwindling options. I too felt at a loss and had no idea of how to respond to the situation. I noticed a Florida Boulevard sign go past. We stayed on that street for a while until she turned on Lobdell. Before long, Charlie spoke up.

"Hey. There's a Whole Food Market coming up, over there. I could use some food."

"Good idea. Maybe we'd think clearer if we're fed," Julia agreed.

Julia parked the car and the three of them went into the grocery. They filled plates from the food bar and sat outside at a picnic table to eat.

"The only way is to go back and talk to those guys, right?" Julia suddenly asked.

Ahh. She has the right idea. Return and test the waters, I told Von.

"Which probably means hand cuffs and getting arrested," Von added.

"Um hum," Charlie said chewing a mouthful. "Ok. So we get arrested and then they call our folks and we get chewed out. What then. Maybe a fine?"

"Who knows. It depends on what they're hiding in that building," Von said. "And how serious they take our being there. Maybe they think we're Russian spies or Jihadists. That could make it serious."

But Charlie might have a point, Von. After all, you are just teenagers. You can't possibly be seen as an actual threat. You're just curious innocent kids. Those guards are smart enough to see that. I strained to keep myself calm. Should I convince them to take on such large guards? I didn't want Von, Julia or Charlie getting hurt.

"What happens if we use Dr. James Howlynd's name?" Julia looked thoughtful for a moment. "We might at least see how they react."

Absolutely. She's thinking, I told Von. *Go back and test the waters.*

"Yeah. And then they slap handcuffs on us," Charlie said throwing his paper plate away.

Von, I really need to do this. But Von stood, threw away his plate and plastic fork and didn't respond. I couldn't panic or pressure these kids too much, so I just backed off and tried to reconsider the situation.

Julia stood, dumped her used plate in a recycle bin and as she did, I noticed a grocery store wall clock that read 3:25 pm. The group began walking to the Bamboo car. Julia unlocked the car and as she did, Von's gaze landed on a woman approaching her own car. He started to look away but I caught the sight of her.

VON! It's her, my wife! I hollered so forcefully that I felt Von jerk. His eyes went back to the woman as she pushed a shopping cart toward her car wearing a small child in a baby carrier strapped to her chest. She was sandy blond, five foot six, of light build with a slightly freckled complexion. As she walked, she looked over at Von and the group for a moment.

Oh hell. You're right. It's her. From the dreams.

Von quickly whispered his discovery to Julia and Charlie.

"That lady? The one with the baby?" Julia asked.

Von nodded, stepped around the front of the car and began walking toward her. As he approached her, memories began exploding in me.

Stephanie! I yelled. God, her name is Stephanie. I remember now. Hurry Von, faster.

"How are you gonna do this?" Julia whispered as she tried to keep up with Von.

"Stay close, ok." Von shot back.

Stephanie stood next to a Subaru loading groceries into the back and I suddenly recognized the car as mine. The loading done, she slammed the gate down and stepped to the back door, opened it, placed the child into a safety seat and began buckling the baby in. The child's name. I needed it. My mind fought to get the child's name, my child's name. Stephanie raised her head out of the car and watched as Von and the group approached.

"Hello," she said anticipating a conversation. Oh, she was just so beautiful.

"Ahh, hi. Are you Stephanie?" Von asked.

Her expression registered surprise. "I'm sorry. Do I know you?"

"No. No, we've never met before, but you're James's wife, right? Got his PhD through MIT, is that right?"

Her brows tensed, her head tilted just a little and I recognized the gesture. I wanted to jump out of Von and kiss her passionately.

"Ok. So who are you?" Stephanie asked as she finished fastening the child in, closed the door and crossed her arms.

Von nodded, smiled and took a deep breath. "Yeah, I'm Von. This is Julia and Charlie. We're from New Orleans. Juniors, ahhh, well actually as of today, seniors in high school there."

You're doing fine Von. Stay calm. Just talk. Keep the conversation going, no matter what. Make her feel safe. Just be yourself. Please don't blow this.

"I see. So school's out. Congratulations. So, how do you know James?" she asked.

"Ahh. Well. I've been having conversations with him lately, the last few days and . . . "

Stephanie stiffened, her arms dropped to her side and her smile evaporated. "You've been talking with James? Lately?"

"Actually, yes. About ten or twelve days now. A while. Ahh he said . . . he said . . . well it's kind of hard to explain but . . . "

"Oh, I'm sure it's hard to explain, since you are a bald-faced liar." Stephanie's jaw muscles tensed and her breathing quickened. "Is this a god-damned joke or something? Who are you people!" She turned quickly and opened the driver's door, faced them again with a more flushed face.

I could use some help here, D.G. I'm fucking this up, I can tell.

Repeat what I tell you, Von. Word for word.

"You and James hiked the Grand Canyon before you were married," Von said following my orders. "You camped at the bottom, on the sands of the Colorado River. You were on top of him when a bat in the night clawed your back. You still have the scar. He told me to tell you that. Just now, he told me to say that."

I could feel Von's stomach trembling, his breathing becoming jerky waiting for Stephanie's response.

For a second, she was quiet, considering his words. Her shoulders relaxed a bit and I prayed that she'd let him speak further with her.

"How did you find that out? We never told anyone about that. How could you possibly . . . know that?"

I scrambled for more information that Stephanie and I would both know but my memories were still sketchy.

"Ok. It's James. He's . . . he's stuck in my head," Von shook his hands desperate to get her to believe him. "About two weeks ago, the three of us were out one night and . . . and . . . this voice . . . well it just . . . landed in my head. At first I called him Director Guy, cause he didn't know who he was. He had no memories, but lately, he's remembering stuff, from his past and . . . and . . . he's led us here. To you. And I think . . ."

"A voice in your head!" Her bottom lip curled under her upper lip and her expression turned to anger. "Look, I don't know how you came up with that, or what your game is here, but you get away from us. Believe me, you don't want to test me on that. You stay the hell away from me and my family." Her anger grew defensive quickly and she was in the car in a flash. The door's lock clicked.

D.G. Give me something man. She's gonna leave.

A new memory came crashing in.

Von, get the group into the Bamboo car, quickly. Hurry. Run.

"We need to be in the car, now," Von blurted as he turned and started running. "D.G. says hurry."

208

Julia and Charlie were right behind him. "What are we doing?" Charlie asked.

"You have to drive Julia, fast. That way," Von said jumping into the back.

Julia swung the Bamboo car out of the parking lot and turned left.

Through Von, I directed Julia back onto Lobdell heading north. The Bamboo car scooted along faster than most traffic around us. I had her take a right on Sevenoaks Avenue.

It's right there on the right, I told Von. It's t*hat beige brick home with the big picture window and the red mailbox out front. Park by the mailbox. She'll be along in a minute. Stay in the car.*

You mean Stephanie? Von asked. *This is where she . . . where you guys live?*

Correct. I recalled it when I saw her get in the Suburu. Her car isn't here yet. Is she coming?

Von checked out the back window as he informed Julia and Charlie the new information.

"But Von. We might just scare Stephanie even worse," Julia protested. "I don't want to freak her out."

"Yeah. We could easily creep her out," Charlie said. "And here she comes."

"But this is where D.G. sent us," Von told them. "I'm just playing his hand."

I remembered more things you can say to her, Von. Memories are coming fast and furious now. Just say what I tell you, just like last time. I think I can convince her. Trust me.

Stephanie swung her car into the drive and pulled up to the

closed garage door. Von and the others got out just as Stephanie opened her car door. When she saw them approaching, she froze.

Von walked to within six feet of her. "D. G. says . . . I mean James. He says he never seduced you. You seduced him. That first time. It's an inside joke between the two of you, right? You tease each other that way."

"Yeah. But we've told that to lots of our friends. You have to be getting this stuff from someone that knows us really well. Maybe Howie Landers. Or Sarah Mintz. Or . . . I don't know. Look. I told you to stay away. And I meant it."

"We're scaring her," Charlie muttered to Von. "I don't like this."

I certainly didn't want to frighten the woman I loved but I couldn't let Von stop. *Tell her this Von, exactly as I recite it.*

"You met in a college Chemistry class," Von nearly hollered nervously. "You were so distracted by James that you made a C in the course. But it was a huge class and seating was alphabetical. The guy seated next to you got an A and the teacher accidently gave that guy's grade to you too, so by a total accident, you got an A. You never told anyone in the department and you kept the A."

Stephanie leaned in a few inches closer to Von, her frown relaxing just a bit, her eyes cringing. She didn't say anything, just stood staring at him. She reached out and opened the back car door, unbuckled her child, lifted him from the car seat and slid the baby into the baby carrier on her chest. She shoved the door closed with her knee and strode toward the front door of the house. Suddenly, she stopped and seemed to be staring at the house. She whirled around, used her electronic key to unlock her car and pointed at Charlie.

"You big guy. Get my groceries. I need them right next to my front door."

Charlie nodded dutifully and moved quickly. Stephanie turned and approached her front door as Charlie carried her bags of food supplies along behind her.

Stick with her Von. Don't give up. Tell her this.

"The two of you broke into a professor's office and planted two video recording devices built to look like a clock radio and a picture frame because the professor was sexually abusing his secretary. You anonymously sent the video files to the head of department and the professor was censured. You both kept it secret. And you haven't told that to anyone."

Stephanie stopped a foot from her front door. She stood facing the door, seemed to be considering his words and then punched her code into the digital door lock. She slowly opened the big oak door and then turned a shoulder toward Von. Her eyes burned at Von. Slowly, she nodded but still didn't speak. She turned to enter the room but then I had Von tell another one.

"It took James nearly six months to convince you that the project could succeed."

Both Charlie and Julia turned toward Von and asked, "What project?"

Von shrugged his shoulders at them and faced Stephanie again.

I don't know the specifics of the project, Von. I only know there is one and it's carried out at that big gray building. I'll need more memories to fill in the blanks. I'm taking a shot in the dark here.

Stephanie slowly turned back and fully faced Von. She took a step closer to him and then another. I could tell by her look that something in her believed something in Von. But I wasn't sure what. Slowly, she backed through the door and spoke as she did.

"You three stay exactly where you are. Do not move. Do not leave. I'll come get the groceries in a minute. Stay."

She closed the door and its lock clicked.

Charlie leaned to his left gazing through the big picture window. "She's calling someone. I can see her inside, talking on her cell."

"Probably the cops," Julia exhaled. She dug the car keys out of her pocket and reached them out to Charlie. "You should take the car and get out of here. If Von and I get arrested, you'll be free to maybe bail us out of jail. Here."

Charlie smiled and stuffed his hands into his pockets. "I'm not going anywhere without you and Von."

Von watched Stephanie pace back and forth in her house, cell phone to her head, talking rapidly, her eyes expanding with emphasis and waving her left arm in the air, palm up. She walked back and forth across the big living room six times, gently patted the sleeping child on the rear, the phone conversation continuing. Finally, she ended the call and looked out the big picture window at them and mouthed the words, 'Stay there,' at them. She then disappeared down a hallway.

"So, D.G. must be remembering a lot more," Charlie said, "I mean if you could say all those things to her."

Von nodded. "Yeah. He's been getting lots of memories since we pulled into the LSU campus. And when we saw her by Whole Foods, the memories really fired up."

Yes, and I'm filing through them as quickly as possible right now, I told Von. *I could tell you the code to that front door digital lock.*

No. No. I don't think we should intrude into the house, Von responded.

You're right, Von. I don't want to scare her. And she hasn't sent us away and that's definitely progress. I think we at least got her attention.

Chapter Eighteen

{I have the authority to jail you so that you have no civil rights at all. No lawyers. No phone calls.}

Julia, Charlie and I stood silently mulling around Stephanie's front door for ten minutes before she showed herself at her picture window, again with her cell phone held against her ear. As she conversed, she gestured with the first finger of her left hand jabbing, pointed at the floor. I tried to figure out what she was saying, to read her lips but she went too fast. She glanced at her wrist watch, nodded and ended the call. Suddenly, the front door swung open. She picked up the groceries Charlie had left by her door, stepped back and slammed the door. After another two minutes, she opened the front door and faced us. I thought she would speak, but she just stood there staring at us with her arms crossed.

On the street came the screeching of tires. Two black SUVs had blocked in the Bamboo car and all doors on both cars swung open. Five large men and one tall woman marched toward us and they didn't look happy. One man wore a US Air Force uniform, the tall woman wore a U.S. Marine Corp uniform, one white-haired man had on a long white lab coat and the other three were the same three security suits at the gray building we had run away from.

"Clip 'em," the woman in the Marine uniform ordered.

A black-suited security guard spun me toward a wall, forced me to lean on it and handcuffed my hands behind my back. When I looked, Julia and Charlie were also handcuffed. The woman Marine looked around the neighborhood and then turned to Stephanie.

"We don't want a scene. Can't have the neighbors calling the city police. We'll need to move everyone inside."

D.G. This is getting scary. What now? I begged.

Easy Von. I recognize these guys. Stay calm. Repeat everything I tell you exactly as I say it.

The three security guys pushed us through the front door and into a nice living room. The big picture window filled the wall to the left of the entrance. The long room held a plush leather couch against the wall opposite the front door. To the right of the couch a long hallway lead to other parts of the house. Off to our left just past the big picture window, the end of the room bore a large fireplace with a marble mantel where a big glass-front grandfather clock ticked away showing 4:05 PM. Two comfortable overstuffed chairs faced the couch. The security suits plopped us down on the sofa and took up positions at either end of it, watching us closely. But something stuck in my mind, something I'd just seen and not given enough attention to. I looked at the fireplace but that wasn't it, the marble mantel either. My eyes went up and down the grandfather clock thinking no, that isn't it, but then I focused more carefully on the face of the clock.

"*D.G.! That clock face. It's the clock we've been standing on, the one in our dreams, I mean, isn't it?*"

"*Why yes. Now that you mention it, that is most decidedly it, Von. In fact that sparks another memory, of how many relatives have almost fought over inheriting that thing. That clock has been in my family four generations. I have to presume that's why my mind used it in those extraordinary dreams we've shared.*"

Stephanie, the woman Marine Major, the Air Force Colonel and the white lab-coated scientist, all stood facing us. For long seconds they just stared. Then the woman Marine motioned toward the other end of the room and their group moved to a kitchen on the other side of a half wall. Their whispering at first wasn't very loud but I made out "high school seniors," "personal stuff that just James and I know," and then her voice grew louder with "knew about the project." The Marine Major questioned Stephanie and slowly walked her further into the kitchen away from us.

Julia's eyes grew large and even more fear filled. Charlie twisted a shoulder back and forth trying to ease the pressure the handcuffs put on his shoulder joints.

D.G. We're in deep shit here. You better have . . .

Patience, Von. Repeat precisely what I tell you. When these people arrived, so did a whole lot of memories about them. I assure you we can make an impression now.

As Stephanie and her whole group approached us, D.G. quickly fed me instructions.

"Major Gwendolyn McManus," I recited quickly following D.G.'s queue. "U.S. Marine Corp, M.D. in Criminology, works in the oversight office of the Secret Service at the Pentagon."

The Major stood peering down at me, dragged up a straight back chair from the kitchen table, sat in it and leaned in close to my face.

"You three are going to tell us everything, and I do mean everything, about how you've gotten your information. I assure you, I have the authority to jail you so that you end up with no civil liberties at all. No lawyers. No phone calls. You would simply disappear. So, first of all, how did you know the personal information about Stephanie? Huh? Who's gonna talk?"

She looked from Julia to me to Charlie. Her hawk eyebrows and set jaw muscles reflected the toughness trained into her mind.

Ok Von, let's try another one, D.G. said, getting me ready for another recitation. *The Air Force Colonel this time.*

"Colonel Randolph Stravieda, U.S. Air Force, PhD physicists, astronaut, masters degree in electrical engineering," I blared out. I watched the Colonel step closer. Stephanie approaching along with him, her brow furrowed, her arms still crossed. They just stared.

Ready Von? One more, D.G. said.

I turned a bit and looked at the scientist guy. "Lawrence Joplande, PhD mechanical engineer, PhD electrical engineer, all from Brown University, employed by DARPA for fourteen years."

Now the scientist joined the other three staring mostly at me.

"I want you to explain, starting now," the Marine Major McManus growled, "Or, I can sit you three in isolation cells on bread and water for as long as this takes."

"Damn it, Von. Tell them. About the voice, about D.G." Julia pleaded. "Tell them." Julia, looking scared, sat almost balled up squeezing her knees together. The Marine Major noticed me looking at Julia and could tell I worried about Julia.

"I'll take this one," Major McManus said grabbing Julia by the arm, standing her up and walking her down the hall.

I couldn't take seeing some big Marine woman hauling Julia off. "No. No. It's not her. It's me. It's all me. She doesn't know anything at all. She can't. He's in ME, NOT HER." I tried to stand but hands came from everywhere and pressed me back onto the couch.

D.G. damn it. Now they're gonna hurt Julia. That woman might beat her up . . .

Relax Von. They're tricking you. I now know enough about that Major and the others to know they won't harm Julia. She'll just question her. Concentrate on Stephanie. She's our ticket. And recite this.

The Air Force Colonel sat down before me and gave me a hard look. Stephanie stood close next to him so I zeroed in on her.

"That digital lock on the front door," I called out, "James installed it. The combination is made up of your birthday, James's birthday and the child's. Nobody else knows that."

Colonel Stravieda glared at me, turned to Stephanie and raised his eyebrows. She caught his look, hesitated just a moment and nodded.

"How did you know that?" the Colonel asked. "Who told you that? Listen son, that lady in the Marine uniform, you don't want to piss her off."

"Julia's right, Von," Charlie spoke up. "You have to tell them where you're getting the information, weird as that'll be. Even if they don't believe you. You gotta start saying it."

"Ok. So here's a question for you," I said following D.G.'s orders for me to recite again. "What happened to James? Is he dead? Is he alive? Where is he or where is his body?"

"I don't think you yet appreciate the situation you've gotten yourself into," the Colonel replied. "We won't give out any information. We have security protocols. See, you're going to give us information. Or else."

"Yeah. Security protocol four, both parts C and D," I said trying to

218

say it just as D.G. had. "Written specifically for the project. Right?"

The Colonel leaned back in his chair, obviously taken by surprise. His eyes narrowed. Stephanie uncrossed her hands and leaned in closer, her eyes wide open. Dr. Joplande stepped up too with a look of confusion.

"How the hell does he keep coming up with information like that?" Joplande cried out.

"It's a voice in his head. If he won't tell you, I will," Charlie cried nervously.

"I don't know, damn it," came Julia's yell from down the hall. "It's a voice in his head. I can't hear it. Go ask him."

A second later, the Marine Major tugged Julia back into the living room and deposited her back on the couch. I noted that the mantle grandfather clock now read 4:35. Through the big picture window across the room from us, the afternoon sunlight took on more of a slanting angle.

"I might have two leads," the tall Marine Major barked. "Karl, you're with me." Major McManus and one of the suited security guards disappeared back down the hall. A moment later, only the Major came back out of the hallway and called back to Karl, "Let me know what you find out."

"So," the Colonel said. "Hearing a little voice in that head of yours, huh?"

Ok Von. Hang on. Now we pick on him, D.G. whispered.

"When's the last time you saw Claudette? You told James and big muscle Lawrence over there why she left you when you all went fly fishing on the Bogue Falaya river six weeks ago," I said to the Colonel.

219

Blaring out personal information had me hoping he wouldn't slug me.

The Colonel's face registered curiosity. He turned and looked at Lawrence, one of the suited security guards standing near the fireplace. Lawrence stepped closer scowling.

"A teenager," Lawrence grumbled. "A fucking teenager knows this? How the hell?"

"This voice is telling you all this?" Stephanie knelt down on the rug next to the Colonel.

I nodded. "Yeah. Like I tried to tell you before. It's the only source I have. I call it Director Guy because he . . . "

No Von. Not yet. Don't go rogue on me. That tactic will fail, I assure you. We have to keep amazing them, overwhelming them, until they are ready to believe you. I have lots more memories flashing up and lots of tricks to pull. Stay with me, Von.

"Did you just stop talking because the voice spoke to you?" Stephanie asked.

No Von. Don't answer that. Tell her this instead.

"You haven't been able to get into the safe, have you?" I blurted at Stephanie. "I can open it. I know where it is. I know the combination. Only James knows that. He designed the safe, installed the locking system, but didn't tell even you how to open it. That's not information you or James had to give up to receive security clearance for the project. James alone knows how to open that safe. He's the voice in my head and he's ready to tell me how to do it."

"What's that all about?" the Colonel asked Stephanie.

Stephanie gave a defensive glance at the Colonel. "Well you know how cautious, really overly cautious, James is. When we had this house built, he had a huge block of cement added to the design of one of the walls. He installed a specially built digital safe within that cement block and set the computerized combination himself. He worried about giving me the combination because he and I usually argue about how secure things have to be around here. He locks doors. I don't. And we fuss with each other about it, so he worried about trusting me with the combination."

"So James is literally the only one that could open it?" The Marine Major asked.

"Yes. I know where it's located but I don't know James's method of opening it," Stephanie shrugged. "Maybe this kid got the architectural plans to the house?"

"Possibly. But that wouldn't have the combination for the lock," Colonel Stravieda muttered as he stood and stepped away.

"Stand up, kid. First of all, you'll find it," the Marine Major snapped.

I stood. D.G. began giving directions and I moved slowly toward the kitchen. One guard, Stephanie, the Major, the Colonel and Dr. Joplande followed along. In the kitchen, D.G. had me approach a tall broom closet.

"In there," I said.

The Major opened the door on a phone booth size closet full of mops, brooms and cleaning supplies.

"I'll need my hands free," I told them.

The Major nodded and the security suit took my cuffs off. Following D.G.'s directions, I emptied the brooms, mops, ironing board and other stuff from the closet. There were thumbscrews at the rear of the closet that allowed the top of a back half-wall to be removed. After removing the thumbscrews, I slid the top half-wall panel out and there, staring back at us, was a heavy black steel door embedded within a solid cement wall. For a second, I felt shock because the steel door was simply blank. It had no combination dial and it didn't have a digital number pad. How could I possibly open the thing? It was just a blank door except for a tiny rectangular slot in the very center of the door. D.G. must have felt my panic.

Not to worry, Von. The solution to this is quite simple. Ask Stephanie for the wifi computer keyboard that operates our T.V. And don't forget the USB toggle that goes with it.

Though Stephanie gave me a curious look when I made the request, she moved from the kitchen to the living room and returned a few seconds later with the keyboard and toggle. Following instructions, I plugged the USB toggle into the small rectangular USB slot in the middle of the door and turned on the keyboard switch. A tiny blue light that I hadn't noticed before turned on at the corner of the safe's door. D.G. then slowly recited a twenty-six letter and number combination, which I typed in. When I hit enter, the door gave a grinding sound and clicked ajar two inches.

"Before you open it," I said cautioning them, "James says the safe contains details of all six mutual funds that he and Stephanie own, their account numbers and passwords, the savings and checking account numbers and passwords and a large amount of cash. It also contains his copies of certain government contracts that he and Stephanie signed when the project began."

I stepped out of the broom closet and now faced five silent

adults. They all held their own version of bewilderment. Stephanie stepped into the broom closet and opened the safe. She moved a few papers around, studied three of them, examined the six piles of cash and then turned and gawked at me. I smiled and launched into a desperate explanation.

"Yeah, see, the voice in my head is James. He just arrived one night. Don't ask me how. He and I haven't been able to figure that out but . . ."

"Shut up!" Major McManus barked, looming over me.

You're a good man, Von. Excellent. We're earning their attention but we must continue. Can't quit now.

Well. I got the handcuffs off. What's next? I asked D.G.

Now we need to press for what happened to me. And I need to know the nature of the project. I'm not getting memories about the project. But I'm pretty sure there's an overview of the project in that safe.

"James wants to know what happened to him," I told the group. "Again, is James dead or alive? Is he buried, jailed or what?"

"Put him back on the couch," the Marine Major snapped.

As the big security guy grabbed me by the arm, Stephanie spoke up. "Wait a minute," she said, still standing in the broom closet. "I need to have Von write down that combination. I'll need to know how to open the safe myself." She stepped from the broom closet, got a pencil and pad from a drawer in the kitchen and stood at a kitchen counter waiting.

Major McManus nodded at the security guard and he released my arm. I walked over to Stephanie and wrote the combination as D.G. recited it to me again. But then I quickly scribbled, 'James needs the project overview.' Stephanie read the note, made a quick glance at me and then over her shoulder to make sure no one else saw what I'd written, tore the note from the pad and stuffed it into her pocket. She gave a slight nod, turned to the guard and repeated, "Put him on the couch."

As the guard hauled me back to the couch, lots of whispering and quiet arguing began between Stephanie, the Major and the Colonel.

"Did you find it?" Julia asked. "Did you open it?"

I nodded.

"Nice," Charlie nodded smiling. "So D.G.'s memories are really sparking."

I nodded. "Yeah. But we're not out of deep shit yet." The sky outside the picture window had gone a deeper orange mixed with purples. Was there a thunderstorm coming? Sunset usually happened later this time of year. If this kept up, darkness would come on quickly.

Karl, the security guard, returned. "Major, the guidance counselor at their school said many of Von's friends have reported Von talking about an extra voice in his head. Strangely, his grades have improved since then. He also said the kid underwent an evaluation with a psychiatrist that specializes in mental voices. And he also underwent a religious exorcism. The priest I talked with confirms the exorcism. He was under the impression the exorcism had succeeded. When I tried to talk to the psychiatrist, a Doctor Kalchavic, he at first refused to divulge any information because of doctor client privileges. So, I sent Marine Sergeant Max Danhurst with two of his Marine MPs to Dr. Kalchavic's office to explain the delicacy of the situation and encourage him to cooperate. Once they talked with him, he provided good Intel on this kid, Von. He stated that he was able to speak with the voice by hypnotizing Von. He also reported that, for the first time in his long career, he failed to control the voice itself. He said that this internal voice seems to be a separate consciousness from Von, himself. That's everything I got so far, Major."

The Major blinked and considered what she'd just heard. "Ok. Let's run with that. Good job, Karl." She turned and began whispering with Stephanie, the Colonel and Dr. Joplande. After a while, they broke the huddle and approached us. This time, it was Dr. Joplande that spoke.

"So, a voice in your head that's independent of you. Right?"

I nodded. "Yeah, and he still wants to know what's happened to him. Is he dead or alive? Where is he?"

"How do you communicate with this voice?" Dr. Joplande asked.

No Von. Those questions are useless and a waste of time. Back to Stephanie. Tell her this.

"Stephanie," I called to get her attention, "when your algorithm solution produced the first successful run of the frequency phaser so that objects would leave and return, you and James celebrated by making love behind the auxiliary battery bank because there were no security cameras back there."

My revelation caught Dr. Joplande off guard. He whirled toward Stephanie. "What! Oh for goodness sakes. Is that true?" he blurted. Stephanie's face went very pink. She tried to hide her grin by raising her hand over her face, but then let her hand fall.

She nodded, a small smile appearing on her face. "I guess I'm caught. Yes. James and I were so excited that we'd succeeded."

"There's only one way I could know all this stuff," I hollered not waiting for D.G. to tell me anything. "James landed in my head. I have no idea how, but the last two weeks has been the craziest of my life and

225

though he's a nice guy, I want my head back with just me in it. You know. I gotta get him out. And he wants out. And you guys gotta help. And you have to help by at least telling me if James is alive or dead."

"Its classified information," the Marine Major butted in. "We don't give out any information. You give information to us. That's the way it works, kid."

Oh yeah, Gwen? Back to Stephanie, Von, D.G. answered and then gave me the information I was to recite next.

"Shit D.G. You want me to say that to her?" I blurted out loud, then realized I'd spoken instead of thought it.

Do it, D.G. insisted.

"James never had that affair with Virginia," I mumbled, afraid of her reaction. "He had it with Joan."

Every eye in the room turned to Stephanie. Her arms slowly fell to her side and she knelt on the rug in front of me looking directly into my eyes. For long moments, she considered what she'd heard.

"Somehow . . . it just might be James in there. Eventually, James always tells me the truth," Stephanie said. "He sometimes hesitates, waits a week or even a month. Like I said, he's cautious, but in due time, it always comes out. But how could James have gotten into . . . in this kid's head?"

"Wait. How do you know it's not this Virginia woman?" Major McManus asked.

"Because Joan and I were close. She's one of my favorite cousins. Joan's mother found out about their affair and told me about it four months ago. I never told James that I knew the truth. I've been waiting to see if he'd come clean. And now, of all times, he has. All the things he's

226

said, all of them exactly correct. No way anyone else could know all those things."

"I have to admit," the Colonel spoke up, "I'm swayed."

"NO. No swaying. We have to be strong here," the Major jumped in. "We have very important security protocols to uphold. We are not handing out information from a top secret project. Let's not forget that."

Stephanie knelt in front of me concentrating on my eyes. She wasn't looking away. Though her eyes stayed focused directly on mine, her head began to turn slowly, a little left and then a little right. I could tell some thought was brewing in her. She nodded.

Julia and Charlie leaned in closer to me, focusing on Stephanie and the heavy look of concentration on her face.

"So, here's an important question for you, Von, Julia and Charlie."

Inside I froze. If she started interrogating me, what if I didn't know the answers?

"When? Exactly when, did this voice show up in your head?" Stephanie asked, leaning in even closer. For a moment the three of us sat silently, thinking back.

"We were out at the railroad spur," Charlie blurted.

"It was night time, though later than it is right now," I said nodding to the darkening sky outside the picture window.

"It was a Tuesday night," Julia added. "Two Tuesdays back, I'm pretty sure."

"Yeah. We had that math test the next day," I added. "Mrs. Dillman dated the test May sixth. So . . . "

"So it was May 5th," Julia called out. "We left at midnight. You complained about the voice in your head about thirty minutes before that."

"So it first spoke to me around 11:30 pm, May 5th," I said.

"Freaking amazing," Stephanie said. She looked up at Colonel Stravieda and then at Dr. Joplande. "That's exactly the time James arrived back unconscious. Those two events coincide."

Unconscious? D.G. mumbled. *Unconscious but still alive? For nearly two weeks now?*

"That IS the exact hour and date," Joplande exclaimed. "I remember that. In fact, I have it right here in my folder." He'd left his folder on the mantle, found it and read over the recorded schedule of past events, checking for himself. Colonel Stravieda and Major McManus moved in close and read over the Joplande's shoulders. Stephanie stood nodding, staring hard at me.

"Sorry. I apologize but I'm beginning to disagree with you, Major MacManus," Stephanie said as tears filled her eyes. "You see, I've lost a lot here. That's my husband in that coma. I've given enough to this project. I've given the most important thing in my life. I've lost more than anyone here!"

In a coma! D.G. screamed. YES! I knew it. I sensed it. That's where that thread leads. Von, repeat this to them now.

"So James is alive," I called out. "That means you probably have his body in the project building basement hospital rooms. James in my head wants to see his body. He demands it."

"Absolutely out of the question," the Major answered. "You aren't going anywhere . . . "

"Why not?" Stephanie hollered, standing and facing the Major. "Isn't this possible? I mean, we were attempting a first. Something that has never ever been accomplished before in the history of the earth. We don't actually know what's feasible. Isn't it possible that James's consciousness veered off and somehow found this kid? James's body in one place, his knowledge . . . his . . . his consciousness in another? How do we know it couldn't happen? We don't have anything else to compare it to because this has never been attempted before."

I got it. I GOT IT. I'VE GOT EVERY BIT OF IT!, D.G. began to yell like a totally raving madman. *I have got it. It's mine. ALL MINE!*

Ok D.G. For goodness sakes. What?

I see my mother's face. And my father's. Everything, D.G. ranted. *I remember it all. Absolutely everything! All my memories are back, Von. We must get into that building. Everything depends on it. I know the project. Hell, I designed and wrote the thing.*

I couldn't help but smile. D.G.'s newfound energy ran through me causing me to rise from slouching to sitting up straight. I took a nice long deep breath.

"Wow," Dr. Joplande mumbled. "And I thought we'd covered all possibilities. Physical evals, psych evals, background vetting, college scores, competitive tests and recommendations for personnel selection, and then the computer coding, all the phaser machinery hand built, the electronics . . . all the thousands of system checks and double checks . . . and we never once considered that space-time transference might split a person apart. There's not one word in the entire project's one hundred and fifty-three thousand page proposal that even touches on any possibility of some kind of separation between body and consciousness. How could we not consider that? I feel completely blindsided."

The Colonel stood facing me, considering Stephanie and

Joplande's words. His eyes going from left to right and back again. His forehead furrowed. "You're right. It isn't anywhere in the proposal write-up. Nobody thought of that, at all."

"But that doesn't mean . . . it's . . . . Just because no one considered it or predicted . . . it doesn't mean that's what occurred," Major McManus said. I mean, I'm not one of you science guys, but that's just simple logic."

"Yeah. It's kind of fifty-fifty," Dr. Joplande answered. "We can't prove it did happen that way and we can't prove it didn't."

They have to take me close to my body, Von. Tell them.

"James wants to see his body, actually wants to touch his body," I said again. "It's his body, after all."

Stephanie looked around at the others. "Has that ever happened? I do math and physics. Has that ever occurred? One person's consciousness in another person?"

"Karl," the Major ordered. "Get that shrink back on the phone and ask him that very question, quickly please." Karl pulled his cell phone from his pocket as he walked away down the hall again.

Ok Von. This time we go after Dr. Joplande. You'll have to listen closely and repeat carefully. OK?

I'll do my best, I answered.

"Lawrence," I said to Dr. Joplande, "You may have been wrong about the guidance system's isotropic coordinates that we fed into Stephanie's algorithm to establish the proper gravitational field. Though you both insisted that James enter in the double eigenvalue[19] for the

---

[19] "Chronological structure of a Godel type universe with negative cosmological constant," by Klaus Behrndt and Markus Possel, https://arxiv.org/pdf/hep-th/0310090.pdf , page 6, Golm, Germany, December, 1, 2003.

return trip, which James used as directed, he feels certain now that it's the wrong value. He believes it's what has caused this situation."

Dr. Joplande leaned in close staring hard at me. Stephanie began to shake her head. The Colonel sat up very erect and glanced at Joplande and Stephanie.

"And now this kid knows not only that it was a very important argument we had in preparing the project," Joplande blurted, "but he is privy to a major value that controls the main steering algorithm? Ok. Ok. Very well. So, what value do you propose in place of the one Stephanie, Colonel Stravieda and I worked out?"

"He says he wants to see his body," I answered. "He says he has lots of critical information that you're gonna need if this project is ever to go forward or even come close to succeeding. He says there are at least eight at fault conditions within the coding and each of those fault things could cause an allover sys . . . ahh . . . an overall system failure. It could affect the frame field settings, over heat the . . . No . . . No, James says you get no more information. He wants to see his body or else he will tell you nothing more."

"But if the double eigenvalue[20] wasn't the correct value to enter into the algorithm, that creates an astounding problem," Dr. Joplande muttered. "That algorithm controls the mirror rotations, the laser beam curvature coordinate system . . . the guidance depends upon . . . why, we would be at a standstill. What other value would cause proper alignment? I'm at a loss."

Stephanie still shook her head. The Colonel stood and faced his team. "The more this kid opens his mouth, the more I . . ."

---

[20] ibid

"James is the only person that could know that," Stephanie called out, her hands flailing the air. "You both remember the effort we put into working out that coding. Security has been incredibly tight. Our computer network isn't hackable because it's never been connected to the Internet or any other network. No one knows this project even exists. The security has been as tight as the Manhattan Project. How else COULD THIS KID KNOW THIS!!"

"Major," Karl said reentering the room. "Dr. Kalchavic, the psychiatrist that treated Von, stated he has never heard of any instance of one person's consciousness entering another person. He doesn't think it possible. Yet, that's exactly how Von's hypnosis impressed him. The voice inside claimed independence and refused to be hypnotized while Von, himself was under hypnosis and completely unconscious."

For long moments, everyone stood looking at Karl.

"Wait a minute," Stephanie whispered. "So this psychiatrist confirms that this kid does actually have a voice in his head? A voice that has its own consciousness? Different from Von's?"

Karl nodded. "Yes. Dr. Kalchavic definitely confirmed that. He spoke with it."

Stephanie froze still facing Karl but everyone else turned and looked at Von.

"Actual confirmation that he does have a voice in his head," Colonel Stravieda said softly.

"And that voice has been saying things that only James would have known. Things that we can confirm," Dr. Joplande added.

For long moments, everyone was silent. But that's when D.G. gave me one more recitation to say.

"And then there's the highly personal value of eighty-three," I called out following D.G.'s directions.

"Ooohh. Nnnoooo!" Stephanie hollered. She spun toward me and put her hands across my mouth. "You hush. Of all the low down dirty . . . I mean, embarrass me no end . . . damn it James. How could you?" The blush across Stephanie's face rose so quickly, I felt shocked. I had no idea what eighty-three meant but it sure had an effect on her. She jerked her hands away from my mouth and covered her own face. "Oh, James, James. Don't . . .you . . . don't . . . ." She turned away, her hand waving a stop sign at me, her mouth opening twice to say more but then saying nothing.

"What's that all about?" Major McManus asked.

"Oh goodness. I'm sorry. That's just too, too personal. But I can tell you, it absolutely has to be James in there. It has to be."

"Stephanie. I'm the head of security," Major McManus growled. "You signed a federal government agreement to divulge all secrets that might affect this project. What is it, this eighty-three thing? You tell me right now."

The two woman's eyes met. Slowly, Stephanie closed her eyes. She then took the Major's hand and led her down the hall so they could talk privately. The Major followed along, leaning over Stephanie, determination written across her face.

"We need to know what value to use in that algorithm," Dr. Joplande said to Colonel Stravieda. "If this kid has James's knowledge, or can somehow fill in that blank, the project could proceed. We'd be able to get past this failure and continue with a second attempt."

Stravieda nodded. "Yeah. I'm beginning to agree. I don't know where the kid's getting the information, but it's accurate. It's well founded. It's known by only one or two other people, all of them in this room. Impossible to prove this kid wrong."

Major McManus and Stephanie walked back into the living room, the Major with a small wry smile across her face.

"Ok. So what's eighty-three?" Joplande insisted. "Is that some value to be place in coding, or what?"

The Major smiled, glanced at Stephanie and then chuckled. "No. No, actually it has no scientific significance at all. It's aaahhh . . . personal." Major McManus not sharing information caused everyone to look at each woman in wonderment.

Stephanie tisked, looked indignant and continued blushing. She muttered, "Damn it James."

"I'm in favor of letting Von see James's body," Dr. Joplande said, "I mean, what harm could it do? Let's be frank here. He's in a coma and if he remains that way long enough, his muscles atrophy and he dies. Letting them see James in a coma really isn't that big a deal."

"I agree completely," Stephanie quickly added. "I don't want to get my hopes up but if Von and his voice can do something, shed light on anything at all, I'm for it. The life of my husband is involved and I say yes, we take them in."

"Agreed," Colonel Stravieda chimed in.

Major McManus put her hands on her hips and slowly gauged the faces of her three associates. "Well, I never thought I'd hear myself say this, but if the three of you are agreed on it, . . . ok then. We take them in through the back entrance. No elevators. We take the stairs right near that entrance, that way they only see the basement hospital. No big secrets there. I'm going to allow you kids to move around without handcuffs, but if you misbehave at all, they go right back on. So act right."

"Ok. We got it," Charlie answered. Julia nodded her agreement.

Chapter Nineteen

{ *We are somewhere out past known human knowledge. And we're guessing.* }

"Excellent. We've earned entrance into the project facility," I told Von. "I'm familiar with that area, the basement hospital. You performed flawlessly, Von. You've done incredibly well, my man."

Von's nerves quaked. His trepidation about entering that massive gray building played on his nerves. Then Stephanie spoke with Juanita on her cell phone.

"Who's that?" Von demanded.

"Easy Von. Juanita is our middle aged Spanish baby sitter. Stephanie needs her to keep an eye on Marky, our child, while she's gone. That's all. Take a deep breath."

Everyone stood around, caught in their own thoughts, barely any conversation happening and then Juanita drove up. After Stephanie made rudimentary arrangements for Marky, everyone moved toward the black SUVs.

The guards stuffed Von and Julia into the back of one SUV and put Charlie, flanked by two large guards, in the back of the other one. Baton Rouge traffic flowed smoothly, the city's night life showed signs lit up along the route and I noticed a bank clock that stated 8:39 pm.

Arriving at the back entrance of the project building in complete darkness, the black SUVs drew close to the building and emptied out. As Von stood there in the parking lot, I concentrated on the silver thread penetrating the building's solid metal back door. The three suited security guards and Major McManus encircled Von, Julia and Charlie. Stephanie, Colonel Stravieda and Dr. Joplande followed. Major McManus swiped a digital pass through an electronic slot and the big metal door slowly slid aside giving access to a long, partially lit hallway. Everyone moved inside the building and the big door slid shut.

"We're taking the down staircase," McManus said pointing, but I already knew that. Everything looked familiar.

At the bottom of the second flight, the thread turned down the long hallway and we were directed along that route. The automated lighting turned on, illuminating more and more of the hallway as we approached. A large picture window along the right side of the hallway allowed us to see into the preliminary medical examination room, but we went past that doorway. A second large window let us look into the heavily equipped medical clinic. I knew this is where they would keep a comatose patient and toward the back of the room was a bed with a person. It was at that very bed that the silver tread ended. It attached to the back of the person lying there, and I sensed right away that it was my body. Something in me jumped with apprehension. I was right here in Von and I was over there, in that hospital bed, all at once. My nerves clamped and Von's nerves tensed too. There was no way either of us could remain calm. His hands began to tremble. We were silent, unable to express anything to each other.

Major McManus looked around, told the three security guys to stand guard in the hallway and secure the door once we were in. She then swiped her pass card through the digital reader. A heavy click allowed the door to be pulled open and everyone but the three guards moved into the room. Stephanie stepped forward quickly approaching the bed ahead of the group. A nurse near the bed turned and said hello. They hugged and Stephanie asked if there were any change. The nurse shook her head. Von took slow cautious steps approaching the bed with Charlie and Julia close behind. As Stephanie stood close to the bed, she scrutinized Von's every move.

Ok D.G. Finally. Here we are, Von said to me. *He is you. The you I saw when we were on LSD. It's definitely that guy. It's you, right? I mean, it's James, right?*

I sensed Von's jittery stomach muscles twitching as he waited for my answer. But, I shook with anxiety looking down upon myself. Obviously, I had not been exercising and so my body looked slack, like it had sunk into the bed an inch or so. My beard, usually well trimmed, looked a bit tattered. I looked older, although my six-foot frame seemed about the right length, my shoulders didn't seem as thick as I remembered. I needed a haircut, or maybe to just comb my hair. My cheeks seemed shrunken and my jaw muscles slacked. But, deep in my eye sockets, a concentration held, as though the coma held secrets to be revealed, or was I just making that up in my head? The problem was that my body was on that bed. I was outside my own body. An out-of-body experience squared. I felt fully alert, but my body showed none of that. I watched for the breath under a rising chest but it showed such slight movement that it only served to worry me more.

Oh goodness, yes, Von. It's me. But, somehow, I'm not there. I'm here, in you. How the hell could I let this, of all things, happen! All that preparation, all the hopes I held going through school, the hundreds of courses throughout college, meeting Stephanie, our life together, the fantastic opportunity this project held and now this. Stuck. Banished from my own being. I must touch him. Please Von, I need your right hand.

I felt Von nod and I took control of his hand. I reached out and touched my arm. My arm I felt right there at the end of these fingers. I was right there. I tried to serge into the hand, through the fingers into my body, to jump the ever-so-slight difference between the skin of Von's fingers and the skin of my arm, his body, our body, but it didn't work. Somehow, my body on the bed and my awareness, here in Von's body, remained separate. I held onto him, trying and trying to get into that body, into my body. Von placed his other hand on James's arm, realizing what I was trying to do. Unfortunately, it didn't help.

"He's trying to . . . move into his body," Von told Stephanie. She nodded. Then I felt Von shake his head and breathe deeper. I felt Julia place her hand on Von's back. Von looked around and I saw everyone silently staring, waiting, maybe even hoping. It was no use. Slowly, I released Von's right hand giving him back control.

I can't. It's no use. I can't. I am profoundly sorry Von. I am unable to leave. To let you have all of yourself to yourself, the way it should be. I can't get out. I cannot . . . I'm trapped. I could not contain my frustration and I began to cry. Von stood very still, tears streaming down his cheeks.

Stephanie put her arms around Von's shoulder. "What's happening? What do you feel?"

Von shook his head but said nothing.

Julia pressed herself against his side and held onto his other shoulder. "Just tell me you're ok. Von. Please."

Von shook his head. "D.G. can't get back in. He's still in me. Says he's trapped."

Both women hugged Von. Both Von and I struggled to breathe. His hands shook and his stomach muscles tensed so that they nearly cramped.

Maybe it's just not the right method, D.G., Von said. *Is there some other way?*

Von, right now, I am completely at a loss. It's like they said earlier, it's never been done before. We are somewhere out past known human knowledge. And we're guessing. And we're guessing wrong.

Without warning, the image of the countdown clock jumped up in front of me, superimposing itself onto the hospital wall and equipment in that area. I was stunned to see that it had only ten minutes remaining. The damn thing had sped up a lot.

Are you seeing that, Von? The clock? I asked.

I could feel his frown, his back straightening and his shoulders dropping.

Yeah. Ten minutes to go. For a few moments, we were both silent. *Well D.G. We won't have time to get back to Margarita. Looks like we're gonna see what that merge is all about. I wish us both luck.*

"So I take it this venture has proved unproductive," Major McManus blared.

Von had no choice but to capitulate, nodded and slowly trudged back toward the door wiping tears from his face. Julia clung to his right side and she moved along with him. Charlie hugged Von and then walked along the other side of him. The Major, the Colonel, Stephanie and Dr. Joplande stood for a moment looking over my body, still unresponsive in the bed. Finally, they turned and followed behind.

I had to shake this depression. I had only tried once to re-enter my body. I must have done something wrong. I wanted to try again and again and again thousands of times till I would succeed. My body was right there. How could I leave? How could I allow myself to get in this predicament? The probability of accomplishing such a project, we'd known the risks, we'd known the chances of success was miniscule. I should have never tried to . . . wait a minute. That's what got me into this state of affairs. And maybe, just maybe, it's what can get me out of . . . .

Von, I have a new plan to get me out of your head. It's risky but we have to try it.

We only have ten minutes. It better be quick, Von responded.

We'll need Charlie to tackle the two guards on the right once we're in the hallway. Clue him in. And be ready to RUN.

I felt Von's shock at my words, but as we approached the door, Von nudged Charlie and gave him a stern look. Charlie caught the look and he peered back, eyes squinting, questioning what Von meant. Von swung his right elbow against his left hand mimicking a football player's block.

"Take out the two on the right in the hallway," Von whispered.

Charlie's eyes widened. He looked through the glass at the guards and then back at Von. Von nodded quickly, "Yeah. Two on the right."

"Alright. Ok." Charlie whispered just before his hand grabbed the door handle.

Two of the three guards stood in the middle of the hall facing the door. The other guard stood a few feet to our left, down the hall in the direction we'd use to go back to the SUVs. Suddenly, Charlie lunged straight at the two, burying one shoulder into the taller guard's midsection and hooking his arm around the other's waist. His weight took them backwards suddenly, knocking them off balance and to the floor, all three of them collapsing in a heap. The third guard immediately jumped in trying to crush down upon Charlie.

Von stepped quickly to the right and backed down the hallway as though he wanted to avoid the fight. Julia still clung to his shoulder. Once Charlie reached up and pulled the third guard down on top of him, Von wheeled around and bolted down the long hallway. Because Julia clung to his side, he dragged her ten feet before she let go.

"What are you doing?" Julia sang out.

But Von's quick running already put him out ahead of her and everyone else by twenty steps.

"Get control of him and slap the cuffs on," the Major bellowed. Von glanced back just long enough to see the look of realization on the Major's face that Von and Julia were at a full run, headed deeper into the project building. "NO!" she screamed and took off running after them. "Karl, you're with me."

Slow down Von. That stairway on the right. Take it. Hurry. Skip the 1st floor and keep going up to the 2nd. Hurry.

Von's running skills kept him well ahead of his pursuers. Once he pressed past the second floor door, I had him head right down that hallway and stop at the second doorway. There he faced a digital number pad.

Press the blue button first, Von. Type in 368942. Then open the door.

He manipulated the key pad quickly and I was thankful for a teenager's reaction time. Julia ran up, breathing hard.

She has to slow them down, I told Von. *Send her back.*

"Julia, block them at the stairway door, quick," Von hollered.

Julia stepped back hesitating, confusion all over her face. "But Von, what ... ?"

"D.G. has another way to get into his body," Von yelled. "Stop them."

Dutifully, she went back and tried to hold the stairway door from being opened. The Major arrived and started yanking against Julia. With the Major and Karl both pulling against Julia, she was yanked through the doorway but managed to entangle herself upon them. They struggled to throw her aside and get by, but it took long enough for the security door in front of Von to open. He jumped inside and slammed it closed.

Now Von, hit that red X below the number pad. He did as I instructed. *Now push the delete key next to it and type in your eight digit birth date.* Again, he responded quickly and the heavy door locked.

Julia's right. What are we doing? Von asked. *They're gonna jail us for running.*

Turn around, I told him. When he did, I felt his surprise. *That is the frequency phaser. That's my ride out of your head.*

Pounding began on the door behind Von as Major McManus realized her pass card wouldn't work. Von turned back to see McManus hollering something against the sound proof door as Karl wrestled a struggling Julia pinning her arms behind her.

We have to completely ignore them now, Von. Now, it's up to you and me and we don't have a lot of time. Move closer to the machine. Von hesitated, frozen in place. He watched as Julia struggled against Karl's strong grip. *Don't worry Von. He knows not to actually harm her. And, if we get this right, it's the answer to everything. Now move to the machine.* Von nodded, turned and approached the frequency phaser. He walked slowly, overwhelmed by the incredible technology around him. His eyes fell upon banks of mainframe computers, ropes of heavy electrical cables running across the floor and up the walls, pulsing lights across control panels that automatically maintained the frequency phaser's multitude of digital functions. I felt his overwhelmed reaction.

What the heck? Von asked. *I've never seen anything like this, all those circuits, computers, gadgets. What the hell goes on in here? And what is that big thing?*

That is our ride, Von. It's the frequency phaser. It moves differently than anything that has ever been invented before.

He nodded, touched one of the mirrors and held onto the guard rail. *All these mirrors. It's like being in a circus fun house. And all these gears and electric motors and . . . wow.*

See the seat in the middle, Von? Follow that little aluminum pathway and sit down. Once you're there, strap in. Hurry, Von! Only eight minutes remains.

Von made his way up the entry ramp, sat in the pilot's chair and figured out how to lock the safety straps around him. His attention moved across the field of complicated technological parts composing the machine around him.

Ok Von. We're almost ready. I need your hand again. Sit back and relax. Using his hand, I initiated the power switch and the frequency phaser began to hum a deep rumbling as though we sat on the back of a whale. I checked coordinates and found that they were still set for the same location as my last transport. I set the timer for its usual duration of one hour. Everything was ready.

Von again looked at the big window in the door where Stephanie and Julia stood side by side, looks of fear on their faces. Behind them Dr.

Joplande and Colonel Stravieda waved and signaled, hollering against the soundless wall. Their gestures told us to stop, not to do this. Major McManus held onto an angry scowl, probably feeling she'd failed in her job. Karl had found a hammer and repeatedly struck the impenetrable glass window.

The frequency phaser's rumbling hum grew louder, and I knew it was building up the reserve of power it would need to operate at peak efficiency. The gears around the pilot seat began to rotate, carrying mirrors with them in circular arcs. With that, Von and I could no longer see anything outside the machine. The chrome coated gears sped up and began to move so fast that a mirrored ball developed all around Von. Once the ball formed completely, rainbow-colored lasers began to flash within the ball, filling it with a pulsing light that ran through the visible light spectrum over and over again. The speed of the light spectrum increased, its rhythm strumming faster and faster, until it turned completely white. A slight vibration began to shake the whole machine and I knew we had seconds before the jump.

Ok. So this is like the thing on Star Trek, right, Von called out above the machine's roar. *The transporter. You know, like 'beam me up Scottie. Right?' So where the hell are we going?*

I chuckled. *Just sit back, hang on and try to relax. This won't take long.*

Chapter Twenty

{But then, I saw the date in the bottom corner of the big screen. D.G. was right. It was eight years ahead.}

The white light went brighter and brighter until I thought it penetrated my bones.

D.G., what the hell is all this, man? I don't know if he heard me or not but he didn't answer. Right away, I wondered if he were gone out of me. Was he back in his body? He said he had another method.

For just an instant, I felt like I had become white light. But then the machine noise faded, the white light grew softer and then a rainbow of pulsating colors returned to fill the eggshell mirror around me. A shiver ran through me even though I wasn't cold. The pulsating spectrum of colors slowed down and finally coasted to a stop. The mirrored ball slowed and separated into its various mirrors attached to all those intermeshing gears. Finally they came to a halt and I realized that this big phaser machine and I had moved. I wasn't in the computer filled control room, not even in the big gray building anymore.

D.G. are you still there?

Not to worry, Von. I'm still right here. And, we've arrived. How do you feel?

I thought about it for a second. *Ahh, yeah. I think I'm ok. Yeah.* I began unbuckling the safety harness and followed the little aluminum pathway down to the floor. I looked around and felt my curiosity fire up. I found that we were in some old dank metal warehouse. The place was huge and completely empty. It was dim inside the building but sunlight came through windows near the top of the twenty foot walls. I could hear traffic outside. All the beams holding the ceiling up looked rusty. Obviously, this place hadn't been used in a while. I turned to look at the phaser machine. Though it had obviously moved itself to an old warehouse somewhere, it looked the same, all chrome gears, mirrors, electric wires, small computer motherboards here and there.

Ok D.G. I need some straight answers. First of all, how much time do we have left on the countdown clock?

Not to worry Von. Because we've transported, the clock is now running almost ten thousand times slower. So, that eight minutes will last a good while yet.

Alright, so how is this beaming somewhere getting you back in your body and out of my head?

It's a two-stage process. First we have to beam away to any other coordinate, which we've now done. It's the beaming back, to our original coordinates, that I'm hoping will place me back into my body and get me out of your consciousness. That part is yet to occur.

OK. And lastly, if we were just beamed somewhere, when I walk out of this warehouse place, where will I be?

Back in New Orleans, Louisiana, Von.

Oh, get out! Really? Man, New Orleans? That ride only took seconds? From Baton Rouge to New Orleans in less than a freakin' minute? I couldn't help but raise my arms and yell. I danced. *YEAH!* How wild.

You may notice some other changes. D.G. said.

Yeah. Fine. Cool. And I started trotting toward a big sliding door. I

247

pushed the big door sideways and sun blared in, lighting up most of the warehouse. I glanced back at the phaser machine all alone in the center of the big floor.

Von, it's ok to look around a bit, but it is essential that you be back in that seat in fifty minutes. The machine is set to send itself back to its original location, the gray project building, in one hour. It is imperative that you are strapped in and ready to go by then, or it would leave you behind and that would be catastrophic. Tell me you understand that.

Sure. Don't worry, D.G. I know New Orleans like the back of my hand. Gotta be back here in fifty minutes. I got it.

I stepped out onto the street and three taxi cabs went by pretty fast. Not only did none of them have drivers, the windshields weren't there to see through. And the front wall of their cars, where a windshield used to be, extended all the way forward to the front bumper. The thing look like a stretched out egg. I thought, Wow, I didn't know New Orleans experimented with driverless taxis. I watched them go by. One of them stopped at the corner and a man got out, unrolled what looked like a small rug, stepped on it, leaned forward and away he went down the street and around the corner of a building. The rug thing had no wheels. It floated above the ground.

Is that what you meant by 'different,' D.G.?

It's a start, Von. Look, it's best I explain right now. I'm glad science is one of your favorite subjects. It might be time for a small review. You've heard of Einstein's theory of relativity, right? Well, he said space and time are the same thing. Space-time. We got here that quickly by warping the space between two places. But, when you warp space, you will automatically warp time also. So, we have traveled eight years into the future.

What? Future? But I thought that phaser thing was a transporter.

Sure, but it mainly transports through time. Both the space and the time it jumps can be independently adjusted. We could have stayed in the project building and gone forward some years, but it's time related efficiency quotient rises when the frequency phaser covers a bit of distance simultaneously.

A freaking time machine? That's what I just rode in? My mind struggled with the whole idea of it.

I suddenly realized that I'd also be seeing the future. "Wow!" I hollered, wheeled around and started down the street. There were department stores on that side of the street and as I strolled by one, a video of me popped up in the department store window wearing a navy blue suit with red tie and fancy white shoes. I turned and watched myself step forward, turn and spin all the way around, showing what I'd look like if I put out the thirty-one Bitcoin cost of the suit. Wait a minute. Bitcoins? I hadn't known of any place in New Orleans that took Bitcoin and . . . wow . . . wonder what happened to dollars?

I kept going and went around a corner. Across the street stood a large Bitcoin bank with a monster video billboard out front. It displayed various stocks scrolling across the huge screen, their current stock price and once in a while, some picture of a news broadcast. I was attracted by a video of military troops taking off in a helicopter, but this helicopter had no rotor blades. Instead, it must have had a hundred small drone blades above it. It looked to be carrying two hundred men and it zoomed away really fast. "These men are being assigned to replace NATO troops in Paraguay," the announcer said. Paraguay? I couldn't remember anything ever happening in Paraguay. And now something required our troops? But then, I saw the date in the bottom corner of the big screen. I blinked and did a double take. D.G. was right. It was eight years ahead.

Wow D.G. Eight years. Takes my breath away.

Exactly. Care to stroll further? Jackson Square is right over that levee.

I turned and trotted over the levee and sure enough, there lay Jackson Square. Much of it looked the same, but I noticed that all the electric and telephone wires above the street were gone and many of the buildings had been reconditioned to look like modernized old buildings. The place was swank. I couldn't help but smile. The artists along the side streets around the square worked on digital boards and most pushed colors around with their fingers on large touch screens. A cop drifted by on some kind of floating disk. I noticed a nickel-size digital implant along the floating cop's jaw bone. He spoke as he moved and another cop on a similar floating board half a block away seemed to talk back to him.

I walked around Jackson Square until I stood in front of St. Louis Cathedral. As I finished looking over one portrait an artist painted of a tourist, I saw Julia going into the cathedral. She wore a very fancy white mini skirt and white high heels. She looked even more beautiful. I'd never seen her so dressed up.

Oh goodness Von. I'm sorry. I didn't know she would be here. You must be extremely careful approaching someone you know from your past, D.G. warned. *And you must be sure you do not meet yourself. If a future version of you shows up, that could be a disaster.*

I nodded that I'd heard him. Yes, I heard him, but this was Julia, the girl I'd secretly loved all my life. And I'd already started walking toward her.

Von. It's best not to approach her. Time travel paradoxes can be very . . . Von?

Sorry D.G. I'll try to be careful. I ran directly toward her. I called to her but she stepped into the church, the door closing behind her. I yanked the door open and bolted through.

"Julia. Hey. It's me. Von"

She wheeled around and gawked at me. Her beauty almost knocked me over. Her green eyes glistened. She had grown another inch or so taller and bore the most perfect figure I'd ever seen. But, she seemed confused. She stepped up to me, reached out and placed her hand on my chest. She pressed harder as though testing what she saw.

"Von? I don't understand. How can you be . . .? How . . . how can you possibly stand here and . . . " She shook her head. "Oh goodness. This is me. This is me . . . I have to be imagining . . . " Her hand went to her neck and I thought she'd faint, so I grabbed her arm to steady her.

"You ok Julia? Yeah, it's me. Von. You remember. From high school, right?" But her arm felt rough and I was dumbstruck discovering that her right arm bore severe scaring that could only have been caused by a fire.

She gently pressed my hand off her arm, turned and walked to a bench along the wall. She sat down, her eyes directed away from me. She sat taking deep breaths.

"What's wrong?" I asked sitting next to her. "You're pale. You ok? What happened to your arm?"

Her eyes rose and for only a moment met mine. "I touched your hand in the casket. It was so cold. I lost you, Von." Her eyes began to read across the floor as she spoke her thoughts. "Your funeral. Charlie's funeral. Oh God. Almost killed me. That damned car fire. I told Charlie it was too late but he went back, fought to get you free of the seat belt . . . that explosion took you both from me."

She bent at the waist and wept. I tried to put my hand on her back but suddenly realized she was saying Charlie, of all people, was dead. My hand hesitated inches from her. Hell, she was saying I was dead. I was dead. My life had ended. I was in a future where I no longer existed. Julia caught her breath, her crying slowing. She slowly sat upright, then stood, inhaled deeply and took a step away.

I sat dumbfounded. Her right arm showed rippled scarring from the top of her hand just past her elbow. Her fingers seemed restricted in their movement, the arm somewhat smaller, shriveled from the blazing accident.

"Oh hell. How can I even think I'm talking to you," she muttered.

Her gaze rose above me and she paced back and forth, turned away from me. She put her arm out leaning on a column, still catching her breath. "I guess I needed this before taking vows. Yeah. Yeah. This kind of makes sense. I've lost you, Von. I have to move on. I have to let go."

Without ever looking back, she let go of the column and steadied herself. I heard her take a deep lung full of air and then she walked away toward the main altar. There, Margarita Paris and a large group of well dressed people greeted her with hugs and kisses. I stood and watched the group assemble into a half circle around Julia and some tuxedo dressed guy I didn't know. They stood together before a priest who recited something about a sacred celebration of holy matrimony. It hurt to admit what I saw before me.

D.G. I mumbled.

Von. I want you to know that I had no idea we would come across Julia. I didn't know that . . .

Yeah. I get that, was all I could say. I stood, walked back outside and slowly wandered through the middle of Jackson Square.

This is one of the dangers of coming into the future, D.G. said. *You never can predict what things will be learned, too suddenly, with no warning, with no time to prepare.*

All I could do was nod. For a full minute, I felt I would faint. I wiped sweat from my forehead and felt small pinpricks of coldness across my skin. I sat on a bench next to a big banana plant watching the pigeons cooing and pecking on the sidewalk.

Von, we've been gone awhile. We should head back to the frequency phaser.

I'm dead, I told D.G. *And Charlie, one of my best friends ever, died trying to save me. Charlie's . . . damnit, Charlie's died in the same fire that killed me.* My stomach muscles pulled me forward, my chest closing down on my thighs and I cried. For long minutes, I couldn't sit up.

I'm sorry Von. The three of you are wonderful people. Nobody deserves this. It wasn't your fault, I'm sure.

You don't know that, D.G. It kind of sounded like I was driving. I wonder if I caused it.

Von. I need you to breathe and calm yourself. We need to start moving toward the frequency phaser. It's time. You can consider all these things later, once we're back in our time.

I stood, shaken, barely feeling the sidewalk below my feet and began to amble past the big Bitcoin bank, past the department stores, back over the levee, toward the warehouse. As I walked over the levee, it hit me.

Wait a minute, D.G. Why should I go back? Back in my time, I'll die. I'll get killed. Some car fire or something. But here, I've jumped past my death. I get to live if I stay here, right?"

Not necessarily, Von. Your presence here could cause a paradox.

What's that?

It means we don't really belong here. We come from another time. If you remained, it would insert an unnatural element into this timeline and that could cause unpredictable complications. You saw how Julia reacted. Suppose your parents saw you. Or Harper and Oma. Or your other friends. They'd see you as coming back from the dead. They'd react in strange ways. I'm telling you, your presence here could upset all kinds of things.

But at least I'd get to live.

There's no guarantee of that either, Von. The disruption in the timeline may work to cause your elimination, the timeline cleaning itself of unnatural elements.

If I go back, can I do something to avoid dying? Can I do something about it?

I don't know, Von. Keep in mind, this whole experiment is a first. We've only done this once before and it went wrong. We don't have enough experience with time travel to answer that question. It may take years to figure that out. I just don't know. But I need you to go back. The return trip is everything. The return trip is my chance to correct the error of our first attempt, the error that placed me into your head. I need you to go back, please. If you don't, I'd be stuck here with you, in your head still. I'd never see Stephanie again. Or my child. Please, Von.

I nodded. He was right. The dream of his son's childbirth flashed through my head. Julia's words about my dying had shocked me so much I'd forgotten the purpose of our being here. I started walking faster, crossed the street and re-entered the big warehouse. The frequency phaser sat glistening in the center of the huge floor, waiting. I slid the big warehouse door closed behind me and walked to the machine.

Ok. We go back. What do I do?

Everything happens just as before. Get into the pilot's seat and strap in. I'll need control of your right hand to set the controls.

As I got situated in the pilot's seat and belted in, I had to ask. *How is this return trip gonna fix anything?*

It all depends on the settings I enter into Stephanie's algorithm. That setting guides the time and place the phaser tracks to. It decides where and when the machine ends up. There are these values known as the eigenvalues. They're rather complicated, but the team and I have been dealing with the first three of these values. On my first return trip, I chose the middle value, the double eigenvalue and entered it into the algorithm. But as you know, it caused an error that moved my consciousness out of my body and into you. I'm hoping that if we get this value correct now, it'll undo that and correct the error. The only way I can ascertain with certainty if that is the correct value is to make the attempt.

So what value will you use this time?

I'm going to use the triple eigenvalue. The machine is very well built and can take the extra strain placed on it by calling for more power. I fear that if I use the single eigenvalue, an under powered phaser might not even get me back. Well, that's my theory.

So, we're taking a big chance here, right?

Yes. But, I've worked it out many times in my head, theoretically, and I think I'm correct. Stephanie and I once debated if the triple eigenvalue should have been used before, but the team agreed on the middle value and I followed orders.

Well D.G., I certainly don't know anything about that. But what about the countdown clock? Will there be any time left?

As we project back, it'll speed up to its usual pace. I think we have a little more than two minutes left. We'll just have to chance it. You ready?

I'm as ready as I'm ever gonna be. Fire it up.

Thank you for trusting me, Von. Thank you for allowing me in. For putting up with me. I owe you . . . everything.

Hey. Don't get all mushy on me, man. Let's just undo this mistake, if we can.

My right hand moved to the control panel, typed in a formula that I had no idea about and then hit the enter key. Next to the keyboard was a green button that simply said, "Go." D.G. hit the button and the frequency phaser began to hum its deep rumbling song again. He had me look a little to the right so he could check coordinates and watch the timer. Everything was happening, or strangely enough, un-happening.

The frequency phaser's rumbling hum grew louder, as it built up reserve power. The incredibly complicated gear set around the pilot seat began to rotate, again arching the mirrors past me in odd circles. They sped up, flying by at such speed that the mirrored ball developed around me again. Once the inner mirrors formed completely, the rainbow of colors started up, lasers flashing in all directions. The ball filled again with the repeating color spectrum. The speed of the light spectrum sped up until everything went completely white. Little vibrations shook the whole machine. Though I tried to settle down, I found my hands digging hard into the padded arm rests of the pilot's seat.

Then, the whiteness of the light grew more intense and broke into spectrums that I wasn't prepared for. Going back in time must be really different because this time I thought I felt every cell of my body becoming different colored light. A completely new sensation, every gene within me went from a red existence, through an orange existence, to a yellow, with an intensity that even my bones felt. Green flushed through me bringing a kind of silence that maybe plants experience. Somehow, I breathed in blue which glowed into indigo and then violet. It was all just too much, something I'd never experienced before. Long moments passed as I tried to remain conscious, but my head fell back against the head rest and I blacked out.

I recall standing again on the countdown clock as it ticked away an extra long second. The next moment, it had changed to the compass. But the compass held three hundred and sixty compass needles, all of them pointing at the center, where I stood. One end of the silver thread rested in my right hand and the other end ran out into space above me. I looked up and there floated D.G., holding the other end of the thread. He yanked hard and the thread slipped from my grasp. I grabbed at it but it flashed out of reach. In an instant, D.G. drifted away taking the whole length of the silver thread with him, disappearing into the black space surrounding the great compass. Immediately, the compass face transformed again to the countdown clock with only one minute left.

Chapter Twenty-One

{ "STEPHANIE." I yelled as loud as I could but it somehow came out barely a whisper. }

I stirred into a fuzzy awareness of air passing somewhere near me. What would make that kind of soft guttural breezy sound? Maybe it wasn't important. Everything was dark. Von obviously had his eyes closed. I hated when that happened. I wanted to know what situation occurred around me but he slept, so I remained unaware. Ah, patience. I tried moving his right hand to see if I could wake him and in response came the sound of paper rustling.

"Oh my god," a woman's voice seemed to panic. "James?"

I felt a hand fall upon Von's right arm and gently shake it. I didn't recognize her voice. She shook Von again and his eyelids made a tiny crack allowing in a sliver of light. The shake made the whistling air sound get stronger and it suddenly hit me that it was the sound of breathing. And then it really hit me. It was MY breathing. I sucked in hard and my lungs inflated fully. I forced an exhale and the sound grew much louder. Abruptly, my eyes popped open. No wonder. Von didn't control them. These were MY eyes. A hand came around and slapped repeatedly at my cheek, followed quickly by a middle-aged woman's face, her eyes as big as she could make them.

"James? Oh my god. Oh my god. Stephanie is gonna be so happy. Oh, I have to call her. Ahh, how do you feel? Don't move. Don't move. We'll have to check you out, ok?"

In an instant I recognized the room around me. I'd only been down here an hour or so before trying to pulse through Von's hand into my own bod . . . that hadn't worked. Wait a minute.

The frequency phaser. Oh hell. I wasn't in Von anymore. It worked. IT WORKED! I'm back in my own . . . in my own wonderful body. And I always thought of myself as a wimp. Oh. A body. What a wonderful thing. That we have our own functioning body to carry us around, to do our bidding, to shake hands and dance and make love and produce offspring. Oh Stephanie. I wanted her, NOW.

"STEPHANIE." I yelled as loud as I could but it somehow came out barely a whisper.

"Yes, she was here just an hour ago," the nurse assured me with one hand on my chest. "I can ring her up. Don't worry. But we have to record your vitals first thing and . . . ahh . . . oh . . . you awoke from the coma at 11:30 pm. I have to write that down."

"I have to get up," I said, my voice growing a bit stronger.

"Oh no. No no. You must remain in bed. Rest. You've been through a terrible ordeal. Why you've been comatose for over two weeks. I doubt you can walk."

I kept moving my head and neck around, trying to swing my weight to the right, to roll out of bed, but nothing would move. I guess I was used to Von moving the body creature but now I had to do it. I concentrated on my left hand and slowly, it crept over my waist and grabbed the restraint bars on the right side of the bed. I tried pulling with my left arm and slowly, my muscles tensed and I began to roll to the right. Once on my side, I draped my left arm over the edge of the bed and felt for the release mechanism to lower the restraint bars. My fingers found the release and the bars shifted lower with a clank. The nurse turned back from writing down my vital signs and found me trying to sit up.

"Oh no no James. You can't. Please don't try to leave the bed. That just won't work dear. Your muscles aren't ready. It'll take getting used to. Physical therapy and all. You know."

I fought, finally got my feet hanging off the edge of the bed and sat with my torso straight up. I managed to smile at her and wiggle a finger at her. She came closer, put her head right in front of me.

"I have to get upstairs," I shouted through a resistant voice that barely made enough sound. "Von's in the phaser and he's probably knocked out. He might be harmed like I was on the first transport. The door's locked and I know the new combination. They can't get to him. Help me get upstairs."

"But the doctor said you were to . . . "

"You like your job? I am the head of this government project. I out rank all those others. Even doctors. I could fire you, see?"

Her head tilted. I watched her eyes glance to the side for only an instant and I could see her reconsider. She moved back and started searching the room. All of a sudden, her face lit up. "Stay here." And she left the room. I waited and a second later she came back with Calhoun, our large janitor that swept and cleaned all three floors by himself. As they approached, I saw Calhoun's smile ignite.

"Why, Mister James. Good to see you, ma' man. We been missing you in the weekly poker games down the hall."

I couldn't help smile. Every time I'd ever passed Calhoun in the hallway or spoke to him on the grounds, a smile automatically jumped onto my face. He was an uncomplicated man with an incredibly kind heart.

"Oh Calhoun," I said, my voice starting to project a bit more. "I'm gonna beat you so bad in that next poker match."

"No, Mister James. You don't know how to handle those flushes. You ain't gonna beat anyone. But I'm glad to see you woke up." And then turning to the nurse, "What do you need me for, dear?"

"Pick him up and place him in this wheelchair. And then help push him to second floor," the nurse said.

Calhoun nodded, slid his big arms around me and glided me gently through the air into the wheelchair. He unlocked the chair and we began to roll along. Calhoun and the nurse made quick work of getting down the hall, into the elevator and up two floors. When the elevator door opened, I could hear the group yelling. I recognized McManus' voice before we came out the elevator.

"He changed the code and there he is right there and we can't even check on him. This is a total breach. How could I fall for some lame story? A voice in his head! Damn it!" McManus yelled at the slightly dented heavy glass door.

As Calhoun rolled me down the hall, the nurse ran ahead to tell the others.

"Stephanie. He's awake. He woke up. He wanted to come up here," the nurse said turning and pointing at me.

Stephanie turned and went silent. The Colonel, Dr. Joplande, Major McManus did likewise. I barely had time to ask Calhoun to stand me up and make sure I stayed standing. Stephanie was at a full run with tears streaming down her cheeks. She crashed into me, her arms wrapping around and squeezing me. If Calhoun hadn't braced me against her collision, Stephanie would have plowed me over. The strength of her hug proved how weak I'd become.

"Oh! Oh goodness. You're awake." Her hands were all over my face and neck making a speedy inspection of me. "Oh, I had lost you James. You were gone. Oh god I miss you. Oh. You're back. Oh, thank goodness you're awake. I love you! I love you so much!" Stephanie's hug clamped around me, nearly squeezing the air from my lungs.

"Goodness, how wonderful to be in your arms again," I whispered.

Colonel Stravieda, Dr. Joplande and Major McManus were only a few steps behind her. They each shook my weak hand and patted me on the back so many times. Karl and the other security guards came over and were quickly followed by Julia and Charlie. Everyone had to take a turn laying hands on me and I rejoiced with them all. Then, I remembered the locked door.

"Julia. Do you know the date Von was born?" She walked up and for a moment looked like she couldn't believe I was speaking to her.

"Wow. Are you Director Guy?" she asked.

I nodded. "Yes. Yeah, I'm D.G. Now listen. Put his birthdate, as an eight digit code, into that door lock. It should open the door. And Julia. You need to be there with me when we check on him. It's important. And Karl, you guys can take the handcuffs off Charlie. I told him to tackle you. That happened on my orders. My apologies."

Julia and McManus were back at the door in a flash. With the code entered, the door opened. We all crowded into the phaser room, even Charlie as he rubbed his freed wrists.

Though my leg muscles burned like the devil, I managed my way up the aluminum ramp. Von lay in the pilot's seat, breathing and very slowly moving his head from side to side. I reached up and lightly slapped his cheek. His eyes barely opened but he focused on me. Then, his face showed surprise and I knew it was beginning to register. His eyes looked to his left and down and I knew he would be calling in his head to D.G. It made me laugh.

"Anybody in there answering?" I asked.

At the sound of my voice, Von's eye's almost exploded.

"Holy shit. You're not in my head anymore?" he said as he began to strain against the safety belts. "You're not in my FREAKING HEAD ANYMORE!" He grabbed both my shoulders and looked down at my arms and chest. "You . . . you woke up. You're in there. Not in here," he hollered pointing at his own head. "You're in there. YOU'RE IN THERE. IT WORKED. It worked. It wor . . . "

Slowly, Julia pressed her shoulder around my left arm and crowded her way in between us. She and Von gazed into each other's eyes and I knew I should move back. I quickly punched in an exit code into the control keyboard and hit enter. The phaser went into shutdown mode and the hum of the big machine quieted completely.

Julia reached out and touched Von's face. "Tell me. Just tell me."

His smile glowed. "Yeah. I'm ok." He took her right arm, looked at it and rubbed his fingers across her smooth skin. "You are perfect." He hooked his arm around her neck, pulled her close and hugged her. They held each other until Dr. Joplande interrupted.

"I think we need to get Von out of there. He's not certified to operate that equipment."

"He didn't operate it. I did," I called out. "Actually, we owe these three young people our thanks, otherwise, I might not be alive right now. It'll take some explaining, but Von and I can delineate the entire experience."

"Delineate?" Von said. He looked at Stephanie. "Does he always use such vocabulary? I'm telling you, your parents had to be dictionaries, D.G."

Stephanie clung with her arms around me, tears streaming down her smile and nodded back.

Chapter Twenty-Two

{ Orange pieces of truck, silver tank trailer, two large tires and an axel unit flew through the air. }

By the time I got out of the phaser's pilot seat and into the hall, the entire group had gone stark raving wild. The swirl of talk began with Dr. Joplande, Colonel Stravieda, and James celebrating that the huge project experiment they'd spent years designing and building had succeeded. Stephanie celebrated that success too, but she did it with her arms around James, never leaving his side, kissing him often. Major McManus stood over to the side, listening, both hands on her hips, amazed that no one seemed interested in security. Her jaw hung open.

And of course, Julia and Charlie had to be reassured that the voice in my head was finally gone. We found a group of chairs in the frequency phaser room and sat together. I told them about my venture into New Orleans eight years in the future. I described the store's digital ad with me in a new suit and how cops levitated along the street and how artists of the future used digital boards of some kind. And then I froze up just looking into Julia's face. I held her hand and just sat there. I just couldn't tell her about our unexpected meeting at the Cathedral. Luckily, James and Stephanie interrupted by dragging up chairs next to us.

"Von. I know you informed your parents that you were going on this trip, but . . . ," James said. Stephanie leaned over and put her hand on my knee.

" . . . but you should call your folks and let them know you're fine.

Reassure them, ok?" Julia nodded her agreement, so I pulled out my cell phone and dialed home.

"Hey Mom. Sorry to call so late. We're in Baton Rouge. Hey, I passed Junior year. How about that?" I said trying to keep an uplifted tone.

"Oh goodness, Von. It's past midnight. It sounds like a party there . . . " she took a minute to yawn and sit up in bed, "but I'm gratified that you passed. And your father told me you'd be taking a jaunt with Julia and Charlie, right? You said Baton Rouge?"

"Yes, that's right. Baton Rouge. Ahh, Mom. Is Dad there? I need to talk to him."

The phone was exchanged and George spoke. "Von?"

"Dad. I'm in Baton Rouge. I came here to get that voice completely out of my head. And I did. It's done. Everything's clear upstairs, ok?"

"Really! How do you feel?"

"It feels good. Really good. I think I'm less nervous. Look Dad. I'm gonna be gone for a few days. Not to worry. Julia and Charlie'll keep an eye on me. Ok? I'll be careful."

"Uh huh. So, you're gonna be a senior? You passed?"

"Yeah Dad. I passed everything."

A few moments of silence went by.

"Yeah. Ok. I reckon you earned it. But Von, you travel safely, understand? Call me if you need anything."

"Yes sir. I got this, Dad. Ya'll sleep well."

As Dad hung up, I closed my cell phone and slid it back into my pocket. Stephanie nodded slowly. It was something in her look. Her

266

happiness showed through every pore of her face. Her love for her husband, newly returned, just glowed. I could almost feel her love. I remember feeling D.G.'s love for her . . . and somehow, it bled through to me. I turned and looked at Julia and nearly broke down crying. She would live, though burned. Charlie smiled at me and put his hand on my shoulder and tears began to flood out of me. I stood and embraced Charlie like I'd never done before. He hugged me back. I cried. Julia stood and wrapped her arms around us both and cried with me. Charlie and I would be gone, dying together. But even though I was stumbling all over my emotions, somehow, I still couldn't tell them.

"Man, Von. And I thought it would be some interesting adventure, some fun little trip, looking for the crazy voice in your brain. Wow, man. You really outdid yourself," Charlie giggled.

Julia wrapped her arms around my neck and squeezed. "Yeah. And that hour you disappeared in that machine about ran me crazy. I thought I'd lost you . . . gone. I can't explain how relieved I am you're back."

She would lose me. She would lose both Charlie and me. I just couldn't get it out. I was going to die and couldn't say it. I smiled for them. I could only hope my smile covered up my worries. I would just celebrate with them and think about all this later. Right now, it was just too much.

Soon everyone drove back to James and Stephanie's house, ordered from an all night pizza joint and a party spontaneously erupted in celebration. Finally, someone pointed out that it was nearly three in the morning. James and Stephanie put us up for the night and I slept with a vengeance. No clock dreams or compasses or threads showed up.

Once James woke us late-sleeping teenagers up, we ate a nice pancake breakfast Stephanie prepared. Colonel Stravieda arrived, this time dressed in civilian clothes and explained we would all need to sit down for hours of debriefing. Dr. Joplande and Major McManus arrived together, had coffee and began conducting an incredibly thorough video camera interview that went on for hours. Everyone stood around, watching the interview with looks of amazement. Everyone asked questions and James and I were able to answer them all, though much of the time it took long explanations. Finally, we had figured it all out. Or at least, James had. The one foggy detail I still felt wouldn't be something I'd talk about, though it struck me that James already knew my question.

By two in the afternoon, we needed to switch over to security issues. Major McManus' biggest concern was that three teenagers had invaded into a secret government DARPA project. She wanted us watched and restricted in our movements. But James had more authority than anyone else in the project. He had been the one that had created the project. He and Stephanie had applied to DARPA and gotten approval, which then brought on Colonel Stravieda and Dr. Joplande. Once the total project was approved and funded, then the government insisted on complete security, and Major McManus joined the group. So, in the end, she would have to consider James' opinions.

"Without Von finding the patience to put up with my presence," James pointed out, "this project would be a total failure. Von, with the help of Julia and Charlie, has assisted us. They have in fact, saved us. And, we can accomplish much more in this regard using a carrot instead of a stick." It took James a few tries to convince Major McManus that there should be no punishment of us "precocious teenagers" and though they argued back and forth for a half hour, eventually, she agreed.

Major McManus did insist that we sign government contracts that bound us to secrecy. But then Julia jumped in and became involved with the negotiations. She wanted to know what the government would do to compensate us for, one, assisting with the success of their project, and, two, for keeping their secrets. We could tell Major McManus' reaction would have been to just jail us, but Colonel Stravieda and Dr. Joplande suggested that DARPA might be able to quietly fund four years of completely free college education at LSU if, of course, we could keep our big mouths shut about the whole escapade. When he said that, Julia, Charlie and I couldn't even move for a few seconds. We exchanged looks and slowly began to nod. "Well yes. I think that might be fair compensation," Julia managed to get out. Oh, hell yeah we signed.

After spending the night again at James and Stephanie's house, we were much closer to meeting all the requirements to be set free. They would need more interviews with me in the months to come and twice a year with Julia and Charlie, checking to see if there were any lingering psychological or physical effects resulting from our involvement in the whole ordeal. We agreed and it dawned on me that we might be able to get long term jobs out of this whole event. Later, James and Stephanie explained that I was the first human to ever successfully time travel, well, without a glitch, that is.

It was just so quiet in my head. I was rejoicing in the new found silence. James and I talked about the relief we were both feeling being able to think and not have anyone else right there to make comment on it. Three times he expressed his desire to visit Margarita Paris to discover how she could grab him while he resided in my mind. We talked for hours, Julia, Charlie and Stephanie right there, amazed at our revelations. James held his baby, Marky, and rocked him as we talked. Marky made some stinky diapers and James walked down the long hallway to change his baby. I saw the opportunity to talk alone with James.

"Are you ok, Von?" he asked as he lay Marky down on the changing table.

"It's really starting to hit me, that Charlie and I will die before long," I mumbled. "I think I can get over the dying part, but losing Julia, losing Charlie, knowing he dies trying to save me. That just bores right through me. And I think about Oma and Harper, about Mom and Dad. I hate leaving them with all that sadness. I hate losing them. I hate losing me. I have lots I want to do in life."

James nodded as he taped the new diaper to Marky's bottom. "The question you asked before was the right one. Can you do anything about it? Can you change the events of the future to avoid that fate? I'm sorry, Von. All that scientific knowledge I've learned over the years won't help answer that question. I just don't know. This one falls to you and you alone. But, I've lived in your head and I saw the way you think, the quickness of your responses, the agility of your mind and I know this. I trust you. I trust you will figure this one out."

James pulled me to him, hugged me and whispered, "Thanks again. You got us to this point. You did it. You carried us, the two of us. I get to be with Stephanie and Marky again, to work on this incredible project again, because of your fortitude. Thank you, Von." He picked up Marky and we walked back to the living room.

By Sunday morning, we were ready to be on the road again. Finally, after we'd talked ourselves nearly deaf, we stood at the curb in front of James and Stephanie's house, about to climb back into the Bamboo car.

"I need to drive," I told Julia and Charlie. They hesitated only a moment and Julia handed me the keys.

"You know, I thought we were going a lot further west," Charlie reminded us.

Julia nodded. "Well, can't we just keep going? Our money hasn't run out yet."

Everyone smiled and climbed in. In just ten minutes, we were back out on Interstate 10 traveling toward Lafayette, going west. The warm late spring breeze whistled through the car, rustling everyone's hair.

"Well, we have a year to decide what to take in college," Charlie hollered from the back seat over the wind and highway noise.

"I'm taking psychology," Julia said which was no surprise to anyone.

"I've gotta learn how to study," I admitted. "Otherwise, I'll flunk out and I doubt the government would appreciate that."

"Well, we got your brain figured out." Charlie smiled. "And don't be telling me to tackle anymore security guys. I about pissed myself. They were mad. Man, I mean angry. We're lucky we're not in jail."

"You really took them down too," I agreed.

"That McManus Major scared me," Julia blurted. "She dragged me down the hall and got me to tell her what school we went to. She wanted to know a lot and I managed to not tell everything, but she was really intimidating."

"I think we did ok," I said, even though Charlie and I were to die. That thought kept coming up in my head. I kept trying to push it aside, but how do you ignore your own death?

I checked the rearview mirror. I looked forward but then an odd motion took my attention into the rearview mirror again. A half mile behind us was a large orange eighteen-wheeler that looked to be switching lanes a lot. I tried to speed up a bit but the accelerator was already to the floor. At sixty-five miles per hour, we weren't going to outrun anyone. Cars went quickly past in the left lane every few seconds. When I checked the rearview a few seconds later, the eighteen-wheeler had cut the distance between us in half. Even in its own lane, it seemed to swerve back and forth.

"Wow. That truck is driving crazy," I told the group.

Charlie turned around and watched the big truck too. "Looks like a tanker truck," Charlie called out.

Julia looked back and watched too. I checked my lane and there was only one car close to us approaching from behind, about to pass us in the left lane. The tanker truck gained on us quickly.

"He's way over the speed limit," Charlie hollered. "He's either drunk or angry."

The eighteen-wheeler's blasting air horn shocked all three of us and I realized that the big truck threatened to collide with both the Bamboo car and the SUV passing us. This guy wasn't slowing down at all. He stayed on his horn, the blaring bugle drilling into my ears. I swerved right, drove out of our lane and onto the asphalt shoulder of the highway. But the big truck barreled ever closer, about to run us over. I steered further right and felt the front wheel contact bare grass and ground. The sound of metal crunching, glass breaking and tires screeching filled the air. I steered all the way onto the grass and even moved over ten feet away from the asphalt shoulder. Our tires dribbled across clumps of grass and uneven ground sending vibrations throughout the car. I hit the brakes and our tires began to skid across the turf and sod. It took quite a distance to get stopped but the Bamboo car finally ground to a halt. We came to rest in a wide grass expanse, completely away from the highway. We opened the doors and stood up to watch as the eighteen-wheeler flew by, its air horn still squalling insults.

"He hit the other car," Charlie announced as he began to cross the road to check on the passengers of the SUV.

On the opposite shoulder sat a gray Ford SUV, its back right corner crushed in, orange paint streaked onto its side. Its red plastic taillight lay scattered across the highway and its back gate window shattered. The owner got out and came around to inspect the damage.

Julia and I walked around the Bamboo car but there were no marks showing any contact. He'd missed us.

"Good idea to go for the grass, Von. At first, I didn't know what you were doing but you kept us safe," Julia said.

I turned to say something to her, but white light invaded from all sides and she turned to the version of Julia eight years in the future. The Bamboo car and grass disappeared, replaced by a cobblestone street with tall black wrought iron fencing, banana trees and the rest of New Orleans' Jackson Square in the background. Julia looked a bit older, more mature and even more beautiful. Her straight blue dress I'd never seen before. Her right hand held an ice cream cone as she stood watching an artist create a digital portrait of a young child. She marveled as he pushed the colors and shapes around on the digital screen, then raised the cone and licked the strawberry ice cream. From behind her, Charlie walked up, his hands jammed into his jean pockets as usual. Julia raised her ice cream cone and Charlie licked the opposite side.

"Man, you always get strawberry," he said smiling.

"Of course. There are no other flavors," she answered with a wiggle.

Charlie looked around. "Where'd Von go?"

"Café de Monde. He and Moby wanted coffee. They'll be right back."

Suddenly, it all changed back in a flash and it was Julia, the senior in high school, again, there next to the Bamboo car resting on the grass expanse next to I-10. I stepped back and shook my head. What was that? That flash? Julia stood watching me, a surprised look on her face.

"Von?" she asked, at first with a serious look but then smiled. "You're freaking out because of a near miss, huh? Here, sit on the trunk and take a few breaths."

I didn't know what to tell her. What should I say? That I'm the guy that finally got over having a voice in my head but now I'm having visions? I just sat on the trunk like she'd suggested. She rubbed my back for a few strokes but must have thought I was ok because she turned and walked across the highway to check on the people in the gray SUV. My gaze fell into the grass as my mind reran the vision I'd just experienced. I wondered about how to interpret such a quick and unexpected mental flash when my cell phone went off.

"Von. It's me," James said. "Did you just have an image of Julia at Jackson Square? Because I did."

I hopped down off the trunk and began pacing. "Wow! Yes. It happened just a few seconds ago. Eating ice cream, right? And a straight blue dress. Watching . . . "

" . . . watching an artist do a digital version of a portrait, right? Like paint with his fingers on a flat screen?" James said and then went on. "Charlie was there. He looked fine."

"Yeah. Exactly. You saw it too?"

"Yes. I was rocking the baby and suddenly, a white flash and then that scene just appeared. What could cause that? Are you guys alright?"

I explained the close call we'd just had with the eighteen-wheeler. As I spoke I noticed Julia and Charlie walking toward me in the grass. A loud explosion came from further up the highway and we all turned toward it. A huge fireball filled the sky in the distance directly over the highway. Orange pieces of truck, silver pieces of tank trailer, two large tires and an axel unit flew through the air.

"What was that?" James asked.

"That eighteen-wheeler. Just blew up, I think."

I turned and reran the vision in my mind.

"James. Her arm holding the ice cream cone. Was it scarred?"

He hesitated for a moment. "No. Both her arms were smooth. And Charlie was there. He looked fine. No burn scars either. They spoke about you, and Moby. She wasn't dressed for a wedding either. Wow. Maybe timelines can be changed. Maybe we just answered your question, Von."

For long moments, neither of us spoke. "I don't know what to say, James."

"Well, we have years to wonder about it. But for right now, I gotta go. Marky is waking up and needs feeding. Look, you drive safely. And check in now and then."

Julia and Charlie stood there, looking at the explosion, safe, all the fire over there in the distance. I could feel my nerves start to unwind, my rib cage expanded a bit more. My breathing relaxed and my mind cleared away tension in one big swoop. A smile began to creep across my face as I watched Julia and Charlie meander across the grass toward me. We were safe and we were together.

We kept going west. With each progressing hour, I relaxed more and more. We stayed with friends in Lafayette, went dancing that night at a Cajun festival and Charlie tied up with this cute girl named Greta. He decided to hang out with her for a few days. Next morning, Julia and I did rock paper scissors to see who'd drive first.

"West dear?" she asked.

I nodded. My mind was quiet, the air moved through me with ease and my muscles didn't strain at all. We churned our way through Texas, marveled at New Mexico deserts and were awed by Santa Fe art museums. In northwestern Arizona, we relished three days of hiking through the bottom of the Grand Canyon and finally came upon a hidden waterfall. Julia totally surprised me by stripping down to nothing and skinny dipping in the crystal clear water. She'd never done that before. Though I couldn't take my eyes off her, I actually hesitated taking off my clothes, till she teased me out of them. I stripped and swam too. She was so beautiful.

Maybe it was being nude, no clothes to hide behind, completely baring ourselves to each other for the first time ever, that somehow shook all the secrets loose from me. As we laid on wet sand letting the sun warm us, I told her finally of meeting her in the future, of the vision I'd had on the I-10 roadside when the eighteen-wheeler just missed us, of the following phone call from James. I told her that I was going with the theory that we had somehow changed our future. She wrapped her arms around my neck and kissed my cheek.

"You know, usually I ask if you're ok," Julia said. "But what I want to know now is, are we ok?"

I nodded, smiled. "Yep," I answered. "And, we've got this incredible new advantage."

Her head tilted a bit, she smiled. "What? What advantage?"

"Well, you see dear, I am no longer a two spirit man."

End

If you enjoyed this novel, I ask that you leave a small review stating that fact at the website page where you purchased it. My thanks.

ABOUT THE AUTHOR

Edward G. Gauthier

I wrote my first poem in 3rd grade elementary school correctly using the word "deft" and have drafted, scribbled, plotted, poemed and essayed ever since.

Writing tendencies:

I tend to explore the psychic dreams and the infinite space of the mind. I am drawn to themes like "the best laid plans of mice and men goes oft awry" or other themes demonstrating mankind's arrogance. We're just so damned full of ourselves, which makes for infinite entertainment. Man running up against his own self-built delusions probably originates from deep within all of us. Life of course is a discovery process. Who am I? What should I do with my life? What is really significant? Today's answer to these questions may not work tomorrow. Things move around. Is change the only constant? Nothing holds still.

A few of the literary influences I've read:

Man and His Symbols by Carl Gustov Jung, Zen Mind Beginner's Mind by Shunryu Suzuki, anything by Kurt Vonnegut, Tabloid Dreams by Robert Olen Butler, Birds of America by Lorrie Moore, Inner Work by Robert Johnson, A Good Man is Hard to Find by Flannery O'Connor, as well as multiple works by Ursula Le Guin, Ray Bradbury, Michael Crichton, Arthur C. Clark, Orson Scott Card, Ernest Hemingway, William Shakespeare and quite a few others.

The absolute best advice I can give to fellow writers:

"Planning to write is not writing. Outlining, researching, talking to people about what you're doing, none of that is writing. Writing is writing."-- E. L. Doctorow